Kathy Page was born in 1958, the youngest of three daughters. She went to the University of York to read English and foreign languages. After receiving her degree, she stayed on in York, becoming increasingly involved in feminism and in painting. She returned to London to find 'work that had its own satisfactions but left me free to write', and chose carpentry. Following a writing course, six of the women in the class started to meet weekly and have done so ever since. Kathy Page has published short stories in *Writing Women*, *Wild Words* and *Eve Before the Holocaust*. She is now at work on her second novel and lives in south London.

Back in the First Person is a remarkable first novel which deals with the far-reaching and too often ignored consequences of rape. For Cath Sheldon the ordeal is not one that can be measured in minutes – the terrifying minutes when Steve, her ex-lover, returns to take what he thinks she 'owes' him – but persists throughout months of police incredulity, medical callousness, legal delays and court-room theatrics. With courage and superb perception, Kathy Page has written a compelling account of the human implications of a very particular kind of violence.

Back in the First Person

Kathy Page

Published by Virago Press Limited 1986
41 William IV Street, London WC2N 4DB

Copyright © Kathy Page 1986

British Library Cataloguing in Publication Data
Page, Kathy
 Back in the first person.
 I. Title
 823'.914[F] PR6066.A3/

 ISBN 0-86068-637-X
 ISBN 0-86068 642 6 Pbk

Typeset by Clerkenwell Graphics and
printed by Anchor Brendon, Tiptree, Essex

For Alex, Dallas, Chantal, Judy, Julia, Margaret and Rosanne who kept me writing and helped in many ways

1

'Get out. Just get out.'

The sound of my own voice fills the room: an utter imperative so sour and loud that it slices the dark like a steel wire looped round an apple and pulled suddenly tight. I stare at the ceiling seeking familiar shadows with which to calm myself, as I used to do when waking from a nightmare.

Beside me, where I won't look, Steve, propped up on one elbow and turned to face me, is momentarily surprised into silence. Then,

'Get out yourself', he says, but my voice has more conviction:

'I mean it, get out, now!'

The articulacy of anger! It seems as if, because he has hit me, shoved me back into that childhood powerlessness which only anger's magic can redeem, I must and can make him vanish. It seems as if I'm saying it, get out, get out, for the first time.

In fact, I've said it before. Three weeks after he moved in I woke up on the sofa with a coat and hearthrug for blankets, feeling so ugly I wanted to be invisible. My limbs were imprisoned and tangled with his so I couldn't leap up, run and hide. I didn't say 'get out' in so many words, I didn't shout, but I asked him to go.

'I don't want this,' I said then, averting my eyes. Soft-faced from sleep, shivering without bedclothes, bewildered at my explanations and contradictions: the sight of him then touched me; I began to think I was stupid to be afraid, to blame him for the discomfort and ignominy of the sofa. The ugliness began to melt; and, catching sight of the curtain, a thin cloth that trapped the sun and sent it through countless tangles of fibres and into the spaces of the weave where it dazzled in the draught like sun-patterns on the sea, I felt suddenly relieved. I threw away my first feelings, and said, laughing,

'No, it doesn't matter, it's just the suddenness, like opening a window because it's stuffy, and then you think you're cold – but it's only the change, you know.'

Still sleepy, he'd smiled and shook his head to say that he didn't, it was a bit poetic for the early morning – but the sound of my words pleased me and led me on. The looseness of his morning face, so different from the daytime one, and for which I supposed that I, and not simply sleep, was responsible, seemed to promise sympathy. So I told him clearly what I meant: that I had only ever 'fucked' – I pronounced the word with conscious abandon, savouring my dominion over its ugliness – with one man before; it had been years ago and, I whispered, 'I hated it. But last night was different', which was the truth. My tongue, having tasted freedom, went greedily on, so that I never noticed he told me no secret in return. I described the panic and the lies my unfashionable distaste for sex had caused me, all mixed up and shaken with a kind of pride in it and a desire to preserve my celibacy at the same time as it humiliated me. I smiled as I spoke, as if I was describing someone else; and we laughed together at my departing self as if it had a funny walk or wore its trousers inside out.

I remember another time, halfway between then and now, when I tried to say 'get out', but my words were sogged with ambiguous tears and mouthed too softly to convince even myself for long. But now –

'Oh for Christ's sake, Cath, you don't know what you're

2

saying,' says Steve, moving impatiently in the bed.

'I'm saying get out,' I shout again – and oh yes, that old anger shoots straight into the bloodstream, an impossibly pure drug which makes my body evaporate into noise, palpitation and a kind of scarlet blindness: it's back again. It brings a reeling of the senses and unearthly concentration of the mind, that anger which comes intermittently and so unexpectedly, always to be forgotten until the next time. It used to possess me as a child when forced to lie in the dark, to eat more or less, to dress in colours I hated, to kiss strong-smelling adults for whom I felt not affection but disgust: 'temper'. The veins around my heart block, the pressure will kill me or it will blind the world, paralyse it for a split second, after which everything will be unrecognisably transformed. Lying on my back in the dark, listening to my breath and the pumping of my blood, I want to prolong my anger for ever, for, so long as it's there, the world is suspended in a state of turbulence for which only I am responsible. After the anger, I know, will come blinding headaches and flashes of colour behind my closed eyes, vomiting, tears to remind me that this feeling of power is illusory. My glands will squirt caustic juices on to the soft tissues within, muscles will jerk involuntarily beneath the parched skin of my face long after the rage has died: as if my body, still helplessly, uselessly, possessed by wrath, were trying to take over where reason and language have failed, its rantings audible only to me, its captive audience. 'Tuesday's child is full of wrath,' my Dad used to tease, 'you take things too much to heart.' The Fury visited me regularly throughout the endless indignities of adolescence, then slipped even out of my memory as I learned that the tainted feelings of disappointment and deceit became, with frequent use, more bearable than the aftermath of an anger that did not transform. And now it's back, grown big in the dark years of hibernation.

'Don't treat me like a child, I'm sick of it. I'm telling you to get out,' I say, my mouth stiff with hatred, and I enjoy

3

both the simplicity and the cruelty of this sentence: it's true too, and there's relief in not trying to understand, not having to do anything more than state facts.

There are memories which say it has not always been so simple, but they play distant and pale before me, enervating as a television in a brightly lit room. I remember I once felt myself becoming addicted to the sense of recognition that came between our hands on each other's skin. I remember being lonely when he went away and there was no one to prevent me from springing out of the suddenly too-big bed, an instant teacher, a spinster woman who came home to unshared meals, voluntary work, marking, and letters to mother. I know I have been frightened for his safety when he went to Africa, to South America, always the most dangerous places in the world where his sort was least welcome and you were a fool to speak out let alone write, naming names and detailing iniquities. Yes, my feelings have been more complicated and my temper asleep, but now even these my own recollections leave me cold, contemptuous even. The years between the times of saying 'get out' have evaporated.

'Get out. Fight a real battle, instead of me,' I say, knocking away even what I've been right to admire.

'So that's it! I apologised, didn't I? I'll say again, I'm sorry. What more can I say? It's not such a big deal.'

I feel my face, it doesn't hurt, it didn't hurt, it was no more than a slap, such as I might have once felt tempted to administer to one of the children in my class on a bad day. But there's more to it than that: a contact of skin on skin which comes from neither curiosity nor love is the prelude to the breaking of an invisible hymen, a penetration that cannot be softened with any kind of pleasure. For a moment, before my anger broke, I felt there was a choice. I held a bottle of pills, unlabelled, but definitely not innocuous. If I took one, I would be taking them for the rest of my life, morning and night swallowing, swallowing. I was, for a second, tempted; because so many people did take them they seemed to promise the fulfilment of something inevitable; they were 'growing up', they were the means of joining 'real life'. But my body takes over, and I cannot swallow: I will not be a person who can be hit, will not have a life scrimped in the shadow of compulsion.

I remember being a child squirming at the dinner table, stomach tight, increasingly nauseous as they moved in closer: 'Eat your food, drink your medicine, it's good for you, there's nothing else, until you eat you won't leave your chair.' Until you swallow you will be deprived of sight and sound and smell and society and sleep and my smile – but still it wasn't worth it, and isn't now. I won't cross that invisible threshold, won't swallow – they would take the spoon and pinch your nose tight until you opened your mouth: and there, as here, the fury bursts, that they will not *let you be*, neither your mind nor your body, they confuse and confiscate and return things later, unrecognisably mangled. And this is what my lover has done, and where anger grows.

'It's not just that. It's everything . . .'

'And, of course, it *must* be my fault! You're like a spoilt child! I remember the last time you said you wanted me out . . .'

He speaks in his political-meeting voice, greased sleek with the knowledge of its next sentence – the one that will expose the weakness, the dishonesty, the stupidity of the opposition, spatter it with eggy ridicule. I shouldn't have offered any kind of explanation. Anger has seeped away and I'm losing again. I've brushed aside the only complaint he would have accepted and now, relieved of that, he is ready to unpick me again. My resistance is not after all righteous anger but neurosis, panic, evasion: weakness.

'It was when you got the sack and decided it was my fault.'

You never mean it, you never mean it, his voice taunts. It *was* your fault, a voice mutters in my head, but I don't trust it anymore. I lie dumb and stiff in the bed, feeling the

5

after-anger sickness, and remembering the last time.

Then, as now, we'd been arguing on and off for days. 'You're wasting your time teaching,' he said, 'turning young minds into factory-fodder and college-fodder, papering over the cracks.' He said I was too cowardly, too fond of my hard-won professional status, 'stinking with compromise'. Always our arguments have been about what I am like: not enough and too much, what I should stop and what I should begin. Like a tree that's been half felled without realising the danger, I'd grown suddenly aware of the chipping and chiselling, now that it had reached the heart-wood; I feared the rope and wedges standing ready. I cried, decided I was nothing, I could not go on, I would die or go mad, and the morning after I was late again, running breathless across the playfields more like a truant than a teacher: I had trained for this and loved it but somehow it was being squeezed thinner and thinner. I was always being late. There were meetings and leaflets to type up, and Steve's articles, taking messages, reading for research. Piles and bins of paper had filled my home and littered my mind. Late also because of making love – or trying to – and arguing, late in the end because of exhaustion.

I was bitter. I remembered how I had loved my work, been ambitious. But now the headmaster considered me just as he considered persistent offenders sent to his white-painted study with its full-size reproduction Mondrians on two walls, venetian blinds on the third, door behind. I was that hateful, humiliated child again. As he spoke I was searching his smooth-shaven face for crevices where hope might hide.

'You seem to have been ill very frequently.' His tone implied something slightly distasteful: the lie we both knew about. There were no cracks in his face; I could not detail the half-understood frustrations and undefined miseries that sapped my strength, could not explain that I could never sleep after making love, and had come to dread my

6

own orgasm, fear my own shadow and my reflection in the glass, how I felt the night clock tick, tick, burrowing through my ear, coiling its spring and mine.

'It's sort of tiredness.'

'Well,' said the eyes bright blue and black on white, like the painting on the wall, 'we all get tired Miss Sheldon . . .' and his face tightened at the fishy dustbin smell of weakness – 'can't cope' – which it was impolite to mention. His clear features were set in a configuration that had an inflexible look about it, as if there never had been and never would be a reason to change, no possibility of collapse or contortion. A face that would not be overwhelmed: but mine, it was wobbling, jibbering on the point of collapse, his next words would puncture its thin membrane and I would be all liquid, bleeding, tears, piss –

Steve said nothing when I told him I had lost my job. He stayed sitting slumped and immovable in the armchair, reminding me of that evening when he had moved in, a posture that then seemed poignant, all splayed and dislocated like a broken doll, but was beginning now to gather itself into something frighteningly solid. He had wanted me to give up teaching in any case.

The bed shifts as he moves a pillow under his elbow and neck, stretches his legs, undaunted by the cold bits at the bottom of the bed as he is by aeroplanes, soldiers, riots and anything I might do or say.

'Well, it's true, isn't it?' he says quietly, 'when something's wrong you just say it's my fault.' And I want to pull the covers over my head – sheets for coolness, blankets for darkness. I hate my silence and my tears and I long to be angry again. But anger's gone, leaving only an ache behind. My anger's a puny muscle, incapable of sustained effort, its tiny strength sapped and lost in the shadows of the times when it has not been there.

I lie still, there's nothing to say, or I can't say it. It's better to keep quiet than to perjure myself, I think.

*

My lover's face in the darkness had a vagueness of shape that went well with the softness of skin; this man's face in the dark has a lack of definition that reminds me that I do not know who he is. My lover's face in the dark had shadowy patches for eyes that were closed to render his body more acute to the sensations of love, that opened to look for my eyes to meet; this man's face in the night has only pits of blackness that would swallow me if I looked. My lover's mouth had spoken without words or with the words of a well-shared secret, it had been wet, it had opened with the pressure of my lips into a secret vaulted cavern away from the noise of the world; this man's mouth is a tooth-barred strongbox full of sticks and stones. I am crying for what has gone.

And this man reaches out to touch me, two hands at my body demanding to be fed, pushing at my skin to get inside, and I know I am right, it is not just desire that's died, but the hope of its ever returning. I push him away, and then I'm standing next to the bed, freezing cold, my muscles stuck in a pillar of affront.

'Get out!'

But I'm already out myself. He laughs, sitting in bed, the hands that tried to touch me pulling the sheets up around him. That bed is mine I think, everything in this flat is mine. I lived here before you came. I let you in. I threw it, and myself, open to you so carelessly years ago; a quiet shuttered room for sitting in that has become an office, a café, a station, a theatre, and soon will have to make way for the street.

'This is my place,' I say.

'Scratch the surface and what do we find?' he sneers. 'You'll be voting Tory in a few years' time and wanting to introduce corporal punishment for theft . . .'

He turns his back and stretches down into the bed.

8

'We're going to Manchester at eight,' he adds. 'It's important, I need some sleep. If you can't sleep in this bed with me, that's your problem.'

In the other room I turn on all the lights, draw the curtains and fiddle with the radio, but it's too late for anything but the pop stations, crackling with interference and swooping from the deafening to the inaudible.

Manchester. Another conference: a dull cold room filled with damp denim, tense with the expectation of scandal, decisions, blood that never materialises. Eyes on the microphone, on papers, on raised hands. Beer and coffee and sleeping bags on the floor. Pages of notes, to be edited on the train, transformed into pages of typing. On and on, exhaustion of judgement and conscience. Beside me indefatigable Steve, whom everyone admires. For his energy. For his uncompromising line, for the spectacle of life dedicated, in words at least, to the publicising of causes, hopes and conflicts that he could never hope to see resolved, fired by a restlessness that could never be satisfied or fulfilled. Part of a larger plan, a sense of History. Relentless. Nothing else worthwhile.

There was a time when I was glad to assist, proud when the articles and features came out and I knew I had improved them, prouder still when once he added my name to his at the bottom, and there it was, the Truth with its photographs and headings, angular, black on white, its prose tightened and blocked into paragraphs and columns, its references, bibliography and dates impeccable, checked by myself. There was a time when I thought he was right, that this was a better thing to do than teaching after all, despite less money and no holidays and the loneliness of watching, writing and recording, despite my feeling so much at sea, at the mercy of any articulate argument, despite something in me that worried whether it was right to try and interfere with places you'd never seen, whether it was right to kill and how could you know – but other people

9

seemed to know the right from the wrong. I wrote everything down, and I longed for each phrase to be the last word, but it never was, and always before me the work of sifting what I had heard or read for small grains of truth.

An activity without landmarks, without permanence, certainty or financial rewards, Steve's journalism has in a few years filled my rented rooms with dictionaries, two typewriters, files and posters, newspapers and photographs, timetables and maps: a sea of paper obliterating the green paint I put up when I – the old Cath, the ex-secretary, the celibate, the teacher of literature with extra qualifications in remedial reading and ESL, the specialist in communication and its difficulties, the believer in Education and its Possibilities, the optimist – moved in. Behind me was the tedium of the typing pool, the prudence of brassières and woollen vests and yoghurt for lunch: before me, useful work, union meetings, long summer holidays, days of thinking and days of talking. I didn't quite know what to expect but I was excited and I painted the flat symphony and forest greens, burnt coffee and cream, burgundy and lily, scarcely caught my breath before I dived. This shabby office-room I am sitting in was my symphony green bedroom. What was a sitting room with the armchair in it became Steve's room then 'the bedroom'. The small room he was meant to have stores books only. Slowly, as habits established themselves, objects have shifted or been thrown away, and new ones arrived to match the new circumstances and the new routine. I didn't carry my clothes back. He has not moved his typewriter from my table where the light is better, the kitchen nearer. Even the dust has settled differently. The lights burn longer at night, and it is not my place anymore, but ours, or even his. And the expectations I had when I moved in? Even though I'm not sure precisely what they were, I know they have not been fulfilled.

I wonder, was the fault mine for not having made my hopes explicit enough?

Once, when I was still a typist, discontented, and rushed

after lunchtime shopping, a shabby old woman came up to the café table where I was finishing my cup of tea, passing by other empty ones. She sat next to me and in a faintly aristocratic accent introduced herself as Elizabeth Paley. I ignored her resentfully, but she spoke on regardless.

'When I was seventy-nine, I went to New Zealand, yes, I flew in the air for twenty-four hours, I stayed in different motels for six months, spent every last penny I owned; I saw every part of that country, and its beauty is incomparable. The lakes . . . the secret caves . . . birds . . . flowers – plants that grow into flowering trees . . . sunsets . . . the scale of it all, breathtaking. Now that was the country I should have lived in, not here. I've never seen such good times, now I never shall again . . .' Perhaps Elizabeth Paley never even went there, just wandered from café to pub, telling her poor imaginings of what her adventures might have been. Maybe, I think, like her, I'll only understand my desires when it's too late.

The Spirit of Adventure: that was what I felt when I first arrived in my Battersea flat, potential buzzing faintly in the new-painted rooms and the lively London streets like the crackling you can hear beneath pylons in a quiet empty field. Why not? I thought in the Spirit of Adventure, when Steve needed a couch to sleep on for a few weeks: I liked him. He had written a column on the literacy project, helped in getting a grant. I admired, even coveted, his articulateness; his politics were unassailable, and no one could, I thought, have called him a hypocrite. Even now. He brought me explanations: why it had been difficult for me to escape from Trent Street, from typing, from the expected marriage and becoming like my mother; why my father's dogged union politics never seemed to get anywhere; why I felt so mixed up for hating where I'd come from while wanting to defend it: the tasteless food and tasteless furniture that had nourished me but seemed then, as he spoke, a badge of deprivation, the trappings of a system of self-perpetuating injustice so huge and horribly

11

efficient that one person could only partially be aware of its iniquities. He's taught me, it's true, how to put a name to some of the forces that hampered me. He's also indicated, somehow, that there is hope: if only there were more like him, people think. St George before the dragon Capital. I've tried to be like him, not with great success.

In a black jacket he arrived with books and typewriter, few other possessions, and I remember thinking, all these dedicated types are like puritans, probably all come from religious families where faith and duty push life daily by infinitesimal inches towards its ultimate solution, where even accidental superfluity is a sin of excess and daily bread would turn dry in your mouth if you had not earned or prayed for it. But the dark clothes hung carelessly on a thin body sent other messages too; they hinted at not wanting to be seen at night, at the pulling of fuses and long nights running down twisting unlit alleys, leather would slow down the blade of a knife at least a little, would not split, would let nothing in on a rainy night. The Spirit of Adventure. Somehow it attached itself to Steven Blake.

It's five o'clock, soon it'll be light. I'm not going to Manchester. He'll go without me, of course, as he went alone in the days when I still left daily for school, my mind filling with schemes and plots for slipping grammar into the minds of word-startled classes, a rising morning noise as I walked the early streets. As he did before he met me. It's only me who has changed what I do. Has my life, I wonder, been so poor that it had nothing to offer? Haven't I shouted my own merits, the treasures of emerging thoughts and transformed memory, as loud as I should have? How have I slipped into something so abject as to become a room someone else lived in? How has he escaped reciprocating? Questions like that bounce off Steven Blake like petty blows from a clenched wall of muscle. He's all zipped up tight in permanence. A consistency grows to his skin with time; with every year his work makes him more like himself

– and still it is true, if only there were more people like him, the world might be a little different.

It is important to change, I think, staring into the lightbulb. Philosophers have written about 'becoming', the continuous imminence of the all-important next-thing-to-happen, daily transformation-of-the-essence-of-being. But they should have minced their words even finer, there are as many ways of 'becoming' as there are of being, and each change brings with it others, consequences that spoil the reckoning page. Halfway along the tendril that circles so perfectly towards its goal, the spirals change direction to balance out the tension: a tendril is not a corkscrew. I no longer miss him, but miss his absence. His closeness is not a comfort but an intrusion. My help is stolen not given; besides, there is little left to offer . . .

'I'll make you an offer,' he said after I got the sack. 'Don't bother looking for another job. I've got more work than I can do on my own . . .'

And all of it important: to refuse would have been cowardice. The Spirit of Enforced Adventure. And I have to admit that, looking at my teaching books – now relegated to the dust-clogged upper shelves – they do not inspire me with a desire to return. That would have been a good beginning, an easy thing to do. But I need time to think. Pick up the pieces, people say, but where are they? Most of my life has been his for so long, an accompaniment that'll feel dull without the theme he's provided.

It was a week after I'd been dismissed that he made that 'offer', refusing all comment until the storm had died down, my private misery worn itself out. Good timing; and he's had a bargain. He's made me drop, he's jiggled and tugged until I dropped without fuss into his waiting hands. This thought is an unpleasant physical shock, like the feeling of falling downstairs that comes at the beginning of anxious sleep.

Very slowly a countertwist has grown in my body, a backwards drag to pleasure, a resistance that's made me cry out and clench my teeth against the power of my own climax; back arched like a dam against the changes he made happen. It grew until it was strong enough to stop the momentum, to stop me falling in his hand that way as well. I haven't made love with him more than once or twice this last year. My problem not his, he said. And, on the sofa, while he sleeps in the bed I ordered him out of, feeling my body dead except for the sensation of coldness, I press my feet into my buttocks in a vain attempt to warm them. I feel still and separate as a granite egg and I grieve for the body I seem to have lost, but also I wonder at its intelligence, for it seems to have known the way things were before the rest of me realised. I wonder about the desire I used to feel for Steve: looked at mechanically, it was a redistribution of blood when certain parts of my body were touched, and I don't know whether the blood rushed to receive pleasure or redistribute pain, nor if the pulse of my orgasm was the rhythm of satisfied desire, or the clutching spasm of panic and defeat.

I pull up the hearthrug, shaking it ineffectually. When I close my eyes I see a screen of red, intermittently obscured by dark blotches inching across.

'We've got to get the train in half an hour.' He's pulled the curtains and stands, a black silhouette in front of me. He's packed, he says, for both of us. There's a faint smell of coffee saying this is the morning. Life goes on, the Conference is important. I blink and turn away from the light. When the doorbell rang and interrupted their raised voices my parents would exchange glances and stretch a skin of cordiality over their quarrel, just strong enough to hold until the visitor could be ushered out. In just the same way hostilities slip from Steve between the table and the bed –

'I'm not coming,' I say. 'Didn't I make it clear?' The hearthrug has deposited its bits in the crevices of my body, but its stiff hessian backing and matted fur seem thick as a wall and leave only my head exposed. Protected, I have the courage for sarcasm, a tactic he particularly despises from me.

I return his glare, unable to prevent a stupid smile stretching my lips: an idiot grin cut off at the neck by the hearthrug. Seeing myself as he must see me is all too easy and imparts a hall of mirrors hysteria.

'You're behaving like a two year-old,' he says, walking to the door.

'I mean what I said!' I shout at the door.

'Get out!'

2

Sally said that my throwing Steve out put her in a difficult position as Steve and Max, the man she lived with, were friends and because she herself sometimes worked with Steve. She was then a press officer for the council's minorities' rights group. Steve, she said (and there was accusation in her voice), had been in a very bad way when he arrived late (he was never usually late) at the Manchester conference.

Sally's betrayals have always shocked me. I reminded myself carefully that, on the other hand, her equally unexpected kindness could delight and wipe away past resentment. These alternations had constituted our relationship since primary school days, when we quarrelled each afternoon and made up each morning. Once she had begged, borrowed or stolen the money for my train ticket to a job interview in Edinburgh, even though she thought the job sounded like a waste of time. I didn't get it anyway. Sally declared she disliked obligations, expectations and demands, and sniffed out even the tiniest one before it was ever a sparkle in the eye. I wanted her to agree with me about Steve, even if only out of uninformed loyalty: fatal. The effort required to seem not to care was numbing. I stared into my glass of wine as if hoping the right things to say would write themselves in its murky glow. I noticed Sally was staring into hers as well. All my life I'd known

Sally, and like a fool I'd not expected us to feel strangers this way again.

'I felt pretty bad myself,' I said feebly. You can't command loyalty I assured myself (they were Sally's words), and particularly not from Sally, whose life seemed to drag helter-skelter after its own tail, the next most important thing in the world always around a corner just out of sight. No time for pause between one action and the next, and no time to waste tidying up the breaks between one passion and the next.

I knew she respected Steve, and so perhaps couldn't afford to see him as a man who might slap a woman in the middle of an argument about why she never wanted to make love to him any more. Dry comfort. I swallowed my wine as if it were beer.

'Yes, but what I'm saying, Cath, is that my reactions are different from how they would be if I only knew one side of the story.'

But you haven't let me tell my side, I thought, and said, on purpose, to insult her vaunted independence of opinion.

'Because of what Max thinks?'

Sally made a sour face.

'Of course not. I'm just warning you, you can't expect me to join in if you feel like doing a character assassination.'

'I wasn't suggesting it.'

One of the reasons I like her is because she's so forthright. Or is it simply that you put up with it so as not to lose a friend? A feeling of my own superfluousness in the lives of people I knew threatened to overwhelm me. My lifelong if intermittent friend, and yet Steve, on the strength of a handful of shared opinions, had a place in her life at least equal, it seemed, to mine. Who amongst the campaign and committee members who had constituted my acquaintance for the last few years would notice if I disappeared unless it adversely affected Steve's timekeeping? It struck me properly for the first time that in throwing Steve out I had scattered everything away, and if I didn't miss him, I might certainly feel lonely enough to imagine that I did. At that moment I decided I would see no one, no one that was, except Sally, who had known me and Steve as a pair.

'Hey Cath,' Sally put down her wine and grasped my arm across the table, 'don't go all monkey faced on me. I was just explaining. Look, I'll get a whole bottle of wine instead of these silly thimblefuls, shall I? Pay day yesterday. Look, it's just a difference of opinion like any other: we've had enough of those over the years, haven't we?'

Weak and babylike I felt, and ready for any kind of second best. I stared at Sally's face: older and more lined than it should have been, large-pored from smoky meetings in small rooms, eyes a bit off-colour from the regular sipping of blood-red wine, cheeks muscular from always having the last word. She wore a dark leather jacket like Steve's, except that it was looser and trimmed with fur. Sally, whose hands cut the air like knives or stroked it like a lover as she spoke. There was a hoarse quality to her voice which made it all the more touching when, as now, it was sanded down a little for tenderness or persuasion.

'OK Sal,' I said, 'but I wasn't going to –'

'I'm just probably not the best person to talk about it with.'

'No . . .'

The glasses were properly filled this time.

'Nice and warm in here, isn't it?'

Like a womb. We can't talk about the awkward present: let's go back in time, let's play 'do you remember?'

'Do you remember, it must be fifteen years ago, when –'

Sharing the last piece of chocolate, snow, no gloves, stuck halfway down the MI –

Snap!

Sally decides to give up school and run away from home to live in Ireland where she's sure her real roots will be. Her face, unlined as yet and strangely slack, is full of hopes

18

(later I was never quite sure if they had been fulfilled or not), her eyes fixed on a green country seen through sea mist, or clear spread as a map from above. Me taking the day off school to see her to the airport, clutching a gift of three pounds saved and stolen, my face molten, drooping, 'I'll write' (shan't see her again) –

Snap!

Three years and two letters later, Sally on the bedsit doorstep, leaves of an enormous plant spreading like an umbrella, big-tooth smile, thinner:
'I'm back –'

Snap! Cheers!

Her accent gone in a fortnight, her money gone in a week, but no matter, she always falls on her feet. Sally and me arm in arm, little dark circles of mouths shouting – shouting together: Stop Racism, shouting Free Ireland, shouting Equal-Opportunities-At-Work, shouting Abortion on Demand –

Snap!

Birthday in the Lake District, New Year on Sally's three-week carrot wine –

Snap!

Yes, we agreed, we always meet up in the end, think the same things by different roads. We're allies, and we don't forget where we came from.
Shake on it, cheers! Snap!
As the memory-drug did its work I felt the hurt thawing: it was partly my fault anyway, I thought: I'd pulled out of the life we'd shared, I'd left Sally on her own. Small wonder, then, that loyalty had shifted, for Sally would have to make adjustments to balance her world, to make it satisfying.
'Do you remember,' Sally was saying, 'the row we had when I told you you should come to the USSR with me?'

'And that time you told me you were going to *try* to get arrested?'

'When you told me I'd be married and returned to the faith by the time I was thirty? Please note, I'm not, you were wrong!'

'When you called me a do-gooder?' The bottle was nearly done.

'You're a bit of a pedant, Cath,' said Sally. 'You've gulped down too much education.'

'You're a sloppy thinker, a thrower-out of babies in the bathwater!'

'But you are clever, I'll admit that,' replied Sally suddenly smooth.

'Patient too.'

Oh yes, it's warm in here, the air's so lazy the smoke hardly moves.

'Patience isn't always a good thing . . . You're braver than I am, always on the move. Impulsive, adventurous. The wine's nearly gone, Sal . . . Sal, you smoke too much.'

'I need to: three deadlines at once, a dozen meetings, a power cut, no sleep for a week: I thrive on it. But take away the ciggies and I'm a gibbering wreck. I need the adrenalin, see? You're more of a cold fish.'

She has a way of making insults friendly; on the other hand, her compliments often made me feel an uneasy need to justify myself.

'I like to keep a grip on things, or I just get lost in the muddle. For instance that community development committee you made me come to –'

'I've been to it this afternoon,' Sally laughed. 'That's why I'm in such a good mood now.'

'All those arguments and little battles going on at the same time, like cat's cradle round and round and inside out for ever, no one coming out with what they really mean: in the end it just seemed senseless.'

'That's what "grass-roots" politics is like you know,

messy: you have to pick your way through the shit.'

'I do know – but then people seem to talk for the sake of it, and –'

'That's true! I do myself sometimes,' she said, opening her eyes wide and trying to stare at her nose, 'it's to drown those mad, mad voices in my head!': letting me off the argument because she'd hurt me earlier. We laughed together for a few seconds, lazy half-gone chuckles and then silence. Sal blew a smoke ring that hung between us, a bent frame around her head, slowly dissolving.

Outside, the smoke from a new cigarette was swallowed instantly by a voracious wind that whipped around corners and into our eyes.

'The parting of the ways,' said Sal, on the corner by the police station. Both of us were folded up with the unseasonable cold, my head hurdy-gurdy inside.

'I think I'm too tired for coffee,' she said, and I was relieved and annoyed at the same time; looked back at the receding glow of her cigarette and felt as I had done all those years ago at the airport, or worse. A sudden sense of the rushing away of time and my life caught me at the throat, I could almost hear it too: an onwards swishing night-whirr of motorway traffic on the road. Steve had been gone a week.

The next day I signed up for voluntary teaching at the adult literacy project, which I had abandoned in favour of Steve's larger causes. Most of the original lot were still there, Dick and Tim and Anne, as well as a new woman called Kim, much younger than the rest of us. These were people who had never known me as Steve's secretary, and there was plenty to keep me busy.

'Your blood circulation won't stop if you sit down for a moment, you know,' Dick remarked, and I laughed, feeling proud of my returning stamina. However, I slept badly. Steve had left me in limbo, the argument's finality unacknowledged. He had simply not returned with the others from Manchester, he hadn't collected anything. He still had a key. Returning as late as possible each evening, I examined the flat for signs that Steve had called with an attention that, despite my seeming enthusiasm, I had not been able to generate in response to the dramas and crises of my work. I couldn't be sure of the place or myself, couldn't believe he had really obeyed my anger, until the last traces of him were gone.

'Are you straightened out yet?' my mother Sara asked me on the phone, the monthly long-distance call strictly limited for reasons of economy to seven minutes.

'If he wanted his things he'd have taken them with him.'

She had never met Steve, and was eager to remove the superfluous presence from our letters and telephone calls.

'If you're taking up that teaching again, you'll want the space for your papers and that, won't you? . . . .'

She thought her daughter was being characteristically feeble minded. If it were her, she would just put everything to one side and leave it by the dustbin.

But I couldn't. Had I been able to overcome my scruples about other people's things, implanted in me by that same mother who now encouraged me to flout them, the real problem was of course not the things themselves but the knowledge that at some point he would come, either to collect them or to reproach me for having disposed of them.

After a fortnight or so, the sight of his socks and underwear and tee shirts all mixed up with mine began to irk me unendurably and so I started packing them into bags, black trousers baggy at the knees and unstretched at the waist, a few tired-looking jumpers. Steve possessed little but the tools of his trade. Even his books were much of a muchness, business not pleasure. His cooking equipment was almost non-existent: I hunted out the aluminium saucepan, knife and mug he had brought with him. Probably he would despise me for such rigour in the returning of possessions, I thought: either he would not be so petty as to want his things back at all, or else he would be of the opinion that the contents of the flat ought to be split more equally since I had more. I added some plates of mine and the electric kettle.

The packing irritated me; I was left doing his business again, a kind of punishment for not having got my house in order when I first felt unhappy. Steve was, I imagined, on a course through life that was describable and obvious. He effortlessly acquired what help he wanted and carried it only for as long as he needed it. But I was surrounded by a welter of props, needs, duties – memories, sentimentality, all expressed literally in a clutter of photographs, bundles of notes and letters, jars with sea shells in them, poems. I had lashed out blind, shouting and weeping with frustration; he, with his eyes calm and far set, negotiated life's obstacles economically, cutting neat as a carpenter, adjusting, finishing, beginning anew. I was fiddling with socks while time ran on.

I started on his books with a feeling of apprehension that soon turned into defiance. They'd frightened me with their long words and endless sentences that I'd learned to manipulate but that left me feeling strained with the effort of trying to latch them on to something concrete. Despite my sweaty labours they still looked clean and new . . . Theories. I thumped them noisily into boxes, remembering the day I had finished the school readers as a child: 'goodbye Janet, goodbye John.' Slam.

Shortly after this I met Sally and a man I didn't know on my doorstep, each carrying a box of books.

'We've come to help Steve move his things,' she said, 'this is the last. Though I don't know why he wants it all, he's supposed to be going to the USA, did you know?'

In a council van parked across the road I could just see Steve, Max at the wheel and a red-haired man I remembered meeting at an anti-imperialist rally. Sally looked uneasy, shifting the weight of the box and glancing repeatedly at the van.

'This is Pete Davies, from Prison Reform'.

I nodded without meeting his eye, feeling acutely hostile. What business had he going into my home, what did he know about it all –

'We must go for a drink or something, a film,' I said, willing Sally to put the box down. 'It's been almost a month since I've seen you, how's everything?'

I wanted to tell her about my own everything: about Paul and Mrs Anderson my one-to-one-pupils, about the thoughts and moods just beginning to brighten the life inside.

'Least said about "everything" the better,' snapped Sally, 'Max is mucking me around. Look, these books are really heavy –'

Put them down, put them down.

'And it's not the best of times, I'm late for a meeting . . .'

She walked down the path behind the man, her shoulders pulled forwards by the weight of the box so that her usually straight-edged body seemed disconcertingly pear shaped.

'Key!' I shouted after her, but she didn't seem to hear. I was angry and jealous that she saw Steve as the injured party, the one she had to help. I noticed the downstairs curtains twitching: Mrs Brown. From upstairs I heard the van doors slamming shut and a few minutes later the engine faded into the distance and then there was a silence that took me back years, to the time before I had known Steve, when the door closed after work and sometimes the stillness and the silence ached so that I would have to put the radio on and ease myself slowly into being on my own.

So he was going to the USA. Like a spider in a big sticky web that I had made for myself, I sat for a while, gloomily tense, feeling the flat vibrate with each move I made. I stirred myself, tidied up a bit and tried to think, as I had promised I would, of ways to raise money for next year's literacy project. My ideas seemed dull, but it was a start.

Living for myself was a skill that had atrophied and it was like picking up a violin after years without practice, all hesitations and horrible noises that wouldn't yet match the music in my head.

3

I sat on the edge of the bath while it ran, every cell of me longing for the water. A muscle in the back of my thigh jerked. I could not look at my body or touch it. The warm water would melt my muscles and wash away the sweat-smell, but would also steam open the sealed envelope of memory; already I must think, think what to do. I turned off the water – sudden silence – and stood feeling the warm steam on my skin. No, this was not the right thing to do. No, I must phone the police.

Far away in another world, a bell rang. Someone would come and help. This was the right thing to do. The voice I spoke with broke like a child's toy. A man said sit tight, we're coming. I knew I must keep calm and remember what had happened, not disturb anything. Evidence, scene of the crime. Crime? Other crimes were not crimes, shop-lifting, fraud, double yellow lines, almost a joke: a crime was what had just happened, to me. He had done it to me.

I could feel it happening again, happening round me like plaster setting. I picked up the phone again, dialled a number to tie myself to the world, but the line swung in the air – side to side, side to side like a pendulum and no one to catch it, no one there. I let go. Whose number had it been anyway? Sally's of course, but I knew she would not be there; I left her at Jean's party: no phone, no phone. Keep calm. From out there they could come and help me, they would, they would – The unused bath water grew cold as I waited.

'Now, let's go back to the beginning again.'

Again! –

'Your statement says: "I saw a man standing in the porch and I was startled. He said, hello Cathy, and I knew it was Steven Blake. I don't know Steven Blake's present address. He asked if he could come in for a cup of tea, and I said yes." Now, Miss, I do believe that "come for a cup of coffee"'

Tea, I said tea –

'late at night is a common enough way of giving someone an invitation to bed, and really no woman could reach the age of, what is it, thirty? without learning that you don't ask a man in for "coffee" at midnight without – '

I didn't ask him, I said, OK, I –

'expecting him to make some kind of . . . advances . . .'

Expect? expect anything – surprised advances anyway no didn't –

The man's lower lip stuck out shiny and swollen, almost purple. Large expanses of whisker-pitted cheek, eyes that hung down sullen, unblinking disbelief. She felt tears gathering and willed them not to flow.

'It wasn't like that, that's all wrong,' was all she could think to say.

It wasn't, it wasn't –

'Then tell me how it was again. Why did you let this man in in the middle of the night?'

No I didn't did I did – let did –

'I hadn't seen him for a year – I was surprised – but relieved that it wasn't a stranger – confused. We parted on bad terms –

What words these? –

'Not friends, I thought maybe –'

Watch it! –

'after all this time there was no reason, we couldn't just

27

talk. I was surprised, I told myself it was silly to say no.'

Did I what did I tell me did I think –

'You let him in? A man who lived with you, a man with whom you had had long-standing conjugal relations? You can't expect me to believe it didn't occur to you that he might stay!'

His face now a caricature of incomprehension.

'It was late at night. Does he have a car?'

'I don't know.'

'When, as far as you knew, at 12.35 he couldn't get home: now let's be frank, it does look very much as if you expected him to stay the night.'

'No!'

'Are you sure you don't know his address?'

No, yes –

'Yes.'

'You knew nothing of his whereabouts?'

'I said I thought he had gone to the USA, but I hadn't seen him for months. I didn't try to find out bec –'

'What do you mean when you say the relationship "went wrong"?'

Why all this far back can't keep track –

'He had affairs? You had another man? He threw you out?'

Stop this. Must say what happened, losing it –

'I don't see why you're asking. What happened is –'

'Everything will be easier if you cooperate; you are making serious allegations, Miss Sheldon, they need substantiating. If I got a fiver for every girl that came in here this time on a Saturday night –'

Saturday. Where was I?

'Well. Did he go or did you go?'

'I asked him to go and then he did.'

'You're sure it wasn't the other way round? Or that you didn't have second thoughts?'

Just answer. Yes, no. It will finish –

'Of course I'm sure.'

There was a pause of several heartbeats long, maybe it was over.

'Now . . . you've been on your own since Steven Blake left you, a year ago, Pretty young woman like yourself; no reason to be alone. Now if he left you causing all that upset and so on, now might it not occur to a woman in that position, if an opportunity presented itself, to get your own back?'

1, 2, 3, 4, 5 –

'He only left because I told him to go.'

And it wouldn't have anyway –

The pace of the questioning suddenly decelerated, as if he was having difficulty understanding answers or in thinking what to ask next. In the pauses between exchanges she became aware that she was too hot in her coat sitting by the radiator with its burnt paint smell mixing with the sweat still on her. If only she could see a doctor, then she could wash, it could all be over. Her throat was so dry it seemed to stick and rub as she swallowed.

'So, if you "threw him out",' he was saying, 'why did you?'

I can't explain –

She couldn't say that, yet how could she answer such a question. It was all too complicated; if she knew why he was asking then she might understand what – but the silence was swelling and splitting in her ears, it was condemning her somehow but she didn't know why.

'We had arguments,' she said,

I sound so stupid –

And her face was wet; whether it was confusion or what had happened or because she couldn't quite think why she'd asked him to leave, just that she wanted it so much but there was something wrong with her if she couldn't say why and she was sodden with sweat, wet and embarrassed like a bad child discovered, but she wasn't and she hadn't done anything. She sniffed, there were no tissues in her pockets.

'All right, Miss Sheldon, would you like a cup of tea?' he said, as if the sniff had been a cue, 'get us a couple of teas!' 'It's not the Ritz here but you can't say the tea's not good.'

They waited for it in silence. He read and re-read the notes he had taken, and the typed statement. He was one of the largest men she had ever seen. She shut her eyes.

'Shouldn't I see a doctor?' Cath asked clearly, her voice almost recognisable. Her strength and her memory came in waves, alternating exhaustion and second wind. He looked up from the notes.

'There's no point in you going to forensic until we're sure what's happened. Was your sex life with Steven Blake satisfactory?'

> Wasn't. But was once. Or is that makebelieve? Stiffened when he touched me. Perhaps you should see a psychiatrist? he said, contemptuous.

'I don't see what that's got to do with it.'

'Did he hit you?'

> I did it, I won –

'Once, but he wasn't violent.'

'Miss Sheldon, you lived with Steven Blake for four years, then decided for no apparent reason that you were incompatible. It looks to me as if you didn't know your mind. Are you sure Mr Blake couldn't be forgiven for getting the wrong idea?'

It was a statement rather than a question.

> Sit tight. Don't think –

There was no thread to what he said. In the time it took for her to draw breath and consider what he'd said, he leapt from a few hours back to a whole year ago, from 'What time do you think' to 'You say in your statement that Mr Blake said' – he shuffled the papers and continued in the tone of a teacher reading aloud silly messages confiscated in class –

' "I'm not going until I've come." '

A voice that poured scorn on the muddledness of truth,

of other people's lives.

'Did he?'

> Wet sharp smell gathering all the rest
> together in its bitterness –

'Yes.'

'Did you "come"?'

'Of course not.'

> As if . . . but was it possible? Did –

'You said penetration took place both in the sitting room and in the bedroom: are you sure?'

'Tell me again what you said on the doorstep when Mr Blake . . .'

'What was he wearing?'

'Would you say you were glad to see him?'

'How long did you wait before . . .'

> Must remember what I said.
> Must remember what I said.

This one was more senior than the first. A slim man with a quiet voice and an unremitting stare. He spoke quickly, steadily throwing new questions down before she had time to unravel the implications of the last. She was so tired and this office was more gently lit, its walls a mellow golden colour rather than white, she might have slept had it not been for the unremitting din of questions, like piecework on a production line, you had to deal with each one as it arrived, or you would be swamped by the pile, nothing you did could stop them coming.

'And at this point too was there penetration?'

'Yes.'

> I told you before, you wrote it down.

'Hm.'

A break in the rhythm: perhaps the end, perhaps there were no more to be asked and answered, the bell would ring and all together everyone could race out of the gates, some on bicycles, some on foot, some in buses, all hurrying away from that awful dripping tap of work.

'You waited a long time before you called us, didn't you?'
>Did I? A calm like sudden snow freezing
>the limbs useless, not even waiting just
>accidentally there. The first person gather-
>ing strength to peer cautiously though
>bullet-shattered shutters after the shoot-up.
>Ominous silence of things hiding in the
>destroyed world outside –

'Did I?'

'What were you doing?'
>– seeing everything in the room, even with
>eyes shut against the light. Green for red,
>light for dark: and patterns too, when I
>tightened the muscles in my eyelids. Some
>cars went by –

'I lay on the bed.'

'What made you get up?'
>– I could tell by the shrinking of my skin
>that I was cold. Opened my eyes and saw
>my feet, still not daring to move –

'I think I was cold.'
>For as long as possible I would be a
>one-eyed blinking camera bolted immobile
>above what had happened, all-seeing but
>incapable of deduction, action, judgement,
>feeling – response of any kind. I would
>swallow these moments of time, my blank-
>ness would absorb them, the room was
>empty but I was emptier. My emptiness
>would expand to encapsulate and preserve
>this beach of time after the catastrophe and
>before its consequences. Later the tidying,
>weeping, the gestures. But now, I would
>never move again –

'For how long?'

'I don't know.'
>– all I know is the bitter smell that comes

from my own sweat, and semen dried stiff
on my skin. I think so he did come then. A
constricted, pungent sweat coming not
from movement but from not being able to
move. From fear. Wetness that has oozed
through my skin. As a child, burying my
nose in the crook of my arm, the smell of
sweat was good, later, aphrodisiac. Nausea.
The smell an overpowering breath, invisible but strong as the wind, its source is
what has happened and one day I will have
to follow it back, I will have to remember it
properly –

'Try to remember exactly what you said to Mr Blake.'

'I can't.' She met his eyes. Was he curious? Angry?
Bored? It was impossible to tell.

'Why didn't you try to get help from the Browns
downstairs?'

'I didn't think of it.'

Bitter bleached face of Mrs Brown peering
out through the thin slit of her chained
door. No dear, we don't involve ourselves
in things like that, I'm sure the government knows best and would you ask your –
looks at Cath's unwedded fingers – husband
to be careful shutting the outer door when
he comes in late. Mr Brown planted
stiff-shouldered by the gate craning his
head to read the stickers on the upstairs
window, shaking his head and going in to
tell –

'I've hardly ever spoken to them.'

'Don't get on with the neighbours, eh?' He looked at his
watch. Bored. 'You can go through there and wait for the
doctor.'

The doctor was coming. It would all be over. She dabbed
at the damp tea stain on her once-white sweater with a

piece of toilet paper. She must not get hysterical. She must think of something calm. Waves beating on an empty beach. Clouds. Count sheep, go to sleep. White, just look at the whiteness of the wall thinking white, white.

You can't cry in here. Get home, have a bath, have a cry. Think of something nice. Swimming. Strawberries. Ironed sheets. Water. What time is it? Morning by now. Soon be over.

Don't count on it. Think of something else, being happy, remember all the details. Dancing barefoot on the carpet, drunk with goodbyes, spilling wine, Jean is saying goodbye by opening her doors to everyone before she leaves and beyond the sadness there's a great joy because things are moving. People have kicked off their shoes and some will go home and some will not.

I shouldn't have gone home, then it
wouldn't have happened.

Seeing Sal, thinking what the hell, what's there to lose, it feels really sad to lose a friend who's still in the same town as well. Sitting next to Sal, so hostile these last months but melted now with gin, her smile was real. 'Makes you think,' she said, 'to mind the ones that stay,' and everyone dancing, the ones that stay, the ones about to go.

And Jean, she had thought, will someday write or even return. Sally will slowly thaw and forgive herself for being hard, things right themselves in the end and there is a thread through my life and friends that stay. A power that slowly digests the hard lumps of grief till finally they are tame and I can drink them like this wine. Yes, I have got it back, the Spirit of Adventure. At least it is all mine, my life I can feel it in me. And she had been glad to walk home alone, feeling it there.

Quite deliberately, though not without effort, Cath stopped the memory there, before the walk home had even started. But then she was back in the immediate past: there was nowhere safe to go.

'Did you come?': the big policeman had asked her that. It

34

was a nonsensical question. Why had he asked did you come? You couldn't come unless it was making love, unless you wanted to, sometimes not even then; you couldn't, surely, come being raped? Couldn't come for a year before they split up: premonition. Like a something inside her that bit against it, though the rest of her had wished she could and she'd shed tears at the sullen intractability of whatever it was, the resistance inside. That was because things went right, somewhere your body knew, even if you kidded yourself. So how could you come when – did he think there was a button, ring three times and she comes running- . . . surely everyone knew now?

But he had come. Maybe it wasn't true then that things had to be right; how could he come when there was hatred, resistance. Cunt stiff, dry with hatred, get out get out, you're not wanted. I hate you: how could he come? But he had. She couldn't have, no, different for men. But how did he feel desire in the face of someone screaming no no, someone shrinking away – even someone indifferent? 'I'm not going till I come', 'I think you owe me something': from that it came, not out of wanting to touch. How did it happen? It was sick. It made a mockery of everything. Men and women different, women never.

Was it a trick question then, why had he asked? To find out if she knew the meaning of the word; or, if she'd said yes, would that have made it not rape: you said no but you must have really wanted to because you came?

Suddenly her confusion solidified into a thought that screamed: just suppose if you came; it would be a million times worse. There would be nothing left if that biting back was beaten down. You would be flattened, there would be no part of you left except a memory that you had not wanted, no proof to yourself that the unbelievable had happened, just a memory and half of you despising the rest – capitulation, betrayal, oh you would never get up off the floor after that. You would die.

There were voices the other side of the door!

'Quite sensible, a teacher – or was. Not the hysterical type,' someone said. A white-coated man and woman walked in, saying nothing. It must be the doctor. The woman stood by the door, the man sat down at the desk and began to read something typed on thin paper that curled over so she could just make it out upside down:

'I was walking home from a small party after midnight. I was alone. I saw.'

The doctor tossed the sheets of paper aside and yawned. After such a long period alone with her thoughts, it was startling when he spoke.

'What is your present occupation, Miss . . .'

The smell on her, picking at her memory. If I could wash I could forget. Sweat. No more where it came from, cold now. Body 90 per cent liquid. Smell of linden trees known to make women faint in summer. Think of trees, the one you know well enough to see in your mind's eye.

'I teach adult literacy on a voluntary basis.'

'How do you support yourself? Social Security? Have you told the DHSS about this voluntary work?'

'Are you the doctor?'

Oak, tannin, mulch of leaves and acorns. Pigs, truffles, hardwood, a deciduous tree. Try to see it . . .

'You have never been married?'

Mountain ash. Patterns of red berries and neat leaves in rows like a patchwork quilt. Silver stem, smattering of berries on the ground, tree shivering with birds come for the fruit.

'No.'

'Generally speaking, are you afraid of men?'

Elm? Dutch elm. Can't see it. Ash tall . . . can't see it.

'Generally speaking, are you afraid of men?'

Poplar, lines in a painting, paint-brush shaped dwindling away to the join of land and sky: perspective trees, thick trunks, deceptive grace branches, stiff point up against the fall of gravity, no shadow, no shade.

'I don't know.'

36

Pine, well-defined patches on distant hills planted even and thick like a rug cast over the soil. Patterns of peaks where the light catches, below, dark and dense as hair. Scots pine, Douglas fir, Christmas tree . . .

'Would you say you were, as a woman, sexually experienced?'

Needles on the floor, smelling of burning and special-baths smell.

'What do you mean? I don't know.'

Writing notes on a small pad of paper as he repeats the question.

'Are you the doctor?' she asks for the second time, and again he does not answer. He has square clumsy hands, not like a doctor's at all. Thick grey hair short as soldiers'. Pale face composed of neat slabs, no signs of stress, no hurrying, no queue of patients waiting outside. Is he a doctor? I must see a doctor, I think I'm bleeding. Is this the doctor that looks at corpses? Pathologist? Forensic? What's the difference?

The woman in white putting plastic on the trestle table under the light. Putting Cath's clothes in a plastic bag. Unsealing disposable plastic gloves for the doctor, they cling to his hands like a surplus skin, they transmit the cold of his hands.

Relax!

Turn over!

Commanding tones, and she has gooseflesh. Scraping on her skin, under her nails, cheek sticking to the plastic, smell and dampness of that sweat, I will wash it away and never let myself smell of sweat again, smell rising like panic, but steady as steam from a boiling pan. I must open my eyes. Feeling in her hair like looking for nits at school, stainless steel comb and smell of opaque disinfectant in a bowl. He has touched her all over except the genitals, leaving there till last. The avoided place grows in significance and shrinks away from the light and from his eye, for surely he will look. That's where it hurt. That's where defined the crime.

'When did you last have sexual intercourse?'

She didn't want to say. She couldn't see why they had to know. Until she knew their reason, she couldn't think what to say. Abnormal perhaps to go so long. What business anyway? Could say she couldn't remember, but then –

'Not recently.'

Could he tell? He made her feel crazy. Important not to seem crazy. Mustn't scream, musn't push the speculum away. It hurt. Mustn't scream. Think of . . .

'When did you stop taking the pill?'

His hand inside her hurt.

'Could you have been pregnant before the alleged incident?'

One hand was still inside her, with the other he ticked off the answers on a form. It happens so often they've printed forms for it. The feeling of metal made her want to scream. It made her think it was a gun – there – where did it come from? But there was silence but for the rustling of cellophane gloves, the scratch of his pen.

'Periods normal?'

Who ever knows if they're normal? The nurse stepped forward with little jars and foil-sealed spatulas.

'Is it painful there?'

She shut her eyes.

'Yes'.

At the family planning clinic where they took cervical smears once in a while the nurses always used to say 'lovely' when they looked inside her. She wondered, lovely in what way? Healthy or beautiful? Was lovely small or was lovely big, lovely for her or lovely for him: it was a silly thing really but nice to be told she was lovely even if it was only to distract you from having the metal eye inside.

'Where did he hold you?'

There were, he told the nurse, bruises on her shoulders and legs, left breast, arms and thighs and more might come later. She could not look at herself to see if what he said was true. The sheet descended gentle. The nurse took blood and scraped the skin on her thighs. She could smell herself again and felt ashamed. It was sensible, the nurse said in a friendly way, not to have washed or changed her clothes.

In the toilet Cath washed under her arms and dried them with paper. The soap seemed to stick. She began to shake and had to go back into the cubicle to sit down. There was no light in there. There was a sanitary towel and two safety pins at the bottom of the clothes in the bag. When she put it on, she noticed there was blood, a small bright patch, in the pants. The clothes were too loose. She avoided the mirror.

It was the one she had seen first.

'It must be morning now,' she said. At least the smell was diminished.

'We'll go over this statement and then you can go,' he said. 'Now let's get this over with, the sooner it's done, the sooner you can go home.'

She held out her hand.

'No,' he said, 'I have to read it aloud.'

STATEMENT

On Saturday evening the thirteenth of November 1981 I was walking home shortly after midnight after attending a party at 56 Blenheim Gardens. As I walked down the path to the outer front door of the first floor flat number 36A Lower Victoria Road where I have lived for the last seven years, I saw the figure of a man standing by the door. There was no light outside. I screamed. But then I recognised him as Steven Blake with whom I lived as man and wife until July 1981. I saw him subsequently on three occasions, once from a distance when his friends came to collect his belongings, once in September when he let himself into the flat and asked me to start the relationship again, and again later in the same month when he passed the allotments in Hargreave Street and asked me to give him some plums which I refused. On no occasion did I give him any reason to believe I was still attracted to him or had in any way changed my mind. I have lived on my own since he left. I have had no contact nor knowledge of his whereabouts since September 1981, though I had thought he intended to visit the USA. He said, "Hello Cath, I thought I'd drop by and see you. Lucky you came back." I was still shocked to see him but also relieved that it wasn't a stranger. I said, "Have you been there long?" He said, "Aren't you going to invite me in for a cup of tea?" I said "It's a bit late isn't it?" He said "I'm only passing through. Come on, for old times' sake: I might be dead next year." We had parted on bad terms and I was pleased that he seemed relaxed and friendly so I let him in. I said, "OK, but not for long." I made some tea. The flat is on the first floor. The door to it enters into the main room. On the left is a door to the kitchen and the bathroom is at the end of the kitchen: to the right is the door to the bedroom. I was in the kitchen with the door open while I made the tea. And Steven Blake was in the main room which I use as a sitting room. He said "You've changed the rooms back." I did not reply. When I brought the tea in he said "Where've you been tonight?" I said that I had been to Jean's goodbye party and that it had been very enjoyable, particularly because I'd met another friend Sally there, who I'd lost contact with. Steven Blake was acquainted with both these people. I said Jean was flying to New York at 6.30 this morning and asked if that was where he had been. He did not answer. He was sitting in the armchair which is by the window and I sat on some cushions on the floor: between the gas fire and the door to the bedroom. He asked for sugar. When I came back with it he was sitting on one of the cushions. The cushions were nearer the fire so I thought that was why he had moved and I sat near to him on one of the cushions. He asked me if I ever felt lonely. I said no. He said he did. I felt awkward and began to move from the cushion but he caught hold of my shoulder and said "You can't wipe me out, you know." I struggled and said that I had not invited him in just so he could have a go at me and if that was the idea then he had better go. I am not sure of the precise words I used. His hands were still on my shoulders and I was trying to get up as I spoke. He said, "I came because I think you owe me something." He succeeded in pushing me backwards and I realised what was happening and I said "You bastard". I was wearing a loosely gathered woollen shirt, ribbed tights, ankle boots and a mohair jumper. He lay on top of me and pulled my

40

tights and pants down to my ankles. I could not move my legs much. He held my upper arms to the floor above my head with one arm and put his mouth over my mouth. He pushed my legs open and penetrated me. It was very painful. I bit his lip and he withdrew his mouth and I shouted "Stop". He laughed. I was very frightened I thought he was demented. He withdrew his penis and pulled me half up by my arms and through to the bedroom and on to the bed. I was crying. He said, "It would hurt less if you wanted me." I said, "I don't." He penetrated me a second time. He said, "I shan't go until I've come." I began to shake. It was very painful. Then he suddenly pulled himself out of me. He said, "Goodbye Cath," and got up adjusting his clothing as he went to the door. I cannot be exact as to the time I arrived home or as to the time this took place but I estimate it was about half an hour since we had come in. I heard him let himself out. I lay on the bed for some time; perhaps another half hour. I think I was in a state of shock. Then I got up and turned the bath on. Then I realised that I should contact the police so I turned off the bath and phoned the police. I also tried to phone a friend, Sally, but there was no reply. So I put a coat on over my skirt and waited for the police to come.'

The flatness of his voice was hard to listen to and she was relieved when he stopped. The words themselves left her unmoved, though she was to remember the statement almost word for word. There was something about it that didn't belong to her: if not exactly hers, the words were ones she had agreed to use, and the sequence of events was as she had remembered it: it seemed more the record of a distant memory of events than an account of something that had happened only hours ago. As with the things her mother said she had done as a child – the words called forth no images but she accepted that they had been hers. She was glad, in a way, that words could not capture, could not contain what had happened.

'Anything you want to add?' he asked.

'No,' she said, and signed.

4

As Cath walked out of the police station the crackling recording of bells from the Holy Land played twice a week by St Matthew's was just finishing. It must be about 8.30 a.m. She stood for a few seconds at the bottom of the steps, feeling lost in her borrowed clothes: the pale-coloured tights, static-laden skirt and clammy acrylic jumper. Not even the shoes were hers. People were entering the station in a steady stream, some obviously workers and plain-clothes police, others heading for the entrance marked Enquiries. No one else was coming out. Sunday, she thought, I wouldn't normally be up. Only Sunday, and she seemed to have been awake for days. Jean's party had been Saturday, it was less than twelve hours since she had left it, yet it seemed thrust back into the nether regions of the past. By now, Jean would be at the airport, possibly even in the sky, her four rooms of clutter reduced to as many suitcases, her visa stamped, her letters of introduction in plastic wallets, her last pound spent and her future, like herself, hanging in the air.

Walking towards the bus stop she thought, they haven't got him, suppose he's still there? But he wouldn't hang around, would he? He'd be scared – but no, he wouldn't, she realised, he wouldn't expect her to call the police.

Calling the police – what had she done?

She shouldn't have. Against her principles. Which?

Against someone's principles. Might make it all worse: already had. Instant reaction. Obey your instincts. Too late now. She must stop bothering and go home. The longer she left it the harder it would be. When she had the motor-bike accident, they said ride again as soon as you can, or you'll never be able to face it again. She never had. Home. There's nowhere else. She could have a bath and put some of her own clothes on.

There was a key in her pocket but, she discovered as she reached the bus stop, no money. Without pausing, she turned around and walked back to the station, in through the door marked Enquiries. Even so early there was a sizeable queue of people: burgled in the night or lost their bikes, have you found my car, what about the insurance, what are the chances, boys, I saw them running down the street. She would wait her turn with her eyes shut to feel less conspicuous. She would think about what to say when the time came. She was wakeful but with no thoughts. Nothing mattered.

'I'll make you a cup of tea, and you can sit there while I tidy up the other room,' said WPC Ingrams, smiling sympathetically as she pulled off her gloves as-a-lady-does with fingers rather than teeth. Cath nodded: she couldn't think of anything to say. WPC Ingrams brought a pot of tea, milk in a jug and one cup.

'Aren't you having one?'

Why, thank you, I will then,' and she went to the kitchen for a second cup.

'I was frightened he might be hanging around,' Cath said for a second time by way of explanation.

'We'll be keeping an eye on you,' said the woman, ordinary-looking and even quite shy if you looked hard enough at her face, cowering and lost in the massive frame of her uniform. Cath almost expected her to draw back the curtains and point out a plain-clothes man parked across the road. What was she thinking, WPC Ingrams, her eyes flickering around the room? Was she looking as one woman looks to see what another is like from how she keeps her home, or was she looking for other clues, reading the disarray that Cath sat with her back to, checking?

'Live on your own?' she asked casually.

'Yes.'

'How do you find it? Don't you get lonely?'

The tone of these remarks was pitched wrongly, the informality seemed somehow inappropriate, too sudden. She couldn't be sure, but the woman's voice seemed to have changed since they got out of the car, to have lost its crispness, its creases, and to be flattened ever so slightly by something to which she could give no more precise a name than 'an accent'.

'One way and another, I'm very busy,' she answered. WPC Ingrams was probably just making an effort to be friendly – and even if she was going to report what had been said, what of it, it was her job after all. But this was a scene Cath had watched on screens so many times before: the clever cop, the clever crook; it made no difference, they got you chatting and then used it to trip you up . . . it was difficult not to feel paranoid, the script had been written, the roles assigned.

'Do *you* live on *your* own?' she asked in an attempt to forestall further questions. It sounded very odd, like a gambit in the first stages of a conversation between wary five-year-olds introduced hopefully by their parents: does your daddy have a car? I'll tell you if you tell me . . .

'I live at home,' said WPC Ingrams, standing up as she spoke. 'I'll go and sort that other room out for you now, not the sort of thing you'll be feeling like tackling, I should think.' She spoke as if she knew what she was talking about, as if it had happened to her. Professional expertise. But no, it was kind nonetheless.

Following her out of the corner of her eye, Cath caught a glimpse of her bedroom through the door: nothing remarkable – a badly rumpled bed, things on the floor – the

44

policewoman shut the door.

This is my home, Cath thought. I live 'at home' too. She let her eyes wander for the first time around the room, cautiously, as if half expecting some pervasive stain, some subtle but unbearable change to have occurred. The other chair was out of place, that was all. WPC Ingrams had set the cushions to rights as soon as they came in. Now she came out for the laundry bag, going straight to it: she must have noticed it under the sink in the kitchen when she made the tea. 'I live at home' – a stupid thing to say, really. Meaning: I don't live on my own and I'm not married. Obviously this officer, like the others she had seen at the station and the Browns down below, didn't think living on your own was quite the right thing to be doing: either you were up to no good or there was something wrong with you so that you had to. Where you lived couldn't be called home until there was someone else in it too.

But it was home. The sitting room had settled back into its own familiarity since Steve left, and she looked round without anxiety at the clear painted walls and the jungle of plants on the window sill. They needed watering, but she didn't feel able to do it with the policewoman still there, nor to start the bath running. I live at home, I live alone. No one there if anything happens. But then, she thought, if I had always lived alone none of it would have happened anyway. She ran her hand across the old-fashioned pink and grey blanket that covered the chair, too tired to do more than tap lightweight thoughts to and fro and listen to their few, tired, diminishing bounces – but acutely aware of the things that surrounded her: the light coming from behind, the shadows in corners, the just-right height of the chair arms, the carpet at her feet flattened and almost slippery from years of her sitting there reading, with her elbows hooked back on to the low seat of the chair. It was all there.

'I've put clean sheets on and tidied up,' said WPC Ingrams without, it seemed, her accent. 'You won't know the difference; you'll be all right, won't you?'

'I really didn't expect –' Cath felt suddenly embarrassed. She couldn't remember why she had asked, wanted, someone to come back with her anyway. 'Thank you, though.'

'Don't forget to see your doctor. And if you don't mind slipping out of those clothes, I can take them straight back to the station: we don't have that many, and could you sign this for your own clothes?'

She didn't want them, but she wrote her name anyway, startled to realise that her signature wasn't hers: it had lapsed back to before the days when she had made herself learn italics at college; it was all loose and overlapped, messy as the back of embroidery, it might be her mother's, anyone's.

She heard WPC Ingrams's steps on the stairs, receding, then silent, then the faint echo of the Browns' bell downstairs and their door rattling its way grudgingly open.

Her ear pressed to the stubble of the carpet, she could hear voices but not words. What would they, what could they say? Had they heard anything? They would say she spoiled their sleep and now she had spoiled their Sunday. They would say they had seen envelopes from the Social Security and also seen her going out early in the morning . . . not lying, just implying. She hated them. There was silence, and she rushed to the window in time to watch, standing back so as not to be seen, WPC Ingrams climbing into her car, walkie-talkie erupting into a blather of meaningless noises. Downstairs they would be watching too.

The bath was so hot it made her skin pink. The water she had run on Saturday night had still been there, cold and pure and comforting somehow that nothing had changed, not really. The bath salts made the water cloudy and she could not see herself, she didn't want to. Gradually, she could not feel either, slipped down so that her knees were up and her face submerged except for the nose. She imagined the water loosening and shifting the sweat smell from her body, like in an advertisement for washing powder. She listened to the ringing in her head and the rasping rushing sounds made by the smallest of movements and the smallest of particles on the smooth surface of the bath, carried direct to her ears in the currents and ripples of water. She sat up and washed her hair, then scrubbed and soaped herself down to the waist, rubbing hard with the flannel and the back brush. Beneath the lather she glimpsed, when she forgot not to look, dark patches that would not wash off. Lying down again she soaped and soaped again between her legs. The water was scummy, little bits of solidified soap and hairs beached on the sides of the bath moving in lazy oscillations on the dull skin that now sealed her bathwater from the air, moving a little slower than the actual movement of the water, like an audience clapping out of time. Get out before letting out the water, or all the dirt you've washed off will stick to your skin again. Queasy, she waited for the bath to drain, cleaned it thoroughly and started another one. This time just water. She lay in the bath as it filled. She lay with her eyes shut tight.

Go to the laundrette, water the plants, buy some milk, cut a cabbage from the allotment on the way to the shop, or maybe on the way back would be better? Sunday paper? Prepare something for Paul's and Mrs Anderson's lessons on Tuesday, there might not be time tomorrow. Get started on the fundraising letters for the literacy project, the ironing, the kitchen floor, the windows, sink: an unstoppable list spilled and coiled itself in her head; and the proper order to put all the things to do – whether to do the outside things first so as not to be caught when it got cold and dark, but then it would be best to get the paper first and the laundry since they were near, and perhaps some groceries, she couldn't remember whether she had gone shopping Friday and where was Egg the cat? It was still only half past ten.

She dressed hurriedly in loose trousers and a thick jumper. She felt stiff and sore between her legs, stretched and displaced inside, but the bleeding seemed to have stopped. She wanted to hurry: there was so much to get done, yet she was forced to walk carefully down the stairs. I'm glad I've got the upstairs flat, though, she thought. Someone could easily come through the window downstairs. The cat ran up immediately and slithered up the stairs while she followed more slowly, feeling the sequence of the muscles tightening and loosening in her legs, feeling tired. 'I'm sorry,' she said, 'you poor thing', filled with absurdly abundant pity for the animal, almost tearful at its ordeal, 'I'll see what's in the fridge.' The cat ran hysterically around the flat, halting briefly on the higher surfaces to stare about it, returning to investigate her progress with the tin opener. She was being so slow, and the stuff smelled worse than usual.

The laundry bag felt heavy; she couldn't get warm. She felt frightened: was there something the matter with her physically? It would be best to stay in. Time had started to race now, and filling the hours seemed less urgent. Even her fingers seemed to have only a fraction of their strength and it was difficult to keep the watering can steady. The cat's high spirits frayed her nerves, she wished it was a fat lazy cat that lay all day in the warmest spot, composed as a piece of sculpture. The wind outside, she wished that would stop too; she wanted to turn the world off. She sat at her desk and began to tidy it, put rubber bands round stacks of envelopes, threw away some old notes to herself and scrap paper she saved but never used. At the back of the desk she found an old cigar box that her father had given to her as a child, years ago, full of things for school: compass, protractor, thick coloured pencils, sharpener and her first fountain pen. She still had that, somewhere. But now, she knew, there were letters in the box. She held it unopened for a long time, caught between the horror-movie fascination of letters and postcards in Steve's small neat writing —

she could almost see them through the box, she could remember phrases – and the desire to throw the box away as far as she could, like someone tortured by but unable to break away from the awful alternations of electric current. She put the box back, finished tidying the desk.

'I can't shut the door,' she said to the man who was standing next to her. But he was gone, and she could see through the crack she was trying to force closed, but which was inching itself wider every huge second, that it was him on the other side, pushing. She put her head down and forced her arms straight, sending the last of her strength out along her arms. The door closed a little and then flew open, knocking her against the wall. There was no one there! In the blind second of shock she had shut her eyes and he had climbed inside her. She could tell because of the pain between her legs. She had lost. He would grow. Sweat, smell of sweat.

She was trying to push the man away, out of her. The man was wearing a uniform – leather jacket, a hat, plastic gloves – she knew it was a uniform because there was a number on it she kept trying to memorise so she could report him. But she couldn't. The smell of sweat was overpowering. Every time she pushed him out a little he pushed back more, it was unstoppable. Get out! She was screaming get out! But only the dryness in her throat came out, and it went on and then something inside her had broken, crumbled away and everything was streaming through the breach, was it blood? And then she knew: an ache in her breasts, a burning on her skin, a stretching inside her, she was coming, but it was transformed into pain, each sensation coarsened into hurt, it was like a heart attack, like strangling – no –

With the light on she sat up stiff in bed, she had been hot, but now her skin tightened into gooseflesh. Had she? She could feel herself and tell, but she couldn't, she couldn't touch herself there. The sheets clung to her, the bed damp, her body exuded again that bitter linden smell. She would not sleep.

Her legs had taken her to the bathroom, she waited for the water to cover her again, the white sides of the bath rearing on either side; it was like being little again, dwarfed by the cliffs of enamel, slowly flooded from above.

'Nervous prostration? Possible hypochondria?' she managed to make out on the card in front of Dr Smith. That would be over three years ago, when she got that awful tiredness before she lost her job. Was it true they taught themselves to write illegibly?

'How did you sleep last night?' he asked.

She had been in the waiting room for nearly two hours and he had treated her to a lecture on making appointments. The air was laced heavily with antiseptic, masking an accumulation of body smells and other chemicals. Perhaps even now he was writing 'hypochondria', or thinking it.

'I'll give you something that should help. And something to keep you on an even keel – a very gentle anti-depressant, I think you'll like it, it's a new one, no side effects, one a day . . .'

It was as if he caught the disappointment on her face and decided to extend the list: 'And you could probably do with some vitamins and iron. Go easy with the iron, or you'll get constipated – we don't want that, do we? You live on your own, don't you?'

That means, of course, that you don't bother to eat. No, I live at home.

'If you haven't had a period in six weeks' time, use this bottle for a morning urine sample, and pop it into the hospital and we'll soon know what's what. Now don't worry, that'll only make it worse: anxiety can stop your periods, you know. You'll be all right. Anything else?'

She had been to the doctor then, and this was it. She had said the word 'rape' coldly, by way of explanation, no

50

tears, no image flickering on the screen. It had all happened to someone else, yet his calm reaction left her inexplicably distressed, as if, had he reacted differently, it would have been possible to comfort and fuss over that somebody else, stroke her and calm her down, put a saucer of cream out for her on the floor. She didn't want to go. She wanted something more than the pills and the screw-top plastic jar with markings down the side: how was she meant to piss in it, anyway?

'The police doctor said something about seeing if any other marks came up . . . but . . .'

He stared at her for a few seconds. 'Wait a moment,' he said, and disappeared down the corridor, to return with the nurse. That used to happen when she was a child, medicals and visits to the doctor meant a morning off school and a day off work for her mother, right until she was sixteen. In case you make up stories about the doctor – what stories, never mind. The nurse, as her mother had done, stood impatient and redundant, clicking her biro in and out as the blood pressures and insulin injections built up in her little office at the end of the corridor.

'So you're taking it to court, are you?' he said as he pressed. 'Does it hurt?' There was a nasty-looking one around her coccyx, he said, and was she imagining it or did his voice sound almost disapproving?

'These cases can be quite a strain, it might be better for you just to try and forget about it – after all, it's done now, so why make yourself suffer even more?' He indicated that she should get dressed. The nurse whisked out of the door without waiting to be told.

'I –'

'When all's said and done, perhaps it's best to put it down to experience.' He gave her an avuncular smile. 'I'll give you a cream for that bruise on the coccyx: the skin's broken. After all, you'll be as right as rain in a couple of days; no scars!'

Was she meant to join in his laughter?

51

'Do you get many –?' she asked.

'Not what you'd call rape,' he said, handing over the sheaf of prescriptions, tapping the intercom for the next patient. Hysteric, your time is up.

'Wait a minute.' She surprised herself, the determination in her voice was quite clear and not a bit hysterical, though she didn't know what she was going to say. 'I'd be happier not to have to wait all that time to know whether I'm pregnant or not – isn't there something . . .'

He looked at her like she should have known about it. Not widely available. But he was writing out another prescription, his lips were pursed, but he was doing it. One in the morning for three days, you'll feel nauseous: that's why we don't like to prescribe these. And then a tiny pause.

'What kind of contraception do you use?'

And 'just in case' – his disbelief flooded through the phrase – he would recommend the pill. The pill that had painted three months of her life nausea green, made the veins in her legs throb. Just in case. The prescriptions screwed in her hand, she walked out without answering. So he would recommend the pill, would he? Was that because it didn't differentiate between sex and rape? Good all-round protection just in case? Less fuss and bother? Were constant side effects worse than a few days' nausea?

The cat inside her had expected cream, stupid beast, but it had got only bile. She would have to starve it to death.

She hesitated outside the surgery, there was nowhere to go but home. She ought to visit someone perhaps, tell them what had happened and be looked after a bit? Cup of tea, stiff drink, good cry, spilt milk and stiff upper lip. But there was nothing really the matter: just stiffness, a headache, a new fact to assimilate, that was all it was. Worse things happen. The cat inside her would spite the world by going anorexic. She would be teaching tomorrow. Tell someone? The thought of the words stuck in her chest. Her mother? Impossible. Sally? Too soon, with the long silence between them only just broken. And it would all be so theatrical. She would have to ease the listener in, broach the subject: 'I hope you don't mind me calling like this but I'm in a bit of a state' – but she wasn't – 'I'm in a bit of a state so' – but she wasn't – 'something awful's happened to me' – but it wasn't that awful, she felt OK. And after the false phrases had dropped from her lips into the startled lap of her chosen victim, what then? What could they say? What could they do? Nothing, of course; and there was too – somewhere in an old cigar box at the back of her mind – a fear of reserve, of disbelief. There was no need to tell. Practical things were best. Some people needed to be always telling their problems, like exorcism, but she wasn't one of them, never had been. She'd buy a better lock. It had been something that came out of the blue, not part of her real life; it was just a few nightmare hours and now everything would go as normal, and very nicely thank you, she'd been thinking only yesterday how well it had turned out since – irritating how her thoughts kept returning to the same place where she wouldn't go. Stop thinking then. Walk faster, get on with it.

Between the four walls of home, she seemed to be waiting. Unnatural quiet hissed in her ears like a crashed wave draining back down the beach, aftermath. Another one coming. Her ears strained, waiting, not impatiently, not for something she wanted, but for something to be over.

It was a good job the Browns weren't in to complain about the drill and the wood dust in the passage. Cath contemplated her handiwork: the neat spy-lens a little tunnel of glass going right through the door to grab and twist the outside, pull it by its edges to her waiting eye; the neat brass chain: more a symbol than a real protection, she had to admit. She sat picking the bits from the bottom stairs on to a piece of newspaper, and feeling less satisfied than she had hoped. What she had put on the door seemed more than anything to shut her in, to barricade her behind a clutter of precautions that might – but you never knew – one day be needed. She'd met him outside and let him in, after all. She locked the door. House locked, heartlocked, tonguelocked. Safe. And throw away the key.

Cath was surprised at the speed and ease with which the police found Steve, almost as if she had expected there to be a protracted search, disguises and hiding, a final desperate struggle at an airport: that was what the movies did for you; but, of course, he wouldn't have been expecting anything. They'd 'picked him up', would she 'drop in' in the morning: suddenly and confusingly procedure seemed to have become informal and almost cheerful.

The police station looked different in daylight, feeble morning sun that squeezed blotty shadows like coffee spills round the bottom of things and showed up the dust. It was shabby in an unexceptional way, and uncomfortable, but far from the windowless Colditz she had remembered it as. She sat opposite Harris, a plain-clothes officer whom she had not seen before, his solid shape topped with wisps of hair silhouetted against the half-drawn blinds. A newspaper and crumbs topped the litter of papers on the desk. Green lights on the row of phones kept flashing, waiting, flashing again with such desperation you could almost make yourself hear the sound, but the switch had been thrown and no one would get through for a while.

'On your way to work?' asked Detective Inspector Harris, a slack gesture towards a smile just visible. 'Won't keep you long.'

There was a lengthy pause.

'As you know, we have traced Mr Blake. And the forensic report has come, it's quite conclusive' – his voice went up a gear – 'fibres found of black cotton on complainant's clothing, subsequently found to correspond with samples taken from the suspect. Fibres of white and brown wool corresponding to complainant's clothing and bed linen also found on suspect as well as hairs . . . small bloodstains corresponding to complainant's blood group but not suspect's found on his underwear, spermatozoa,' he coughed and put the report down only half read. 'All this tallies with the medical evidence, minor bruises, lacerations and so on . . .'

It was as if he was trying to bestow upon her as a reward the truth of her own story. His tone was both congratulatory and self-congratulating. Scrapings from your body do not contradict what you say happened to it, eureka! There was something assumed about this misplaced complicity, and suddenly she felt anxious.

'So you can see, we might well have a case.'

'Might?'

'Calls himself a revolutionary something or other, doesn't he, Mr Blake?' (That was like the movies, the way they never answered or listened.)

'Er – socialist.' (It's a common enough word.)

'A journalist, isn't he?'

'Yes, but –'

'You said that you didn't know where he had been since September . . .' He was staring hard at her.

'Yes. I thought he was going to America, but I don't know if he did not. I just knew he wasn't around anymore.' How many times those words had spoken themselves.

'You had mutual friends – surely one of them would have told you what he was doing?'

'I seemed to lose touch with them. I changed my work, you see, when he went.'

'Been nothing of his in the papers for a while, has there?'

She had stopped reading the journals and six-page newspapers that had used to litter the flat – she had stopped reading even the ones she had used to read before she knew him. Pages packed with tight columns of print, black, white and red, hard-edged graphics, and photographs of people shouting. Somehow the effort of defusing that intensity of important words, messily bound round and round, their meanings like loose string on a hastily wrapped parcel, had ceased to be worthwhile. It was frightening how you could change, how something you had considered fundamental would wither away in a few weeks, forcing you to realise that you had done the thing not for its own value but because of an ulterior motive or a misunderstanding or a duty that had ceased to compel. Momentarily she felt guilty.

'I don't know,' she said.

'Well, I can tell you, Miss Sheldon, he wasn't in the USA, he was in Belfast. "Research for a series of articles", he said, but declined to produce the articles or to say how he supported himself . . . not a very pleasant character, all in all.'

Harris twitched another smile, managing to keep it in shape longer than the first one. What had all this to do with her case?

Harris's manner was so different from that of the officers only a few nights ago: suddenly her own credibility and motives, which seemed so much at issue, were no longer under the microscope; more, she felt, because they were for some reason now irrelevant than because they had been accepted. There was another lengthy pause.

'You wouldn't,' he said, 'have any idea what he might be doing in Belfast?'

'No, I told you . . .'

'You said, I think, that you used to help him write these articles, that you shared some of the same interests . . .'

'Well, yes, but I've lost contact, I –'

Was that it then: just another way of telling her she was lying or unreliable. You've been mixed up with this nasty politics, how can we be expected to believe you, was that it? Surely not, but –

'Well, Miss Sheldon, the position is, as far as your complaint goes, we would *like* to prosecute. Mr Blake has obviously been unable to deny that intercouse took place, but declares that there was no element of force. There's only one piece of corroborative evidence –' (What's 'corroborative'?) – 'from the couple downstairs who heard you shouting, even that's a bit dubious –' (How?) 'Now, if the case comes to court, character evidence will be important, you could say decisive . . .'

Speaking very slowly as if the meanings of his words would require time for her to appreciate, 'As I said, character evidence will be very important. Now, I'm writing a report for our solicitor to assess the case, and any information you can provide about Mr Blake would, in a way, add to the weight of the case. Evidence is what it boils down to, no hope of conviction without evidence.'

He picked up a pen to hold as he examined some papers, not looking at her at all during this last sentence. I've made my offer and I shan't look at you while you're making up your mind: a strange kind of politeness – but what was the offer, exactly? What does he think I can tell him? And what has it got to do with what happened? She told himself, when in doubt keep quiet, wait and count. And what was 'Evidence: Steven Blake used to make bombs in my kitchen and took an Irish correspondence course, therefore he must be a rapist' – does he expect me to make something up? Had she misunderstood?

'I don't know what you mean. Isn't there evidence of force anyway?'

And the man on the other side of the desk who might have been a doctor, spy, magistrate, cold eyes and a pen mightier than the sword, glanced up briefly then flicked the switch on his row of telephones.

'I'll submit the report as it stands then,' he said coldly, 'and let you know if we decide to prosecute.'

The phones began to ring.

Cath walked away from the police station as quickly as she could. She must be slipping into paranoia, she thought. Must have got it wrong, have a persecution complex. Hadn't the man been saying: you say something about

Steven Blake and it will help your case? Or maybe he'd meant: 'We'll prosecute if you can tell us something so that we can charge him with another offence as well.' But why? Did they want to bring her case as a way of getting him for something else they suspected but couldn't prove? Oh, it was silly, unbelievable. A journalist who raped his ex-girlfriend; it wasn't gangster stuff, lacked scope for deals, false trials, grass and supergrass. Testing her? Tripping her? Cheating her? But why? Whodunnit? What? And why should they bother, wasn't it straightforward enough? What was corroborative anyway? He never did anything they could get him for: Christ, she'd followed him like a dog for long enough, she'd have known. She must have got it wrong. Police corruption: OK, but not over something like this, not just on the off-chance or just for fun, there could be no point.

What had he said exactly? 'Might have a case', 'would like to', 'not a very pleasant character' and then that stuck-on smile that said, 'so we both have our reasons for getting him?' Why? And then, she remembered: 'Kicks on the job. Steven Blake exposes appalling routine violence in the metropolitan police force.' Of course, it must be that. Christ! maybe they had beaten him up? The thought horrified her, it would be her fault. Then she dismissed it. That article had appeared years ago; it had just come out when he moved in with her. She remembered him making a joke about it because he and his old flatmate had had a fight and he had lost, there was nothing for it but to move out. The quarrels had been about money. 'I'd've needed police protection to stay there any longer,' he said, and it was funny because the article had just come out.

But no, she thought, this is life, not a film. Not an article, even. They'd probably not even read it. Ingrained paranoia afflicting even the most law-abiding when they have dealings with the police, start imagining, apologising, checking and double checking. Entrenched guilt from undiscovered childhood thefts: pennies out of the milk-money, catch me please.

The article, she remembered, had shocked her: 'Violence sometimes resulting in permanent injury is used as a matter of course in the questioning, or rather the interrogation, of certain types of suspect . . .' There were cases, dates, names. She'd believed it then, and more so now. What would Inspector Harris do if he knew that? Suddenly refuse to accept her story? Call her a 'nasty piece of work' and find something to charge her with? Strenuously Cath shepherded her panicking thoughts back together again. He hadn't said anything; it was her imagination going helter-skelter, lack of sleep. He had simply called her in to see if there was anything to add. Nothing to add. That was that. For a few seconds she succeeded in holding her mind completely empty –

'Stupid cunt!' and red metal skimmed inches from her, for a blink of time everything was in shadow, a cold wind that could have been steel whipped up her skirt. She stumbled back on to the kerb, bumping into someone, and feeling the heavy and isolating disapproval of the other waiting pedestrians. She was smiling stupidly. Her fault. The wait at the crossing seemed interminable. She crossed slowly with the crowd, but wanted to run, desperate for the safety and familiarity of the Project office: the geraniums, the mixed batch of donated chairs, filing cabinets, inky stencils hung up to dry, notes and notices, books and coffee: things she knew about and dealt with competently. At this time of the morning the only person likely to be there was Kim: little big-eyed Kim who made her feel old, and, although she had worked with her for some months now, awkward. Kim: friendly, hardworking, cheerful – and yet she so much preferred tongue-tied Anne who was often irritating and incompetent under pressure. Kim, who had said right from the start that she would only teach women (and no one had argued, because she was so good at it), spoke to Dick and Tim as little as possible because, she said, they didn't listen properly. Cath knew what she meant, but still felt out of sympathy. She imagined Kim felt that, being women, they should get on with each other or be allies, just like that. Such automatic, indiscriminate friendliness made Cath feel stiff and hostile. These things, relatively easy to admit, were however only the tiny top growth of something that went much deeper: a pervasive jealousy that she could admit to herself only rarely, and never for long enough to think her way out of. Kim's almost childlike skin sunned itself appreciatively beneath her sunburst of whitegold hair, proclaiming its intimate con- nection with the healthy tissues beneath; likewise the words that came to her lips seemed in perfect concord with her heart and mind. Looking at her, Cath had often found herself uncomfortably aware of her own face: big-boned and almost dramatic, yet somehow at odds with itself, spoiled and puckered with an effort she couldn't quite name – 'getting older' was the easy explanation, but she knew Kim's face would age without that happening to it.

'Am I getting on your nerves?' she'd once asked Cath, suddenly, in the middle of a careful description of a science fiction novel she had read, and Cath, cowardly, had said 'no'.

'We're having a party for women at my house, would you like to come?' she'd said only a few weeks ago, and Cath had found herself barely restraining a riot of resentful thoughts: Oh, thank you for realising I'm one too, I suppose you think I've never heard of 'sisterhood'; I could tell you, people had to work for things you take for granted – Christ! 'take for granted' – what a thing to think, but that, ghastly and unsayable, was half of it. If she'd been born a few years later might she have been more like Kim? Would she have had that frightening ability to speak her mind? Or even now, could she? No. It was personalities, difference irreconcilable. That business about 'sisterhood' too wasn't as simple as it seemed, for what had happened to her version of it? It was an uneasy word, one of the snaps she and Sally got out to remind themselves they could be

60

friends; half-buried guilt, sense of failure; dull feeling. Kim sparkled, resilient, decked in a tinsel glitter of hope and progress, armed with an ability to challenge, to maintain her position effortlessly in hostile or supportive environments alike, and, 'Got it on a plate', Cath would think, hating herself as she did so and knowing it might well not be true. Argues so damned hard about one little word –

'Cath, this sentence about electricians, I think you should put "he or she", not just "he"' – because she'd never had anything worse to bother about (but the truth was she had been right there, it had to be admitted). Damn Kim, but do the best not to let it show –

'Morning', said Cath, flushing and walking straight past Kim's desk to the bookshelves.

'You OK?' called Kim, now invisible, and Cath replied, 'Fine, busy though'.

One by one Cath rejected books: *The Psychological Implications of Long-term Illiteracy* . . . *Alternatives to Grammar*, titles that didn't inspire. *One to One Methods, Basic Dictionary for the Late Reader*: none of it would help with the fundraising letters, and she'd already read most of them in any case. Had Inspector Harris really suggested? No. Yes. Hell, she needed advice, an answer to stop all this running in circles wondering what people meant and what would happen next. She would make an appointment at the Law Centre. She stared at the shelves resentfully and for a few seconds hated everything she was or ever had been involved in, wanted to sweep the whole of her life away in one gesture and start off again, blank. She seemed to have spent so much of her time cramming herself with ideas that she respected because they had been published; she'd struggled to absorb them because someone else had struggled, she imagined, to set them down, and someone else had recommended the book: her father, the paper, college, Steve. The hours it took you to discover that the whole book would give you no more than the first chapter were gone for ever.

At least her pupils seemed to have a healthier, more functional attitude to reading than she'd had. She reached for the Project's last report, which she'd written herself, and realised that her hand was shaking. Something the matter? 'Nerves', said her mother's voice, disapproving. What's worrying you then? Nothing.

(Was that policeman really saying . . . should I have said . . . How long is it all going to last? What happens next? How can I tell Mum? She won't know what to say, but I'll have to . . . the Browns don't like me, perhaps they'll refuse to give evidence . . . Could I make them? Have they locked him up? What next, what happens next? I ought to be doing something. Shouldn't I have a solicitor? What happens next?) Her hand shook still and she felt as if she was made of glass and she could shatter, fall off the shelf and shatter, if the rumbling of questions and the thin wail of anxiety, muffled but all the more enervating for that, wasn't silenced or dispersed. 'At least you've got plenty to do to keep your mind off it,' she told herself. 'Get on with it. Look at the books again. Think of ways of putting it, headings, justifications. Don't give in, keep busy.' But she couldn't: the alternative to anxiety was frustration. Cath swallowed something bitter. 'Keep it down.' But it rose again, a smell more than a taste, pushing up behind her nostrils. She would not, must not, be sick.

Pale blue pastic bowl on sheet of newspaper on the floor, smelling of the grey disinfectant Aunty May poured weekly down the outside drain.

'Now be sick in that.' Acid surging in her throat, creeping up after each swallow, burning as it goes, but she won't be sick, not with someone looking.

'Can't.'

Big dry hand on her neck.

'Just try, bend down, get it up: you'll feel better after.'

Didn't want the burning in her throat, taste already leaking up. The smell. Stuck her stomach out to make room for it, must keep it down.

'Open your mouth and put your finger in, that'll help. Can't have you being sick in the car now, can we? Open your mouth at least . . .'

Spasm. The awful creeping rushing unstoppable out, scouring, insides ballooning and shrinking like a gasping lung. There's some in my nose.

'Good girl.'

But really she was cross, because of missing the bowl. The back of Cath's eyes hurt; she wanted to hide. Mingling of strong smells, soap, grey stuff, vomit, Aunty May's cologne that scalded. No time to change, all in a hurry. Mustn't cry.

'Better now.'

Never let it show again. Don't let on if you're feeling sick. Keep it down, wait till there's no one there, clean it up.

Cath struggled desperately as she stood pretending to read; it was only a matter of time, it would escape, she'd better be careful, keep quiet, shut herself in the toilet, she didn't want any mess. Her whole body stiff with effort, Cath subdued the sick feeling, stood glaring over the bookstand at Kim, now in the grip of a violent desire to heave the whole gulletful of festering emotions at her, start shouting and blustering and blaming. She controlled herself. None of this was anything to do with Kim. And Kim was perfectly OK really. She wasn't sure, she couldn't in her mind peel off all the differences between them to tell what was important about Kim, what was her character, but she had no right to – She was afraid of Kim. Kim worked intently at the files and booklets on the biggest desk – the one that had been donated by Midland Bank. Cath felt she was going to burst or explode. There were two neat rows of badges on Kim's jumper: her beliefs, loves and hatreds ranked, it seemed to Cath, like medals or wedding money worn in the hair. Cath wanted to shock her, to test and challenge her.

She found herself asking:

'Kim, d'you know anything about the legal procedure in rape cases?'

Kim's smile leapt to her face; like an eager pet's, Cath thought, bile burning the back of her throat. Glad to be approached. She put her pen down.

'Well, you can imagine, it's pretty awful from start to finish – the woman must be lying, the man forgiven for unquenchable lust – the judge is a man of course. There was one in the paper yesterday –'

The toothbrush hair was whiter and shorter than ever, looked more like some sort of halo than hair, a stiff blazoning of youth, luck, confidence. She's trying to educate me again. There's more to women's rights than equal pay and abortions, she's saying, as if I came out of the Ark. She doesn't even realise I'm talking about myself.

'Hold on! I meant what to do, what happens? Actually, it happened to me last weekend.'

Suddenly drama struck. Kim was halfway to her feet as if to vault over the desk and whisk a chair beneath Cath, enfold her in her arms, rock her like a child. But Cath was sitting already, four feet away in the tapestry-covered armchair by the door, dry-eyed and calm and absent as her reflection or a photograph. Kim's shock and desperation lent her confidence: as Kim panicked, so she felt her sense of control proportionately greater.

'But are you all right?' Kim repeated.

Cath's antagonism towards her was subsiding. Perhaps, she thought, she ought to help her somehow, tell her about it instead of provoking all this emotion and then refusing to accept it. But it was not in her to do it: Kim's shocked face and offering of cigarettes made her feel so solid, so self-contained – and almost contemptuous. Made her feel better. She was unmoved and calm, yet it was her, after all, that it had happened to: this implied that she was equipped to bear it. There was a temptation to be cruel, to extinguish Kim by converting her sympathy to pain or anger – that would make herself even stronger and nothing would matter. Slowly, this time, Kim was getting up again to come over.

'I'm OK, I just wanted information,' said Cath, suddenly frightened not of what had happened but quite simply of Kim, who lowered herself back into her swivel chair, her face all jumbled up with the effort of packing her feelings back into a box suddenly too small, and trying to think straight at the same time. I think she's really upset. I think she's really trying, thought Cath guiltily. But how she wanted that coldness, that arrogance that came from watching Kim twitch and fizzle in front of her! She doesn't know anything, she thought. The best person to work all this out is me. Law Centre, library. Solicitor.

'I could ask someone tonight,' said Kim, 'or I could give you her number to ring, she works on an emergency line for rape victims. I'm sure they could help.'

'I –' began Cath, and she had been going to say 'I'm not a rape victim' but that was ridiculous, she was. Had been. Raped. 'I've heard of them, but really I just wanted some information,' she said, and took the card Kim offered. Just what she ought to have expected. 'Thanks.'

Packing some books quickly into her bag, busying herself signing them out, desperate suddenly to get away from Kim before she began to feel small and swamped again.

'They'd be able to tell you anything you want to know. And if there's anything you want, at any time –' Kim's raw voice just behind her made her jump. 'Any kind of support or ringing people up or . . .' the voice persisted, relentlessly undermining the strength she had so recently stolen from it.

'Yes. OK. Thanks.' It was as if she had managed to pass her panic on to Kim like a disease in a child's tag game, but there was no real relief, only suspense, and you soon got it back. She wouldn't do that again, it only made it worse in the end. Tears half squeezed out, quivered. Be practical. That was a rotten thing to do, serves you right.

5

'What do you mean – not necessary?'

'I can't do anything about it, it's the way the law is: you don't have your own solicitor or barrister in a rape case. It does seem a bit crazy,' said the wispyhaired man in the Law Centre. His name 'Roger' was written on a tag clipped to his lapel, next to a small silver cannabis leaf. He spoke as if that was the end of the matter and he was glad for once to be confronted with something he could do nothing about. After waiting three hours in the crowded, leaflet-littered ante-room it was difficult to believe that this was all she could get. Cath stared at Roger as if she had suddenly realised her purse had been stolen and she must check again: it must be there, in my pocket, in my bag, in the police station, in the Law Centre, I've just dropped it somewhere, missed something someone said. It's all a mistake.

'The police should've explained all this to you, but you know what they're like. D'you want to make a complaint? There's this new committee now, monitoring the way police deal with members of the public.'

'But if I've got to wait until they decide whether to bring the case and if, as you said, I'll be having their solicitor . . . it doesn't sound a good idea, then.'

'Well I hadn't thought about it like that,' said Roger, 'but I suppose, if you're being *pragmatic* about it, probably not. But on the other hand, you won't probably ever see the solicitor, and the barrister only briefly just before, so there wouldn't be any hassle there . . .' He smiled brightly, encouragingly. 'And, of course, if people don't complain when they get bad treatment from the police, then it'll never change. This committee I'm on . . .'

Cath realised again that she wasn't exactly sure where a solicitor finished and a barrister began. How was it possible that they wouldn't meet her, either of them? How could it be that no one told her anything, that she had nothing to do with any of it, no choice about anything, no representatives?

'But surely there must be some help I can get?' she said. Roger drummed his fingers on the table and put a hole puncher that had been on the desk into one of the drawers.

'Er, hang on a minute,' he said, and reached for one of a row of books behind him. 'It's difficult to explain simply . . . somewhere in here it says . . . Yes, here we are . . .' After skimming a couple of pages, he shut the book and looked up, suddenly confident.

'What happens is the police bring the case. They're the ones doing the prosecuting, not the woman – that is, not you. Do you see? It's not you that's bringing the case, it's the police. And you're one of their witnesses. So you can't have your *own* solicitor, because you're only a witness. Do you see now?' He seemed pleased that the book had confirmed his original version, like a doctor too glad to have his diagnosis confirmed to be sorry that the patient was fatally ill.

'But supposing I'd rather bring the case myself. Could I do that? Could I get legal aid?'

'Oh no, you can't do that.'

'Well, how much would it cost then?'

'No, I meant you just can't do that at all.'

An increasing weight of confusion kept her pressed to the sticky vinyl chair; it distended and clotted blood and mind so that it was impossible to organise even something as trivial and automatic as getting up and putting on her coat. His sentences were clear enough, but something prevented her from understanding. What he said was so alien and so distressing that she could not absorb it, it just piled up round her and on top of her.

'I'm afraid it's after closing now,' prompted Roger.

Cath sat silent, still unable to move. It was like a dream of being paralysed. Roger looked apprehensive.

'What I could maybe do,' he said speaking hesitantly now, his eyes straying to the door, the clock, his desk top, 'is put you in touch with a barrister who'd be able to give you a bit more detail about what's likely to happen in court: how to put yourself over, what sort of things they'll ask — that sort of thing. There's a guy called Salter on our board of sponsors: a "socialist" earning twenty thousand a year who donates the odd hour of his time to salve his conscience —' He laughed, and there was a small pause while he waited for her to laugh as well. 'Well. If I gave him a ring and told him all about you, then you could get in contact by the end of the week. That would be the best thing. But you understand, don't you, that he won't actually have anything to do with your case at all: he won't be representing you?'

She understood what he was saying. But she was sure he must have got something wrong. She tried to remember things she knew about courts and the law. How many times you saw in the papers that so and so was acquitted, at such and such a court five youths were sentenced, without knowing what it actually meant. It was only the results you knew about. There was nothing coherent about it, it was like snakes and ladders, every which way at the throw of a dice; no she didn't understand. But she got up and thanked Roger, copied Salter's number into her book.

She would buy some meat and some beer for supper. Look after herself: when in doubt a sensible thing to do. Couldn't go wrong. In the butcher's she felt sick at the smells of

68

bleach and sawdust, stomach sick at the thought of the food that would do her good.

'I don't know if I can stand it,' she thought. The mother that lurked in her skull frowned. Ought she to tell someone? The thin white bag of meat was ballooning out at the corners: blood. She held it away from her. Who though? How? She caught sight of herself in a shop window, tall woman with messy hair holding a bag of blood. Going mad. Best talk to someone, she prescribed abstractly, as if in response to a third-hand story about someone else.

Lost-and-found Sally, why not tell her? What are friends for, but for comfort? But Sally had said: 'Don't expect me to join you in running him down. Perhaps I'm not the best person to discuss it with.' And Sally carried his books for him, too busy to meet Cath, too busy to speak. But that was history, wasn't it? At Jean's party not long ago, she had promised to visit – they had talked from dusk to dark like old times, as if Sal had come back safe from a journey, prepared for the time being to let her friend be as important as higher causes. Sally then? I tried to tell her as soon as it happened, I phoned but she wasn't there. Couldn't be expected to be there, silly. But. Don't I trust her then? No. Yes. Not the point. Imagine:

'Sally, he raped me': wouldn't it all come back just the same, why shouldn't it? And Sally might say, her mouth puckered with disgust,

'What! You called the pigs?', she might say,

'Don't expect me to take sides', might say,

'I don't believe you, what do you mean?'

'Surely you could have done something? Kicked him in the balls or something?'

After a few glasses of wine she might say,

'Cath, have you been feeling OK, I mean, living on your own for so long and not seeing anyone except that literacy lot?'

I'm afraid she'll hurt me. And if she did, if she said:

69

'Come on Cath, don't exaggerate, don't get it out of proportion –' Would she say something like that? If she did, reconciliation would be impossible ever again, it would be a breaking point at which years of friendship would be separated off into nostalgia, continuity cut dead like a worm in half, but not to grow again. A friend I used to have. It had been nothing to say to Kim 'it happened to me last night': she'd wanted to force Kim, push her to a point to see if there was anything worth having, to punish her, no – either way, it didn't matter. Kim was friendly, but she was indifferent to, no, she disliked Kim. There had been nothing to lose; with Sally the stakes were too high.

'If you beg when you need, you won't get': her mother's voice confirmed her decision. There wasn't a way to tell without begging sympathy, or seeming to. Sal might say nothing, nothing at all, just silence, pretend she hadn't heard. She herself might sit there and the words shape themselves on her lips but with no sound coming out. Her tongue might trip her up, she might find herself making a joke about it, might find herself crying . . .

Sally was hard. People said so, admiring. And she was hard when she was with Sally, but it wasn't quite real.

'Come on Cath, you look miserable as sin. Race you to the bus stop.' She'd pull you out of it, cuff and charm you back to cheerfulness. Succeed because you're grateful she's tried. 'Don't brood.' Just like mother. But for this that wouldn't be enough. To tell her would be an ultimatum and a begging letter all at once. This is it: prove we're not set and stilted, prove you're my friend, last chance, oh please, please do. She didn't think she could do it, please – no.

'Mrs Brown!' The upright figure half paused, then continued down the path. 'Mrs Brown.' Cath ran, the bag of blood bumping against her thigh, and caught up with her just as she reached the front door. Outer door step and tiled passage a shared responsibility, but Mrs Brown did it more often. Cath noticed footprints on the red and white tiles, a little flurry of them at the bottom of the stairs: hers. Mrs Brown put down her shopping bag and turned to face her, back to her front door as if guarding it.

'I just wanted to say, I'm very sorry about the disturbance the other night . . .' Mrs Brown's eyes, passionless but determined, glinted from behind her pale-rimmed spectacles, a face evenly, decorously aged, somehow held back from life, immune. She took breath as if for a very long sentence, then said, 'It wasn't our being woken up that was the trouble: we're used to that, after all . . . it was all the to-do in the morning. The police! We've never had dealings with the police, and I can tell you, we don't want to start now. Did you know we may have to go to court? As I said, I can't see why, it was nothing to do with us . . .'

They would go then; unwillingly, but they would go! She smiled with relief.

'I'm sorry Mrs Brown, but it wasn't really my fault.'

Mrs Brown's eyes and her silence denied this assertion. What did they hear? What did they tell the police? What did the police tell them?

'If it comes to going to court, I'm sure it will only take a few minutes to say . . .'

'Scarce seems worth the trouble,' said Mrs Brown, refusing to reveal what it was they would say. 'The lady policeman asked what sort of impression we'd got of that – your man that used to live up there. Times change, I said, but I wouldn't think much of a man that'd move in with a woman instead of doing the decent thing. But then that's only our opinion, and I know we're in the minority these days . . .' She snapped open her bag, hunting for her keys. 'One thing leads to another,' she said, looking down in her bag. 'You might have known . . . not that that excuses him of course.'

None of the child left in Mrs Brown; everything confirmed everything else and you couldn't make her smile. Universe shrunk to the size of a front room. Cath wondered if they had ever had children and guessed not. She knew nothing about them. Mr Brown she'd only ever seen, a large man, never without a jacket.

'Well I'm glad you were in that night –' Where else would they be, the Browns? 'And grateful about going to court. Nice to know there's someone down there,' said Cath, despising herself. Mrs Brown moved half a step closer, a faint, hygienic whiff of lavender water.

'I might as well tell you now, I suppose . . . Mr Brown and I will be moving next month. We're buying. At our age you want some privacy – and round here, well . . . it's changed. Gartforth Road we're going to. A detached house, built just after the war. So I couldn't tell you who'll be down here. He's having some repairs done I think.' Mrs Brown bent down hurriedly to pick up her shopping, as if the barely concealed excitement, the faint wash of pink beneath the powder on her face which relaying this information had caused, was somehow shameful.

'Well, it was good of you to apologise,' she added, almost pleasant, from the safe side of her threshold.

'Mr Brown and I', thought Cath, like the queen: my husband and I. 'We' wasn't good enough: could be me and my sister, me and the cat. Her mother had taught her to say when a man tried to chat her up – what are you doing here then? – 'I'm waiting for my boyfriend.' A way of saying 'I'm spoken for, I'm safe': and it worked, it was a little wall between you and the world, a thick man's overcoat enveloping your shoulders, shielding you from the night and others' eyes. Cath shivered. Perhaps Mrs Brown was frightened of moving after all these years. Perhaps that was what made her want to reiterate the safety she had earned in marriage to Mr Brown, a steady regular man rarely seen, and never in casual dress.

But I live alone. Not, they say, at home.

She had eaten, and now she would work. There was a design to be done for the project's poster, a letter to the Rowntree Trust asking for funds . . . Dear trustees, I am

72

writing to tell you about the excellent work we in the Battersea Literacy Project . . . unfortunately . . . in the hope . . . substantial . . . and there was the first instalment of her pupil Mrs Anderson's autobiography which she had agreed could be posted to her in between lessons so that the whole hour wasn't taken up with it. Cath scoured the burnt liver pan carefully. The cooker was a mess too, but you couldn't spend the whole evening cleaning up after just one meal, for one person, living alone. Her hands had gone bleached and puffy from the scouring powder. She stared at them flipping languidly in the opaque dishwater like a pair of unhealthy fish. The telephone made her jump.

'Hello Cath – not disturbing you am I? I thought you might like to go out for a drink, somewhere up by the river, I've forgotten the name, but I've been there before it's never crowded, and there's a lift, I got your number in the centre, I hope you don't mind . . .'

'Who? –'

'Oh sorry. It's Kim. There's about four of us going, and . . .'

Cath let her talk on, her own vocal cords twisted into an impossibly complicated knot of embarrassment, panic and guilt.

'Kim, I've got a lot of work to do tonight: the poster, fundraising, and Mrs Anderson's stuff.'

'That's OK, I just –'

'Kim, if it's because of what I told you – I might have been abrupt, the thing is I don't actually want to talk about it. I don't know what came over me, I nearly got run over on the way to the office, but really, I'm perfectly all right now, and I don't want to talk about it, it was nice of you to ask me and to be so sympathetic but there's absolutely no need, you see. I'm sorry.'

'I –'

'I'll have to go, I think I left the water running.'

Sorry, sorry, what's the use. Cath hung up, abandoned

the pan and sat down at her desk. Turned the radio off: work. But work to be done alone in a curtained room seemed suddenly uninviting. She got up and altered the light. Evenings were too long in winter. She missed the everyday clatter of the typewriter, and writing by hand made her feel self-conscious, like being in a history-book picture of someone illustrating a manuscript. She tried to list all the disadvantages of illiteracy, obvious and less obvious. Shame was one thing nearly all her students had felt. No matter what you say, people thought you were stupid if you couldn't read, and you ended up believing them . . . There are notices in stations, post offices even, Mrs Anderson had informed her, scandalised, stuck on a pole in front of a field in the Lake District: you didn't know what to do, it might be a minefield, a right of way, a bull or free-range eggs. Not reading meant you could only do certain jobs, always unskilled, and often the reason you'd not learned to read was that you'd had to start work when you should have been at school. 'Shame' she wrote under the heading 'Rowntree Trust', and then 'poverty trap'. The words looked clumsy, rheumatic. Not reading made you dependent on those to whom you'd confessed your inability. They read your letters and there was no privacy; they translated whole columns of the newspaper into a single sentence. They wanted you to do something for them in return. The phone rang again: she hesitated, ignored it, unwilling to interrupt the slow swell of thoughts beginning. Thought's a narcotic, and memory too.

Cath remembered being stranded alone in Paris for an afternoon, how she'd sat in cafés with her ears straining but still hearing only sing-song babble, fretting with questions she couldn't ask. In her own language she could say, 'Excuse me, I think you've given me the wrong change', and the tone of her voice would also say, 'I'm not saying you're a thief, we all make mistakes.' But here, deprived not only of implication, of sarcasm and subtlety, but of even the most basic words, she had to hold out her change in her hand and raise her eyebrows, then be unable to understand the explanation; be thought insulting, mad or stupid. It takes years to become good enough at a language to be able to interpret tones of voice, read between the lines . . . So reading and writing was like another language altogether, her students were attempting something she herself had been too daunted to try –

The phone rang again, on and on. She tried to drown it out, wrote down 'alienation from culture', pressing hard. The non-reader was silenced and powerless, could neither understand nor affect what was going on: was disenfranchised. Not so long ago the skills of literacy were reserved as a privilege of the rich and the religious. The congregation would sit spellbound but uncomprehending through Latin services, relieved perhaps that they had learned at least to recognise the rises and falls of the voice that meant to stand or kneel . . . A release of tension in the back of her neck told her that the ringing had stopped. If it began again she would answer it. It might be Sally, she'd promised to call within the week of the party, but then she'd been drunk: it was more likely Kim again.

'History of', she wrote. Make your mark here, the squire would say, and someone had signed away their cottage or their daughter in return for a sack of adulterated corn. If you couldn't understand procedure you had no choice but to trust. All dissent evaporated like a curl of incense. Cath imagined the white faces of hungry peasants in a huge stone cathedral, a fat purple-robed priest with his gold-edged book of Latin words heavy as a weapon, the pen is mightier than the sword, and above it all the cheerful mockeries of painted frescoes and the shifting glow from coloured glass. There's nothing wrong with the centre's work, she thought suddenly, Steve and that lot always belittled it, do-gooding – but really, you could say it was revolutionary in a way, it gives people the means.

She pushed aside the letter to draft tomorrow, and opened a thick envelope from Mrs Anderson. There were seven sheets of blue-lined notepaper, the letters neatly formed but some of them were backwards, and there were whole paragraphs where scarcely a word was spelled correctly. To straightjacket Mrs Anderson's account of her life into any normal kind of order would be utterly impossible. The events were all jumbled together, just like the letters and words themselves: no consistency, no thread, no chronology. It took her almost an hour to get it into basic shape. Then she took it over to the cushions and began re-reading carefully.

'The best years of my life were in the war. War is meant to be such a terrible thing but I must say I don't know if I've ever felt better before or since . . .'

She had heard much of it before, but Cath found herself re-reading intently, and not as a teacher. Certain phrases and sentences seemed to carry a weight of experience, familiar without being her own. In no sense a chronological beginning and little concerned with childhood, 'Chapter One' awoke in Cath memories of stories she had overheard as a child: half-understood hints as to the nature of the passions and rituals determining the adult world to be puzzled over and pieced together and decorated with her own imagining, much as she'd dressed dolls and built them first of all rooms, then streets and cities as their lives grew in scope.

'My first marriage was not –' a capital 'C' was followed by a squiggle of the pen. 'Arthur was called up straight away and died in the first month of the war. As my mother said, he wouldn't have been the man for me. Now my second, Joe Martin, I met when I was working on the ferries: an American from California. That was a marriage of love. I wore his ring, though we never did get to the registry office, as we said in those days it was just as good and saved money. If your man hadn't been killed or gone off with someone else by the end of the war, you could always get a proper service then. Well, Joe, he only ever sent me one letter after the war, and that was to say he'd married some blue-eyed Miss America, he hoped I didn't mind. And me all set to pack and go out there to settle down. This country was miserable after the war. I did get to California later, but that's another story.'

Cath remembered listening from under the table in the kitchen to her mother and aunts talk, and lying with her ears pressed to the floorboards trying to decipher a quarrel between her parents that had woken her up. It was this sort of thing they had been talking about, exciting-sounding events summarised in a few simple but cryptic phrases.

The night Mrs Anderson's father hit her mother she, as a girl of ten, had decided then and there that no one would ever do that to her, though later she'd found out she couldn't stop them but she could make them suffer afterwards. Cath flicked through the pages. The determined pressure of Mrs Anderson's pen embossed the reverse side of each; the physical act of writing alone must have been about an hour a page and yet the neat unjoined letters bore no sign, no scars, of the impatience Mrs Anderson expressed so frequently in their lessons. It was probably a copy, or even a second copy. Cath marvelled both at the effort it had cost Mrs Anderson, and the effect it had had on her. Why should a rambling account of someone else's life be so particularly interesting – especially when she had other work to do? The man in the park, soldiers, sailors, guns, bombs and food . . . correcting the spelling had been easy enough, but with the grammar and the order of things Cath was torn between being a teacher and a listener.

'So then I thought, I'll be darned if I let something like that stop me, you only live once, and seeing how I'd been left in the lurch things couldn't get any worse. So I stayed at the dark end of the platform, quiet as a mouse, and just as the train starts moving I jumped on. It was all a mistake though, because –'

She picked up the phone after its first bleep. A call-box call.

'Hello', she said.

There was a moment's silence and then a muffled outburst of laughter, suddenly stifled as a hand went over the receiver.

'Who is it?'

Laughter was audible again, more than one voice, but restrained. Someone drew breath loudly, blew a raspberry, started again:

'Hello –'

The voice started out deep but reverted almost immediately to the scratchy tones of an adolescent boy: 'Hello – sexy!' The laughter hooted and splattered. For a second she saw them, four or five kids crammed in a housing estate phone-box, smoking fags with fingers and thumbs, craned together over the receiver.

'W-what have you got on underneath?' the squeaky little voice was garbling, tripping over itself, 'I hope it's nothing, because I'm going to come round and –'

Cath smashed the receiver down, then picked it up again to leave it off the hook. Kids, just kids. She stood still a few seconds, her breathing stuck and the room straining to fall back in time. Her hand was tight round the receiver just as it had been after – abruptly she left go, disconnecting a dangerous circuit. Kids – they couldn't get in here anyway, she said aloud, her voice reassuringly unruffled.

6

The eagerness Cath felt as she approached the library was familiar. You could study your way out of most things, she'd discovered at training college; there was a peculiar pleasure in forcing frayed nerves to knit together in a concerted effort to get to the bottom of something, a grim satisfaction that she was capable of making time that could not be happy at least useful. The card index, the books to be read whole and digested, notes taken, summarised, condensed; an original thought to be wrested from the mass of other people's: none of that could be done without a concentration that ruled out what her mother called 'self-pity'. She'd brought a new notepad, black and red pens, coins for photocopies.

The reference library was full and the atmosphere was of desperate concentration; people of all ages, some of them in suits and ties, heads down and wide-eyed under the fluorescent light. It was only just ten but they looked as if they could have been in there for hours. When she had last come to this library there had been only a sparse population of eccentrics and aged newspaper readers, perhaps the odd group of school children giggling and shuffling over a project. A sign of the times: unemployment, she thought, everyone hauling themselves on to the next qualification or requalification, passing exams in their spare time and reading the specialist journals for vacancies no one else would have thought to look for. Perhaps, had she been born a little later, her mother would actually have encouraged her to immolate herself in libraries instead of seeing her professional ambitions as a useless and slightly shameful obsession. But there you are, she'd got the sack anyway, given up. Cath searched the packed tables for a seat. The air was tired and heavy, laced with smells of felt markers and cough sweets that caught in the back of her throat. She made her way to the section marked 'Law', and then, because none of the titles – *Criminal Procedure, Revisions of Statutes* – seemed precise enough, to the card index.

There was nothing under rape! Not even a single card. She glanced at the information desk where a small pinched-looking man sat almost obscured by the sign curtly informing readers that there was no toilet in the library and seats could not be reserved. His forehead screwed itself rhythmically in and out of a frown as he conducted a conversation on the phone in a whisper that only emphasised his irritation. With his spare hand he was gluing forms into the front of new books. Cath felt she knew him from somewhere – perhaps from a parents' meeting or a school committee. When he pressed the phone down and looked up she turned quickly back to the index in case he should recognise her. Impossible to go up and whisper excuse me, where could I find books on rape? Impossible, stupid, but impossible. She leafed carefully through thick swatches of grimy cards under Law. Bibliographies, supplements, dictionaries, histories. She took down references for Criminal Law, Criminal Investigation and Crime. Somewhere amongst those she must find it. The librarian came up and stood next to her, filing stiff new cards laundered and unread in amongst the dirty ones. Criminal Law directed her to Sex: it couldn't be right, surely? She hesitated by the draw marked 'S' feeling the librarian's irritable gaze. Perhaps it was he who had done it: classified rape with 'sexual behaviour related to income', 'sex, literary themes', 'sex: humorous', and the 'biology of human sexual response'. The inconsistency of it, she thought. They put pictures of naked women on packets of peanuts, they'll print the most private of details in a newspaper, but they'll cover a box of tampons with brown paper and sellotape and in libraries they'll file rape with sex, humorous. SEXUAL OFFENCES, there it was. Case history of Jack the Ripper, Rehabilitation of Sex Offenders, Sociology of Sex Crimes, Incest and Family Break up . . . here and there she gleaned a reference back to the dictionaries and statute books she had rejected initially, but there was obviously not going to be just one book containing all she wanted to know.

Finally she sat down, squeezed between an elderly woman reading *Country Life* and an anaemic-looking schoolgirl copying someone else's history notes. The books made an impressive pile with their gold-embossed spines, black and olive-green bindings. She tried to sort her questions into the sort of categories likely to be in the indexes. Was it really true she was only a witness? What would she be asked? How long would it take, could she appeal?: these massive books heavy with years must surely have the answers, if only she could find them. Finding out for herself: so much clearer and calmer than asking for other people's help, tears and misunderstandings. Crisis Centres: what a thing to call them when what you needed was to keep yourself calm, and it in perspective. Facts, just the facts. Treat it like a piece of research. Nonetheless, muscles somewhere in her chest clenched as she pulled the first book towards her, disturbing its ticklish smell of paper dust. Sheaves of paper made loud slapping sounds as she tried to find her place. There were two markers for each book, one for the text and one for the index. The first she tried was numbered, ordered in chapters and sections and paragraphs in the text, but only with page numbers in the index. However, there were fourteen pages numbered 2587 in the text.

81

The first heading halted her.

'*Offences against the Persons of Individuals*' – an individual then possessed her person like a pair of shoes to wear or a house to live in. So what was the distinction between offences against the person and offences against property? But with the next heading: '*Subsection: Sexual Offences*', the distinction had slipped away, dissolved into an adjective: I charge you with offending me sexually. By sex? With sex? In my sex? Unless it meant 'offences against sex'? However it translated, what had happened to her did not fit into this category any better than it deserved to be hidden in the 'shameful' section of the library catalogue where she – who it had happened to – could scarcely find it. What had been 'offended' – and that word was wrong too – was not her sex but something deeper inside her that might be reached by sex but was not distinct from it: a secret invisible skeleton that had used to sustain her as home does, or friends, unremarkable till its loss is felt. And yet it would not have been so bad, say, to have been hit; she could have endured more pain in an assault directed at her body in a blind general way. That would be 'an assault against the person of an individual', somehow external to the thing inside that Steve had smashed. But what he had done to her was an assault on an individual, inseparably inescapably her. Stop rambling, she ordered herself, forcing her eyes back to the page.

'*Unsolicited Matter Describing Human Sexual Techniques*'.

Surely what happened to her was not with these? Just because that part of her had been touched she was to be put amongst this sordid trafficking? It was like describing all plants bearing red berries as species of tomato.

But why was that part unknown, and unnamed so vulnerable? Because it was a way inside her, a last hidden refuge halfway between the skin that everybody saw and the life inside that no one should touch unless invited? Or was it only learned symbolism that made it so special? Should she not think like the doctor, no real harm done, just bruises and scratches that the body effortlessly washes away or clots together, no worse than childhood's grazes on the knee? Why such lingering pain, such a fermenting of frightening questions, and dull dread of comfortless answers?

The pages, cream coloured and unblemished by pencil or fingermarks, thin but dense with no hint of transparency, stared her out. She felt as if she were trespassing.

'Form of Indictment for a rape: AB on the – day of – 19 – had unlawful sexual intercourse with CD who at the time of the said intercourse did not consent to it or being reckless as to whether she consented.'

That was it. Her eyes criss-crossed the pages as a lone newcomer scans the faces at a party hoping to see someone she knows or someone else alone. But no one had invited her here, and the paragraphs closed in on themselves, sending her away to other sections to get lost and distracted by exotic but vaguely familiar phrases: malice aforethought, hearsay, diminshed responsibility, a year and a day, not with intent.

Abortion was in 'Offences Against the Person', next to Murder. Suicide was one too, so an individual didn't really even possess her person. Whose was it then? The question was, she felt, in some way relevant to her case. The legal language bewildered her, carried her off on an endless weaving process, doubling and redoubling back on itself. Perhaps the person belonged to the state, or the crown, or her parents, or society, even God. She shut the book and pushed it away from her, causing the table to shudder and the *Country Life* woman to transfer her magazine from table to lap. She took the next book, resolving to be methodical.

'Rapuit et Carnaliter Cognovit'.

'Raptus is when a man hath carnal knowledge of a woman by force or against her will';

'Forcible sexual intercourse with a man not his wife';

'The carnal knowledge of any woman above the age of ten

83

years against her will and without her consent'.

Rape too it seemed was variously defined and who it could afflict moved inch by inch with the changing centuries, two back one forward.

'Carnal knowledge without her conscious permission not being extorted by force or fear of immediate bodily harm; but if such permission is given the fact that it was obtained by fraud or that the woman did not understand the nature of the act is immaterial.'

Unconscious permission? And to whom was it immaterial, oh god, what was going to happen?

'It is an indictable offence for a man to rape a woman.'

Write everything down. Treat it as a piece of research.

'Subsection: cross-examination of the complainant' – that's me.

'Cross examination' she copied *'with a view to showing that she consented does not involve an imputation of her character . . .'* What? Surely it implied she was lying? Cath paused for a long time, trying to work out how the end of this sentence could justify its beginning. The upside-downedness of it was frightening.

' . . . since by alleging consent the accused is doing no more than denying one of the elements of the charge.'

She held that in her mind, in case it fitted in with something else.

' . . . the defendant, if called, may not on that ground be cross-examined on previous convictions or bad character.

'The defence is not allowed to say: "the woman is a prostitute" but after a proper foundation has been laid in cross-examination a defence witness may be called to say: "I say she is a prostitute because of so and so." '

There followed several pages on the relevance of the woman's being a prostitute, and how it could and could not 'properly' be established whether she was one. There was a quotation from a famous judge:

'We live in an age when it is hard to say where promiscuity ends and prostitution begins, and it may be unnecessary to

decide on which side of the dividing line the particular conduct falls which a man charged with rape may wish to prove. Evidence which proves that a woman is in the habit of habitually submitting her body to different men without discriminating, whether for pay or not, would seem to be admissible.'

She read it over again; it made her want to cry.

'A woman is in the habit of habitually submitting her body to different men without discrimination': there was something so contemptuous about it; the words' length and supposed technicality served only to emphasise a vast hatred, some kind of twisted Victorian loathing trying to hide behind them, a kind of madness almost.

'Rape of a woman'

'Rape of a prostitute' – as if prostitutes weren't women, she thought, as if they didn't have persons – *'thorough corroboration of the evidence of the prosecutrix.'*

'Corroboration', she wrote, and forced her eyes back to the page, *'is not essential in law. It is, in practice, always looked for, and it is the established practice to warn the jury against the danger of acting on her uncorroborated testimony.'*

The Browns: she'd never thought she'd need them. Cath continued to flick through the little stack of pages. There seemed to be nothing of use at all. Certain frequently used words stuck in her mind and rankled or confused. 'Submitting', for instance, submitting her body – that seemed to imply capitulation, surrender, and yet at the same time it could be used as evidence that force had not been used. And 'submitting to carnal knowledge': it all tied itself in knots. How could you submit to someone else's *knowledge?* Being known: biblical. *'Connection with a woman of weak intellect'*, *'connection by false pretences'*, *'connection by personating husband'* – how did connection differ from carnal knowledge or from rape, it sounded a mutual kind of thing, but it could be anything.

If she had been accused of rape, she thought, these books, despite their archaic phrases and unpunctuated sentences, might have been of some use: they would have told, for instance, how to accuse the complainant of promiscuity so habitual that consent wasn't an issue without actually saying it himself; it would have been explained how far consent as a legal idea could actually deviate from what an ordinary person might imagine:

'Consent to a course of action does not imply a mature understanding of the consequences of that course of action, but merely a willingness that it should take place.'

To a man accused of rape the books would have held out hope. It was *'established practice to warn the jury against the danger of her uncorroborated testimony'* – and yet how could his simple assertion that actually he believed that she consented possibly be substantiated, corroborated? Was there a difference between 'proved' and 'corroborated'?

Now, every new sentence she read raised a doubt or a question of some kind which seemed to threaten or qualify the tiny pile of facts she thought she had managed to establish: that she could be asked about her sexual relationship with Steve, that he could argue that she consented and it had to be corroborated that she didn't – and that was the Browns, and the medical evidence, but even that she wasn't sure of, because, she supposed, that didn't 'prove' that she hadn't consented. How could you really prove a rape? No one else was there when it happened. She took up *Principles of English Law*. The 'burden of proof' was on the prosecution. There were different kinds of proof as well as different kinds of evidence: admissible and inadmissible, and different kinds of corroboration, too, were acceptable under different kinds of circumstances and depending on which side was offering them and what sort of thing they corroborated. Occasionally there was an 'element of doubt' as to exactly what was allowed, and 'precedents' were quoted, one judge's arbitrary decision defying the honeycombing of categories and exceptions with a single pronouncement:

'It is well known that women in particular, and small boys, are liable to be untruthful and invent stories', one of them had

said, and now that would be woven into the law, enshrined perhaps in the green book she had yet to open: *The Encyclopedia of Forms and Precedents*.

There didn't seem to be anything about her side being able to ask him anything, not that she could think what might be asked – but that was how she had always imagined the law conducted: examination and cross-examination, two speeches at the end, balance scales as the emblem of justice. But nothing was so clear. Cath craved some release from the frustration the books engendered – to slam them resoundingly shut, get up overturning her chair, shout something and walk out leaving the swing doors grasping air behind her.

'*The judge must use clear and simple language that will convey without any doubt to the jury that there is danger in convicting on the complainant's uncorroborated evidence.*'

Her head throbbed. She shut the book quietly, then carefully replaced the books, AUA–STA, MA–PU, the easy, soothing logic of alphabetical order and same-size books, volumes all in a line. She felt so stupid. The rows of spines, calm and immovable, concealed an incoherent writhing of hints and qualifications. It was early closing day for the reference library; she ought to see if there was anything downstairs that she could read at home.

The wide staircase seemed to swoon and lurch: too much small print. She took it carefully on the outside curve, stopping to stare at the exhibition of framed prints hung each one a step lower than the rest. A watermill, puffy clusters of trees, cliffs and a storm at sea: they seemed like scenes from another planet.

'*The aggression is specifically directed against the mother-figure . . . the very violence of the attack bears the stamp of immaturity . . . the urge arises spontaneously and cannot be assuaged . . .*'

She rammed *The Psychology of Rapists* contemptuously back on the shelf. That kind of stuff was easy to dismiss, at least you could see what they were saying. *Neurosis and*

87

Crime, Sex Crimes: more of the same in them, you could tell from the covers. But suppose, she thought, that what meaning is actually buried in those reference books of Law, tangled over with that never-ending growth of Latinate words and forest of sub-clauses – supposing, it's actually as simple and dismissible as the rubbish here? They say the Law's an Ass. You can't afford to think that. There was another book: *Against our Will.* She'd heard of it somewhere. She opened it at random and read:

'All houses without exception were plundered. Three hundred and fifty cases of rape had been registered, neither children nor old women of sixty were spared. After . . . the little girls were thrown down the water closets.'

Despite the thick public-building heat of the library, Cath felt very cold. For a few seconds she hung on to the book like it was a rope that burned and cut and yet was at the same time the only thing between her and a flailing into waiting oblivion. Then she put it in her carrier bag and walked straight out of the library.

Outside Cath walked slowly in the purple and orange glare of city dusk.

You could see it as a stupid, impossible, crushing waste of time and pull out now, or alternatively, as some kind of challenge or enquiry to be pursued, she thought to herself coolly, as if giving uselessly honest advice to a friend in distress. Yes, I sympathise, what a terrible dilemma! Either you do or you don't, let's face it. She walked along with her mac over her shoulders even though it was cold, and when she tripped over a beer can she turned the trip into a kick and then stood still for a few moments, paralysed by the difficulty of the decision and her resentment at having to make it.

I hate the city, you can't see the stars, when did I last see stars? Fat chance of going away, unless I get a proper job. I wish I could afford a proper coat as well. What a day. I've got to walk home now, walk somewhere at any rate. Tired.

Self-pity.

Cowardice.

But I just want to forget it.

But she knew she wouldn't be able to: like a tedious book not worth abandoning because the suspicion that you ought to have gone through with it would cumulatively poison your thoughts and fill the time you had snatched from it.

I'll have to ring that barrister.

So she'd risen to the occasion, picked up the gauntlet. But rather than firing her with resolution this brought a dull sense of resignation like boarded windows on a rainy day, a misery like the hunger that is not starvation but a hankering after taste, succulence, abandon and choice.

Cath stared up at the lighted window of the upstairs flat Sally shared with Max. She would just visit, perhaps talk about it, perhaps not. Play it by ear. The important thing was to keep the lines open, not have another argument. Grown women like little girls at school walking home in dudgeon, making friends in the morning. 'Oversensitive' – how often over the last week she'd caught herself talking in her mother's voice, the one that had always irritated her.

Max answered the door, his hair newly cut shorter and all wedged around his face in a parody of carelessness. In contrast to the obvious grooming that had gone into achieving the haircut, the lower half of his face was blotched unevenly with stubble.

'She's not here.' He stared at her, momentarily surprised, then irritated.

'Do you know where she is then? I'd really like to see her tonight.'

'I'd've thought you might be the one to tell me that. Haven't seen her for a week. All her stuff's still here. You could tell her, if she's really going, I'd appreciate it if she'd come and clear it out. I want to get someone else in, I don't like living on my own: too expensive for a start. And if she doesn't get it soon, I'll ditch it anyway.'

'Max, I can't tell her anything. I don't know where she is

– and it's only a week, you can't just – it's her –'

'It's absolutely typical,' said Max. 'You should know, you've known her longer than me.'

'Did you have a row? What happened? Don't you have *any* idea where –?'

'Nope,' said Max, now looking above her head across the road. 'Look, it's cold standing out here, don't you want to come in?' His eyes returned to her face. 'I was going to pop round and see if you knew anything about it, but I got the impression you didn't want anything to do with any of us since you fell out with Steve.'

Did he know? No, he must mean since Steve moved out, that was all. Helped him move out, friend of his. But perhaps he did know – no reason why Steve, wherever he was – Locker-room gossip. 'Went round to see her, I mean, I reckon she owned me something . . .' No, that was teenage stuff. 'But you know, the bitch is taking me to court.' She didn't want to know anyway, just get away.

'No thanks.'

Max's indifference seemed to have changed within a sentence, he was insistent now.

'Come on, have a coffee, or a glass of wine. I've got some people in.'

'No thanks.'

Where would she go? Home? Look for Sally? Impossible, she might be anywhere, anywhere in the world; everyone had scattered themselves, she had no friends left, no one there, there never was.

'Why not? You're not going to wander the streets looking for her, are you?'

He knew, she was sure. But that was paranoia. The mocking manner was nothing out of the ordinary, that was how he talked. She was getting hysterical. People, she ought to go in, see people.

'Just a quick drink.'

He pulled the door right back as she spoke, flattening himself exaggeratedly against the wall as if to let a very large person pass.

'Quite safe, I assure you.'

It was too late, she was in now.

The handful of people seemed like a crowd in the tiny sitting room: a red-headed man she remembered from the Racism in Education Committee was talking quietly with a middle-aged man who kept fiddling with the sleeves of his jumper; two women were half-heartedly reading newspapers, one of them looked vaguely familiar.

'Cath,' Max announced to the room, but he did not tell her their names. 'I'll get a bottle of plonk. Why doesn't someone put a record on?' Cath felt herself blushing. She hadn't done that for years. She sat down abruptly on the sofa without taking off her coat. The room was tidier than when Sally was there. Where was she then? She took the glass of wine. The room seemed to be regrouping itself in response to her entry, the two women put down their papers and pulled their cushions nearer, one of them putting her arm round the red-haired man, the other leaning towards Max, but not touching.

'Well –' Cath said, at the same time as the red-haired man asked,

'How –'

'How's the literacy project then?'

'Everything's going well except for funding,' she replied. 'We're having to go begging to Quakers and Tories and all sorts. Still –'

'Milk them dry, milk them dry,' said the red-haired man, which was what Tim had said.

'I've thought of volunteering for the literacy teaching,' said the woman with him. 'Do you need people? Is it difficult? How many hours a week would I need to put in?'

Cath told her, aware that she was quoting from one of the publicity leaflets she had written, but it didn't matter, she was almost enjoying herself, feeling a bit lightheaded from the wine and nervousness, but she was glad she had come in.

'The trouble with all this,' interrupted the older-looking man, who had a slight paunch, 'is it's all so damn band-aid, just clearing up the casualties of an abysmal education system. Now I think the energy should go into changing the system, not patching it up.' He had turned to face her. His features were all puckered up in animation. He thinks he's said something original, thought Cath, noticing out of the corner of her eye that Max and the woman in the denim trousersuit whose name she didn't know had yielded to the inevitable consequences of the looks that had been passing between them and begun to whisper in each other's ears, finishing each communication with a kiss. Is that who he wants to move in, she wondered. Is that why Sally went? He can't throw her out, it's in her name. Is he showing me so that I'll tell her; why hasn't she told me, why? What does she know, where on earth – The argument continued lazily – pit, pat, but, chicken and egg if you say that then you must – between herself, red hair, and the man next to her whose name was Andrew. It was an argument worn smooth with use, and on another occasion she might have been bored with it, sought to break out of it or to resolve its polarities; but tonight, she realised, she was glad of it, sitting in the warm wine-smelling room knowing what had to be said next, feeling it all a little distant, a little unreal, distracting but not demanding, like knitting or washing up. The woman with the red-haired man was tired, snuggling up to him, opening her eyes briefly from time to time as he spoke.

'Do you think you will come?' Cath asked her suddenly, she didn't want her to go to sleep, leaving her alone with the impasse argument. Without opening her eyes the woman nodded slowly in time to the music. There was a long silence. Ah well. Cath began to button up her coat, feeling drowsy. She would sleep well tonight.

'Why not take your coat off and stay a bit longer . . . coffee?' said Andrew, and five pairs of dazed eyes seemed to be waiting for her answer.

'No, I've got to get up early,' she said, still with the well-worn script. Someone would say, why not phone for a taxi. Four pairs of eyes slid back where they had come from. But Andrew's stayed on her face. She did up her belt.

'Don't go,' said Andrew, putting one arm around her shoulder, the other hand heavily on her thigh. A half scream half shout had forced its way out of her throat before she could get it back and she was standing up. A red patch burned on Andrew's sallow face, everyone sitting up suddenly straight, the room completely changed around, woken up as if a light had been turned on.

'You'd better be careful Andrew,' Max's slow voice cruised through the shocked bright silence, aware of eyes upon it and enjoying them, 'or she'll have you up before the magistrates.'

'What do you mean?' Cath spat, looking from face to face: Max's denim-dressed woman and red-hair were smiling, Andrew beginning to look angry. Max shook his head slowly from side to side, making loud clucking noises.

'You're lucky she doesn't want you,' he said, 'the last –'

'Shut up,' said a voice she didn't know she had, a hiss not loud but thin and swift as a thrown knife. There was a slight change in his eyes, no longer flickering, no longer wide to draw in his audience, they narrowed and fixed on her.

'For fuck's sake. Can't you take a joke?' he said. 'Steve was right, you –' he stopped. She picked up her bag and was halfway to the door.

'If you try and take over this flat,' she shouted, 'I'll write to the council and tell them!'

Oh what a fool. Who else knew? Cath walked as quickly as she could down the path, trying not to run. Like sudden things that scare you as a child, false teeth, bodies of mice, old man in a garden where you thought you were alone. She thought of Max knowing what had happened and telling, and was profoundly shocked – it left her not knowing what to do, overwhelmed by an embarrassment and a vulnerability that demanded flight, that made her have to get away and pretend it hadn't happened. It was like returning as a child to the secret place on the building site where there should be nothing but the grass flattened for her own body, shrivelled remains of daisy chains, sweet papers and the ring she buried to keep it safe: a bottle, cigarette stubs, someone's been here, might come again, any minute now. But that was a pleasant place and this was not. Why care? There was nothing to cherish in this memory. Ought to want to spread it around as far as possible, get rid of it, get it worn out and used to, gone. But the thing was, she realised, that would be no good unless they took it as it was. Even if she could tell it as it was, and that – well, the words did not come – the words that should have told it all, it didn't fit, it said nothing. The effort of searching for the right one, of sketching and shading the alluding that would have to come from inside, too much it would hurt, not worth it. I've been raped: it meant what the listener chose it to mean, it was hardly a word at all, guaranteed nothing in the way of response.

'She's been raped', 'I raped her': would he have said that or would he have said, 'We did it on the floor', or I 'fucked her', 'She struggled a bit but I fucked her. Hard. On the floor. Teach her to throw me out.' If he said that it wouldn't be rape, not at all, and Max would have nodded, yes, one of those everyday things. Forcible sexual intercourse with a woman not his wife: she'd almost been his wife, hadn't she, but for the bourgeois bits of paper, the promise to honour and cherish? So he couldn't have raped her. Just hard on the floor, struggled a bit, teach her to throw me out. So she hadn't been raped; you couldn't just say you had. Whys and wherefores. At court, not just proving it happened but proving what it was as well. Till death do us part, once is for ever.

Perhaps Sally knew? But then, surely she would have . . . she wouldn't think it wasn't rape? Please. But then they wouldn't have told her it was. Just a fuck, why mention it? Taking Steve to court, what does she think she's up to? When did he tell, about rape or about the case? Or maybe no one else heard . . . everyone knew except the people she wished she could tell.

Common currency. Made it seem what they wanted, trampled on secrets and sore spots, read your letters, went where they shouldn't be and shuffled it all up so that your own words came back to you warped by another's use, all silly and blinking exposed in the light, all bent and useless taken without asking. Nothing you could do. Still they were yours, better if they'd just taken them and that was that. But they came back, turned vicious. Your job to sort it out, if you could. Keep quiet. Don't panic. Spilt milk.

7

'I'm wanted at court? Already?'

'Just the Magistrates' Court. For charging.' The desk sergeant's toneless voice kept receding into inaudibility as if he was turning his head away from the receiver. He'd said 'court': what was she supposed to think? She swallowed, and held her free hand very still in her lap, watching it. 'It'll only be for half an hour or so. Bit of a formality. The High Court's different, that could be in six months, nine . . . Now, there's a few details to fill in for the paperwork, we can do that now.'

'Six months!'

'Nothing we can do about it, that's the clerk of the court.' The line spluttered and clicked as if in sympathy with the speaker's irritation.

'Who am I speaking to?'

'640. Is it a "C" or a "K"? Place of birth? Support Liverpool myself . . . daytime phone . . . don't want to frighten you in the middle of the night, do we? Are you planning to leave the area in the next six months? No holidays? Dear me. Let me know if you do, won't you? That's all. Didn't hurt, did it?'

'Wait a minute: I wanted to know, what are you doing with him? I'm worried in case . . .'

There was a pause, shuffling, muttered consultation, then she thought she'd been cut off.

'He's not being held, Miss Sheldon, but you're quite all right, he's not living locally any more.'

'But what do you mean, how far away?'

'I can tell you too far for him to be paying you any visits.'

'But he knows where I live!'

'It never happens twice, not once they've been caught. No need to worry, like I said.'

'When will I know the date of the actual hearing?'

'Give them a couple of months, they'll have some idea then. Like I said, a law unto themselves that lot. Anything else?'

Patience beat its way heavily down the line, like tired footsteps, grudging. No, they didn't know when exactly she must see the magistrate. But it would be 'soon'.

'Anything else, Miss?'

'Yes . . . No.'

It had started now, for real. Cath sat on the floor by the phone imagining what that might mean: a custodial sentence. If she wanted the prosecution, then she must also want a person shut in a small room without a view, too alone or too together as the case might be. Two years? Ten? Two months? She had no idea. Remission or the possibility of remission, 'good behaviour'; that would be an extra humiliation; and no music, no train journeys, no friends. Brutality perhaps, other prisoners . . . No, she didn't want that.

The cat climbed on to her stomach, kneading and purring vigorously. She rubbed between its ears, feeling the skull-bones beneath its warm fur. She got up suddenly, leaving it to stalk off disgruntled. Of course she didn't want that. But that's what you're after, that's what might happen if . . . That's the whole point. Your one-time lover shut in a box because of you, that's what the whole thing's about. What is it then? If I don't want his suffering, what do I want? Why not just say: I know it was a crime, but I'm alive, forget about it. Forget about him, and get on with life?

This question seemed, bafflingly, inappropriate. Suppose there was a different kind of sentence, one more obviously an eye for an eye, something to make him think: would she want that? Could she watch it (shouldn't eat meat unless you could kill it yourself)? Have him raped back: what would she think of that? As a punishment? As a way of making him know what he'd done? It'd hurt, it'd humiliate, but more than anything it would make him angry, far too angry to compare, identify or regret. And how long would it hurt anyway? He'd flick a switch inside himself and return to the life awaiting him, eager, concerned and outraged that such a thing had been done to Steven Blake who's never late and never lets down. It would be in no way the same, would serve neither as lesson nor punishment. Why was she too stunned for proper anger? Why couldn't she flick a switch? Why was he so damn solid, his skin hide, hers a membrane? It wasn't the same for men. She remembered thinking that in the police station. Where were those feelings of panic and dissolution? He'd never understood. She supposed that kind of secret struggle had been absent from his experience since he was a child: playground bullies, classroom tyranny, the utter misery of suffering force – if it had ever been there at all. It was a part of his life he'd refused to resurrect for her, and now perhaps so long gone that he wouldn't recognise it.

The first argument they'd ever had had been about that kind of incomprehension. They'd gone to Spain for a holiday. In a crowded tourist bar by the beach he had left her to get drinks. A man said something to her in Spanish and she didn't answer.

'Not Spanish, you are English,' he'd said, smiling broadly; her eyes searched resentfully for Steve, one of the indistinguishable among the crush of denim shirts at the bar. She was too hot, but felt unable to take off her sweatshirt while the man was looking at her so pointedly.

'You are English,' he'd repeated, taking a step to one side to prevent her gaze escaping from his face. There was a twisting in her stomach as she hung suspended between anger and guilt. Her instinct was to cut him dead, insult him in English since he was making such a point of using it. But remember, people here are more open, strike up conversation at the drop of a hat . . . He muttered something in Spanish and smiled some more, a huge glistening smile that teetered on the edge of the insulting. *What* was it he'd said? Noisy, red, hot – all the bars were cheap, why had they come to this one, the most crowded? Despite her mistrust she was straining towards him, trying to catch a phrase that would make things clear and allow her to react.

'I don't understand,' she'd said coldly and stared at the wall to the left of him. There was a boiling feeling in her guts as if her frustration had been reduced to a thick residue that splattered and clung and burned inside. This was not the first time it had happened.

'You would like a drink?' He took a step left, cutting off her view of the wall, face still pulled into its wet-toothed smile. No. His expression of enthusiastic friendliness didn't falter.

'Come to the discotheque with me, very nice, very near,' he said, bending down and putting his hand on top of hers. She withdrew her hand with a force that would have made an effective blow but, as it was, left her pulled backward, off balance and unsettled physically like a person holding back vomit.

'Go away,' she pulled the guidebook out of her pocket and pretended to read it. Instinct told her the moment he had gone. Steve was just sitting down with their drinks when she looked up, big glasses with bits of orange floating.

'I'd like to get out of here, a bloke was being a real nuisance.'

'But he won't bother you, not with me here.'

Steve had taken her hand and again she'd snatched hers away, with only a little less vehemence than a few minutes previously.

'How would you feel if you had to have a bleeding bodyguard just to sit and have a drink? They just force you to pay attention to them –' That sense of being locked in a box, held casually at gunpoint, how could she explain that?

'Mmmm, but they're like that here. It doesn't mean anything.'

'I don't like it.'

Her rage had coagulated, a thick layer precariously suspended in her upper stomach, floating like fat on yesterday's gravy.

But the night he'd raped her he'd known those feelings existed in her, even if he couldn't ever share them. He'd known and that was why he'd done it. Blood rushed to Cath's face, half anger half remembered fear, a little embarrassment even, that someone could know so well where she was weak, stare at what no one was meant to see, and hit the bullseye of pain. He had punished her for telling him to get out. Was it simply that she now wanted to punish him in turn, in which case it would go on for ever . . .

'I think you owe me something.'

If there was any debt, the way to discharge it, now, would be to drop charges. Bury the hatchet. That was the burden . . . and the evidence all against her if she did it – but she didn't owe! What could she owe? She'd shared her life and helped with his, she'd let him into her home – even if eventually she'd sent him away from it, he'd been there. And why did people always remember just the last thing you did, never the history, never the reasons and the whys and wherefores? She'd thrown open the doors, read his books like a good child eating meat, fat, gristle and all, ate it all. With respect Mr Blake, I typed your prose and put the colons in, even wrote words that had your name at the bottom; as a means to your ends I swallowed, swallowed, swallowed – and so to sickness in the end. I don't owe you a thing. What could I owe you except to say when I had had

100

enough? I did that. What need then, what weakness had she fed without recognising? What was it that, when removed, led to such a sense of righteous deprivation that he felt he could smash into her like that? And how could someone who had so much find themselves owed to?

Blood pushed heavily in her veins, a confused surging between rage and bewilderment.

'I'm not going until I've come.'

Hurt his pride? It was some kind of revenge for something: vindication of the rights of man. Pass the parcel backwards, it gets bigger every time. Getting too big to pass on now.

She half sensed in herself bottomless anger that she could not touch, it would burn like a lake of petrol. There seemed nowhere to put it but into the case, whatever its outcome, however inappropriate – nowhere. Was that why she was doing it? Was that a good enough reason? If he was found guilty – not sentenced, even – that would be enough, she thought. My pain would be legitimate, my story truth: that would be an end to it and I could simply acknowledge the facts, say I had been raped and it was wrong. A fact.

But you know that anyway! Does it take twelve strangers to convince you a fact is a fact? Pathetic. What does it matter how many other people agree with you?

It does, it does. I want it to be admitted, to be said that it was wrong. I want it disapproved of. Steven Blake, you shouldn't have done that, you'll be looked at askance by those who know you from now on. Damn whether you change, whether you learn, whether or not your imagination can be stretched to understand the precise flavour of what you did. I want some consensus, something to be seen to be done – or said would be enough. I want to be vindicated and then I can forget. I want you to carry the Burden of Proof, it's got heavy with all this passing to and fro. You'll survive.

I can't think of any other way.

✳

'Mr Salter's very busy.'

'I was told to ring.'

'I see, and who advised you to consult Mr Salter?' The woman's voice was positively purring with politeness; she would have the satisfaction, Cath thought, of knowing that no one could ever criticise her 'manner'. It was irritating, it made you feel small, but no one could fault it.

'Roger something or other from the –'

'I see. Is it Legal Aid then, Miss Sheldon?'

And it made you answer back in the same way.

'No. Roger has contacted Mr Salter on my behalf, and suggested I phone as soon as possible.'

It was like the interview she'd had at the unemployment office when she got the sack: put things the right way and pretend that nothing matters anyway.

'And what is it you want to see Mr Salter about?'

'It's personal. I've got to be a witness.'

'Uh, huh. Miss Sheldon, Friday is a very, very bad day. I really don't think I can interrupt Mr Salter when he's seeing clients. I think it would be best to give him a message and for you to try again on Monday, between 9.45 and 10.15, if you haven't heard by then.'

It wasn't possible to make an appointment. The receptionist enquired as to when the case Cath was involved in was coming to court and implied politely that there was really no hurry, then, was there?

'I'll give Him your message.'

There was a capital H in him, and what would He be like, when she got to see him? Cath feared the worst: he would be like a television caricature of a GP, he would listen with an air of indulgence and say, nothing to worry about dear, nothing at all. But she couldn't afford to think that: he was the sum total of the help she could get. But not until Monday. Damn the woman.

If she'd stayed typing instead of going to college, that would have been the pinnacle of her career, legal secretary, personal assistant, will of iron and perfect manner. Similar to a butler. On impulse, she decided to phone her mother.

'You know it's not six yet?'

'No? Well I shan't be long.'

'How are you then?'

'All right. But –'

But. Afterwards, Cath stared at the receiver, her nerves jangling for the satisfaction which telling her mother had not brought her. She felt incompetent. It was her fault. The words that might have made her mother respond as she had wanted had hidden as she opened her mouth, and the ones that had come out were enemies. I went to the police, she'd said, and I'm seeing a barrister, and I've been back to work, yes, fine, she'd said. She'd wanted comfort but left no space for it. She'd not wanted melodrama: she'd certainly escaped that. Her mother had asked if she'd seen a doctor and again if she was feeling all right. And would she like a break, come and visit May and John? Or – No, I'm fine Mum, the words had said, partly, even, because that was how her mother would want her to be, not liking fuss. They had agreed that Steve was a bastard, and Cath assured the miles-away woman who couldn't see her face that she was so all right she wouldn't have bothered to mention it if it wasn't for the fact that it would come up in court. No use, they agreed, in making it worse by getting worked up.

Telling, but not telling (good girl doesn't make a fuss). I'll never be able to tell anyone Cath thought, I couldn't tell my mother. She didn't really want to, anyway. That was it. Look after yourself. Yes. Your Health is the Most Important Thing. Yes. For the first time she had not argued the point.

If she had described it more, said what he said and how it had happened, instead of using that dead and debased newspaper-word, would her mother then have been shocked, angry? If she had been, perhaps that would have made Cath desperate, perhaps it would have been worse? Or because she'd been shocked, her mother might have been annoyed, convinced Cath must have done something to make it happen: wrong kind of friends, living in sin, wrong kind of interests, bad sort, stupid. What could she have said to –

She was dialling Salter's office again, her fingers moving too quickly for the dial. On the third attempt she was connected to an answer-phone. Was that his voice, then? 'If you need to contact me urgently, I must stress urgently, my home number . . .' She took down the number and listened through again, partly to check, and partly to find out what she could from the way he spoke. He sounded very young: moneyed-graduate voice, slow, slightly ironic. It wasn't really urgent, especially, she supposed, since she wasn't a 'client'. She ought not to rub him up the wrong way. But she dialled the home number, half expecting no reply.

'This is his wife speaking.' Just changing his shirt and having a sherry, the voice said. My Husband and I. Busy man. Soufflé. Quiet evening. Together. Ruined.

'It's important.'

Wives, everywhere, safe as houses, safe as a wife she thought. 'You live alone' people said. Rich and poor, eveywhere wives. Polished nails on white hands shielding him from unwanted calls: a minor service considering the protection received. The line had gone all muffled. She hated wives and husbands. If I was a wife, she thought, would I –

'Salter here.'

Yes, he remembered – Roger saying something about it. He told her about the management committee, and what a good idea the whole thing was. Yes, Roger *had* told him about her. The law was confusing for the layman. He could give her a run through the court procedure, a bit of practice. He talked about the English Education System and how it prepared no one for Life, Income Tax, the Law, Business, none of it was on the curriculum in state schools, and despite his convictions he was going to send his little boys – but they must get back to the point.

'Ever been in a school play?'

Cath had been wondering for some time if he was drunk and didn't know what to say.

'Never mind. You might as well try to get copies of your statements from the police: though I don't fancy your chances. Probably "lost" them by now. You do understand – though I can give you a bit of advice, I shan't be representing you?' Cutlery tinkled in the background and a baby cried. Cath's flat felt cold and damp. 'Good, well, try and remember what you said in your statement. Write it down. Come and see me in my office, next Wednesday. Six. And we'll make a start.'

Tuesdays were always busy teaching Paul and Mrs Anderson, so she set herself up with an egg on toast for breakfast, spearing the yolk with a crust and spattering the tacky yellow with pepper. She scanned the local paper for something that might interest Paul but it was all planning permissions, corruption in the council housing department, a new centre for pensioners, Michael wins scholarship . . . . more Mrs Anderson's cup of tea, really, but then she didn't need any encouragement. Already she was buying books in the certainty that she would be able to read them; *Techniques of Novel Writing*, *What This Katy Did* by Katie Boyle, *Travels in Tibet with a Donkey* waited on the mantelpiece for when, as Mrs A put it, I can curl up with a book. She heard the postman scrabbling with the letterbox: 'post person' Kim would correct. It might be Sally had decided to let her know she was alive, or Jean had arrived in New York – but there was only a form from the DHSS because she'd forgotten to sign on, and a blue-enveloped second-class stamped letter from her mother. Her mother's letters were never long and the bold handwriting hurried her through it four words a line like an impatient walker dragging a child by the hand. Of course I'm all right she said aloud, putting her plate resoundingly in the sink. Why didn't you ask when I wasn't?

It was going to be sunny. In a way Paul didn't need to read. However many times she went to his home, the tiny streets at right angles to each other never failed to confuse her sense of direction. But Paul could find his way anywhere he had been once. Winchester Street? Easy, he'd say. Turn right here and keep on till there's a tobacconist with Swiss knives in the window and turn left, then left again where the 133 goes. Now where the houses get bigger and there's alleys between, take the alley by number 68. And the penknives would be hidden away in a far dusty corner of the window, the 133 stop an unmarked request – she would be lost. But Paul could get anywhere: like being blind or deaf, she supposed, the other senses sharpened themselves to compensate.

And the mental effort inside his head every time he went somewhere new. Told at school he was incapable of learning; now would I have done a thing like that? No. Perhaps? Maps and diaries and calendars and lists and notes: always forgetting, always getting lost, stopping to consult. No great advertisement for literacy when you come to think of it. Would he lose all that when he learned to read? No, she decided, it's too much part of him. Her mother learned reading at school but now read only newspapers and letters, necessary things, not pleasure and addiction, and she had Paul's acuteness: remembered recipes, birthdays, appointments, addresses, dress sizes. Probably how dependent you became was proportional to how much it could be useful to you in the first place.

'I want to write a letter,' he announced, 'to my brother. He's gone home. To Jamaica. The one with the rings and the big car: he just sold it and went, always said he'd take me but he didn't he took his girl instead.' No, he didn't know where to start.

'Dear Everard' he wrote slowly, glancing up between the two words. He could do that much weeks ago. The table was cluttered with bits of a radio that he had been mending for his cousin for the last month, small parts carefully separated on to lids and matchboxes. The whole lot was laid out in a sequence that meant, he said, that he would be able to put it together in five minutes, easy, as soon as he got the missing part. The pen had stuck after 'Everard'.

'What are you going to say, then?'

'First you should have told our mother that you were going because she looked for you for three days before Leroy got through on the phone. And then, you always said you'd take me. I wouldn't mind but it aint good for a brother to break his word and I don't think Julie is the girl for you. I haven't got another job yet but I'm fixing a car for someone. If you can get me some kind of job I'll come over, easy. Everyone's OK but like I said Mum's really mad so you better get in touch – get on that phone no matter how much it costs.'

'Let's have a look,' he said, peering at Cath's scribbled notes, a gleam in his eyes.

'I'm not going to tell you any of it till you've tried.' Laughing, she snatched the paper away. Saying the words with all the letters in slow motion, watching Paul's huge eyes staring, straying from the letters slowly appearing on the blue airmail paper in front of him to one with her notes on, laughing some more – she felt she was really over it all now.

'What was it made you want to read and write?' she asked over the coffee that was thick and sweet not from sugar but from the condensed milk, whole crates of which stood in the corner by the fridge. But Paul just raised his shoulders and opened his eyes wide in incomprehension.

'I dunno. It's not as if you need to read, there's always someone will do it for you . . . but I do like the lessons.' Lazy, just like me, she thought, no need to read; no need to remember because you can read. No need to because everyone can. Everyone's naturally lazy. Why else the toothbrush you promise nightly to replace, the lying in bed wondering whether it is burning you can smell, speculating even as to what you would do if there was a fire? Then, out of the blue he said:

'There's black people don't like white people and women don't like men. But the truth is hardly no one likes anyone.' The cigarette he was playing with broke. 'Lack of communication,' he said carefully. 'Most communication goes on with reading so I reckon I'd better learn.'

Reading, he kept very still, his hands on his knees, the book flat on the table. He stopped for whole minutes before difficult words, too proud to guess or sound the letters out. The whole of his thickish body locked so that he could concentrate on the page.

Outside there was a light wind and a scrubbed look to everything. Paul walked with her to the postbox, giving directions to the high street. Freed from the cramping effort of fiddling with letters and words, he raced and capered, pulling off his hat and bowing exaggeratedly to some of his mother's friends, crossing the road to creep up behind one of his own and take the paintbrush from his hands. After he was gone, Cath went on spelling to herself, concocting mnemonics and explanations for the 'ph' in telephone and the 'b' in plumber. This work was good she thought: no exams and no classroom and an almost free choice of who you taught. People you liked and who wanted to learn: I want to read this book, I want to write to my brother, I want to read to my granddaughter – you could see the sense of it. But no money, of course. It was true: work took your mind off problems. The case was a long way off and she needn't think of it except, of course, for seeing Salter. For a moment her interview with him loomed large like a speck of dust on the eyelash blurring her sight. She willed it away. There was no need to think about anything till it happened. Already yesterday's anxiety seemed part of a former existence: the rape itself was almost something that

108

hadn't happened to her. She congratulated herself, secretly.

Cath searched the high street unsuccessfully for a café she had been in once and had remembered for the generosity of its sandwich fillings, her mind pleasantly distracted. Were things, she wondered, really more difficult to learn as you got older, or was it just that people became more selective and more economical of their efforts, more adept at assessing whether it was worth filling their minds with alphabets and facts? Whereas children have dustbin minds: coin collecting, poster sticking, train spotting point-scoring, minds that gobbled facts like sweets – but no, already she had forgotten, slipped into stereotypes, for in fact there were a lot of kids who said there's no point, who sealed their minds off and resisted all learning, at school anyway. 'Good learners' in the classroom, perhaps they were the ones who just didn't guess what would become of them or what was required of them, except that in a general way it was better to be good at things than bad? Or, as she had been, were they perhaps fired by a vague idea that education was the key to something, something better, but were unaware of the market value of knowledge, and of their own real needs and interests?

The train of thought was comfortingly endless. She could feel it like a person talking, unstoppable; a lonely person endlessly prolonging a cup of coffee, giving good entertainment in the hope of being asked to stay or come another time. She took her thoughts for a beer and a sandwich, grateful.

'So many people,' said Mrs Anderson, not for the first time, 'have told me that I ought to write a book, and I never said but the true reason I didn't was because I couldn't actually write – except my name, that is.'

Mrs Anderson professed not a mere inability to save but an actual distrust of saving; she preferred a bird in the hand to two in the bush, and for someone living on a widow's pension her flat was surprisingly luxurious. There were pale coloured wall-to-wall carpets, a large walnut-veneered television, a microwave oven and a profusion of fluffy rugs and china figures. She poured Cath the usual tumblerful of port and gestured to the biscuit tin. She had cleaned the windows since Cath last came and bought potted cyclamens flowering profusely in several shades of pink. Their petals were smooth as pampered skin, firm and yet fragile. They seemed to be more of an exposure than a display. Cath felt faintly uncomfortable with their combination of flamboyance and weakness, as she had done when Anne Marie, her room mate for the first term at college, had decorated her side of the room with exaggeratedly worded love letters from her boyfriend.

Smoothing the cuticles back from her nails as she spoke, Mrs A told Cath of a projected holiday to Paris to be taken in the company of her surviving brother, ten years younger than herself and of ill-defined but spasmodically lucrative employment. He had bought her ticket and implied that he would pay for everything as well.

'Not a word for nearly two years – and then this: Paris in the spring. I'd like to know where that one gets his money from . . .' She laughed, a searing Woodbine laugh accompanied by thumping on the chest and another sip of port.

'Duty free,' said Cath, joining in the conspiracy to postpone the frustration and temper that beginning the lesson would bring.

'I'll get you some nice scent,' said Mrs A unexpectedly. She was almost reclined on the sofa, her legs crossed and stretched along it, at her back several brocade cushions the same colour as the glass of port she held firmly in the hand resting along the top of the sofa. She was a short woman, but not thin. At her age, she said, a woman shouldn't wear too much make-up, especially under artificial light. Lipstick perhaps, and powder, but scent, that was something you could always wear. She held out her wrist for Cath to smell.

*

'I can't remember the bloody words long enough to write them down or look at all the letters. I just can't.'

She stared at Cath angrily and Cath felt guilty, held for the duration of the lesson personally responsible for delaying the appearance of Mrs Anderson's autobiography. Growing old.

'I want to write everything down before I forget it. My sister was like that: one minute clear as a bell, the next she couldn't even recognise me.'

How could a grown woman with a book to write waste her time with words that didn't spell themselves with their own rules? Said, dead, red, three, free, men; might bite: it was all holding her up and yet she had to do it. She wrote: 'Lissen my girl, my mother sed when I was three.' 'Said.' But then there was 'dead' and 'read'. 'Three' but then there was 'me'. List, listen glisten.

Staring at the spellings and trying to justify why the same sound looked a different way: rules with exceptions – by, before, but not ever – except – it seemed to Cath that between them they created whole cosmologies that lived for only an instant before they were superseded, toppled by a new exception discovered. And in between, Mrs Anderson picked out choice morsels of her life that were to become an autobiography, offering them as one child might offer another the cherries prised from Dundee cake.

'I pulled the communication cord,' she might say, or, 'I just turned the key in the lock and left them there. I walked up to the manager and said: "That's not fair, and if you can't understand that, you shouldn't be managing this place." My last husband couldn't do it unless he wore something, oh, how I hated them, but of course, it was all there was then. Don't have to worry now, of course.'

Cath was content to accept all that was offered, to feast on intimacy and the excitement of work. Only occasionally she wondered if it was fair that she only said things about words and never about herself, considering how much of what might normally be considered personal information

111

Mrs Anderson showered her with.

'Had to talk him out of it, and that took some doing, I can tell you, sat on a park bench in the middle of January, dying to go to the loo.'

'Had to have an abortion, a real one, not like they get nowadays. They didn't half make me suffer. You know, I shouted at that doctor, you're treating me like an animal! Didn't let anyone near me after that. Have you ever had an abortion?'

'No,' said Cath, answering the question, but not the invitation. 'Spell things like they sound until you've learned, as long as you can sound it out, we'll know what it means.'

'But that's no good for a book. I've got to write properly.'

Right. Write. She wrote carefully. Write a book about her experiences. A simple thing, really, once you can read and so long as you remember what they were.

She must have fallen asleep and dreamed. But the knocking didn't go away. It had got dark and she had no idea of the time. She took her shoes off and walked down the stairs as carefully as she could: amazing how much noise she must normally make – hands squeaking on the rail, feet slipping and bumping in a hurry, breathing, shouting, OK I'm coming. Now there was only the very slightest brush of her feet on the carpet and no one would hear that.

She didn't quite know why she was creeping down her own stairs, slinking down without a sound, tiptoe through the tulips, hands out to steady her both sides of the stairs. Halfway down there was another bout of knocking, but she continued at the same pace, too bad if they go before I'm there; a strange feeling of power you had from being invisible, choosing your moment to appear or even whether to appear at all. Carefully she brought her eye to the spy lens. Difficult not to feel they could see your eye from the other side, magnified and jelly-like suddenly appearing in the middle of the door.

Cath started. But, no, it wasn't Steve, she realised almost immediately. It was a man though, long-legged, growing and shrinking alarmingly as he shifted from foot to foot: it was Max. The figure loomed and widened as he leaned forward to knock again – very loud. She could see the vibration in the door. Held her breath. Why had he come?

'Cath!'

Suddenly she didn't feel safe anymore. But the thick door and its extra lock were there and the lights were off. Couldn't know she was in. Unless he'd watched her go in: hours ago, that was ridiculous. Even so, she crouched down, just in case it was possible to see her shape through the spy glass. There was silence. Perhaps he had gone, leaving the outer door open, he always wore trainers. No, she could hear him breathing. Was that possible or was she imagining it? She couldn't let him in, not after . . . He knew. Why was he coming then? Perhaps to apologise? He wouldn't. They'd never really got on. Perhaps it was news of Sally? That was it, she was back –

She almost opened the door. If she was certain that was it, she could open it on the chain. What kind of news? And if she was back she would come herself. Never sent messages. Bad news then, accident: Cath's hand was almost on the lock. Would the chain hold? Silly. No. If it was urgent he would push a note through the door or telephone later. If it was urgent, he would have phoned anyway, for quickness. Slowly she raised herself, her knee joints cracking, her legs afire with pins and needles. She wouldn't answer. The lens distorted so much that you couldn't make out the expression on his face. Remarkable you could recognise anyone at all; it must be things like clothes and hair she supposed. When would he go, for heaven's sake?

Suddenly the small prick of light with the picture in it just disappeared. She almost screamed in the sudden dark behind the door at the bottom of the stairs, and then she saw the shape of a hand dwindling away and heard the bang of the outer door, steps on the path. Was it laughter she heard? And what had happened, had he put his finger over the lens? Known she was there? How? Why had he come?

8

Cath sat in the quiet of Salter's office.

'They said they'd send a copy of the statement, but it hasn't come. But I think I can remember it almost perfectly. It's odd – I seem to remember the statement more clearly than what happened. If you see what I mean, the actual –' She stopped herself. What was she saying to him? It didn't sound right or wise to be saying that the statement and the actual events weren't consistent. She was babbling as if he was a therapist or hairdresser; hearing herself, the confidence bright and sharp as new clothes that had girded her as she walked up the stairs, that feeling of being an efficient secretary dealing with someone else's business, vanished in a sickening little eddy of self-consciousness. Like the last dregs of waste down the plug. Luckily he didn't seem to have noticed anything. But what had she meant: was there a difference between her statement and what had happened? Had she lied and forgotten it? That piece of paper, she had seen it written and read it and heard it and there was nothing else there, was there? She felt her skin suddenly damp, trying to recall, to see beyond the statement that had printed itself on her mind, but there was nothing.

'Tell me a bit about yourself,' Salter asked.

No, there was nothing. The paper statement grasped what had happened, maybe it left out the intangible but there was nothing more. Glancing up she saw that he had put aside the paper and pushed his chair back, one knee up and a small note pad balanced on it. She couldn't really look at him properly. She couldn't think what to say, it was like smiling for a photograph.

'Er, I work in adult literacy. Voluntarily, that is. Really, I'm unemployed. I used to be a secondary school teacher. I like the literacy project. There's not just the teaching, but organisation and writing up reports and fundraising –' I'm not like this, I'm not, she thought, my voice doesn't sqeak, I don't babble. Interrupt me, stop me . . . he wanted to, she could tell from his face.

'How old are you?' he asked.

'Thirty-one.'

'Have you ever been married?'

'University education?'

'Parents?'

So it was a kind of CV that he wanted, then.

'Have you had many men friends?'

No, it wasn't. Did he mean friends or lovers?

'No,' she said to be on the safe side.

'Contrary to what you might think, that won't necessarily stand in your favour.' He was still writing. 'There was a case a couple of years ago where the defence argued that the girlfriend had been . . .er . . . celibate for so long that she was obviously unbalanced – in fact I think she was a virgin, about thirty – they said she was torn between her natural instincts and a repressive neurosis which made her pretend afterwards it was rape: guilt, you see. He was acquitted. Modern psychology has changed a lot in the courts, a lot of people who would've been convicted thirty years ago aren't these days.'

'The Psychology of Sex Offenders,' she thought, remembering the books in the lending library, 'Neurosis and Crime.'

'Mind you, it cuts both ways,' he added, but she noticed that he didn't provide any example to back up this

116

assertion. His slow voice had been almost animated as he spoke: professional enthusiasm she supposed, but she also wondered if 'the defence' he spoke of had been him; if so, was he proud of the argument? He had told her after all that he was primarily a 'defence specialist'.

'I know they can ask about my relationship with him before,' she said, 'but what sort of thing . . .'

'Anything. Anything at all. A question such as "Did you sleep with anyone between the night he left and the incident?" would probably be allowed even, on the grounds of relevance. But your answer could not be disputed or contradicted. But how you answered that question would be important, and counsel for defence will have in his head what he can make of any answer you give, before you give it even. So you see, the important thing is to present yourself as a coherent character whose motives are intelligible to the average man and as such would earn his approval. Nothing extreme, nothing peculiar. In this case especially. The facts are clear enough from what you say of the police and medical evidence: it's character that will count. And, of course, luck,' he added.

'Now, there's two things I can do for you, first I can draw up a kind of sketch: guidelines as to what to emphasise, and what to play down, that's something you can keep reading and assimilate. So, for instance, if I said it was important to emphasise that you were not given to drunkenness and all-night parties, when counsel puts to you: "Where had you been prior to the alleged incident?" you reply, "I had been to a supper party given by my friend Jean because she was leaving the country the next day" rather than "to a party". Do you see?'

Cath nodded. She didn't know if she would read his sketch or not; she shouldn't have to: her story was true, it wasn't her who had to play games and wriggle out of something. Shouldn't be. The words I'm innocent came to her mind, as if she had been accused of something. She fought against the realisation but it was impossible to resist:

Salter was indeed trying to prepare her for the time when she would be accused, when it would be her trial.

'And I'll ask you a lot of questions in order to get the sketch together, so that will give you practice in answering clearly and guessing what counsel wants you to say and how you can answer the question without giving him what he wants: and we can iron out any little wrinkles in your story . . .'

He spoke only in paragraphs, nothing or a lot.

'What I'll do next,' he continued, 'is go over this version of the statement and what you've told me and get it typed up for you. Next time you come we can start with that as a basis. Three or four appointments should do it: and there's no hurry, of course, though we want to get the basics sorted out before you forget any of the details.'

That's all there is, she thought, that's my statement. There are no details, they've gone, sunk in quicksand never to be retrieved. Don't try. Don't dare.

'Actually I'm surprised they're taking this to court, I really am. There's not much to go on, not much at all.'

Cath's tongue had died, sands filled her mouth. His words piled themselves up in her head, he could say anything and she wouldn't react to it, just store it as she had stored the statement, carry it home wobbling inside her and put it somewhere till she could bear to get it out later. She stared at the wood of Salter's desk, red with a swirling of dark grain and knots, like two liquids stirred together: what was that? Rosewood? Mahogany? Tulipwood? Strips of light came through the linen blinds and caught a thin day-old fall of dust drifting above the polish. Beneath all the surfaces, applied and accidental, what would the wood feel like?

'Unless, of course, they want him for something else. That's always possible. There was a case I remember when the prosecution managed to circumvent the previous conviction rule that normally protects the defence's character . . .'

He had been staring at something not in the room, his head tilted slightly back; suddenly he relaxed his legs so that the chair rocked forwards on to all four legs and he leaned forward at the desk – a square of arms and shoulders, his head lowered and staring at her.

'Do you think that's likely?' he asked. That was what it would be like in court; a gathering of the opponent's strength, settling the body into the deadliest attitude, pause and the question launched. You cannot move to avoid it, you have no armour, you must take it straight on and unprepared except for the clenching of your muscles.

'I know he wrote some articles about the police. He's always been – er – anti-establishment, but I don't think he's ever done anything they could get him for, just things he wrote.' She might as well tell him about that business with Harris. 'As a matter of fact –' she began, but he interrupted.

'Did your name appear on any of these articles, the ones about the police or any other particularly controversial ones?'

'No'. How far would his sympathy go, she wondered. Would he help her whatever he thought of her and her life just because Roger had referred her? Why should he? Was he really as he seemed, fascinated by the complexities of his own profession but objective, disinterested? Permutations and possibilities and loopholes – a board game that you could make a career of, a rare occupation where the childhood qualities of audacity, deceit, white-lying were prized and encouraged rather than bred out; argue the hind leg off a donkey: it would make no difference what he thought of her once the argument started. But she suspected that somewhere there must be an allegiance to the processes of Law and Justice, an ultimate reverence for those thick books he had, presumably, struggled with until they welcomed him into the fold, a belief in Society and the superior quality of the British Police Force – and if he thought she did not share this belief and respect, would he not treat her differently, help her less? Or could these

119

barristers cut themselves off, pour passion into the defence of a murderer: at the flip of a coin, defence, prosecution? She wished it was a proper arrangement and she could pay him, pay him so much that he would wipe away all his secret values and direct his cunning purely in her interests. As it was, she was in receipt of a favour, she couldn't argue, she could accept but not expect.

'We'll have to deal with all that in case something comes up.'

There was a thick leather diary on his desk, he took a smaller matching one from his pocket.

'A month's time, or six weeks, that should do.' He wrote in fountain pen with great care: there was a kind of sensuality in his expensive paraphernalia that reminded her of other people's bathrooms, of Mrs Anderson's living room. Some people, she thought, choose objects to say the things they wouldn't say in so many words. There was something attractive in the tulipwood and leather, linen and parchment, but it was all mixed up with a strange kind of power she had not often encountered before, not brute force, not the power of crowds, but the silent heavy-duty power of an intelligent, rich man at a desk, unchallenged. For although he might daily intervene in other people's lives, not one of them would ever be in a position to touch his own. He need only say to his receptionist-wife, after all, no calls tonight and she would add the final touch to his invisible armour. Cath shuddered a little.

'If you remember anything that might be useful, write it down.'

She had been there exactly half an hour though it had seemed much longer. And she'd forgotten to ask him about the Magistrates' Court.

Steve would be at the Magistrates' Court.

She'd taken one of the red sleeping pills the night before, and one of the tranquillisers in the morning. The doctor had said she'd have to take those for a couple of weeks before they had any effect, they were special ones that weren't addictive. But she didn't believe that, even one would probably do something; she did feel very calm, but whether that came from the pills or herself was impossible to tell.

So this was the Magistrates' Court.

It was just like a large office, almost informal. Informal, because it was 'only a formality'. They were all waiting for him. What if he didn't come? Suddenly she was sure he wouldn't, not unless they brought him. She leaned back in the wooden chair deliberately enjoying her lack of anxiety and groundless conviction that it was going to be all right. The police officer who had come was the one who had interviewed her first, she thought, but he was now polite and almost solicitous, so different that she couldn't be quite sure. She looked sideways at him and suppressed a smile: he was studying his notebook like a schoolboy before an exam. Big fish humbled by bigger fish, she thought, and looked at the clock. Another twenty minutes had gone – half an hour late: he wasn't going to come. Who was that man next to the policeman? Perhaps it was her solicitor or barrister, no, not hers, the police one. She was only a witness, that was it.

The two men beside her got up at a signal from someone standing in the doorway at the other end of the room. Then the policeman came back for her.

'What's happening?'

'He hasn't come, it doesn't matter. The magistrate will see you now and him when he arrives. You needn't have been required in the first place.'

'Are you Miss Catherine Sheldon?'

'Is this your statement made to the police?'

'Is it the truth to the best of your recollection then and now?'

That was all. She could go, leaving them with forms to complete. She walked away on air, glad for the first time to be a mere witness, comforted that the statement would suffice: she need not even read it, she would recognise it from now on from the bent corner at the top left and the slight turquoise tint of the paper. It had been written in panic and pain but now it had saved her: the power of the written word, signed and stamped.

A fat cheque came from the Rowntree Trust, and the entire project went to celebrate in the Fox. Kim left after the first round, squeezing Cath's shoulder briefly as she did. This year the project would clear its rent and rates, next year it might be able to restock on books, increase publicity and even pay someone a wage. Everyone was buying Cath drinks for writing the application.

'Amazing,' said Tim for the third time, spreading his fingers and rolling his eyes. 'Don't know how she did it. Mind you, I saw that letter, it would've frightened me, more like a dissertation than a letter!'

Cath smiled without amusement. I'm exhausted she thought, giving a name to the inappropriate feeling of misery and indifference spreading through her, slow and sure as an ink blot. She was glad about the money of course, yet at the same time the success of her efforts seemed not to satisfy but rather to emphasise the feeling of blankness that had been with her for weeks.

'And I think,' continued Tim, turning to look at her, 'that if we decide to have a paid co-ordinator, it ought to be Cath. She's done so much lately, I think it should be recognised.'

Smiles and picking up of glasses.

'Of course,' said Dick. A flush of satisfaction and maybe relief softened the faces of the small gathering humped over the too-low table. Cath felt big and awkward.

'As long as she wanted to,' said Anne, glancing rapidly at Cath before leaving her seat, ostensibly to go to the toilet, but Cath knew it was really out of nerves and embarrassment at having spoken. She watched her slip into the door marked Ladies and emerge with her face settled only seconds later. Why was the woman so nervous in groups? It seemed an odd reaction to a divorce which, after all, happened five years ago. She was all right if you got her on your own. Cath was pretty sure she didn't want to be co-ordinator, paid or unpaid. She felt grateful to Anne for pointing this out. That was how she'd got the job fundraising, by thinking she wanted to do it because it was presented as a privilege.

'I don't know what I'll be wanting to do next year,' she said, 'but really it's the teaching I'm interested in, that's what I am – a teacher.'

'It could be part time, needn't stop you teaching, in fact it'd be better if it didn't,' Tim interrupted hurriedly, 'but I do think we need someone.'

'We may not be able to afford it anyway,' said Cath. 'There's no point in discussing it.'

A couple of Tim's friends, already half drunk and laughing at the slightest provocation, joined them, and Anne said she must go home as the babysitter had to go early. Cath envied her the excuse; she couldn't really leave since half of the point of the celebration was to thank her. Dick finished carefully giving the news to the newcomers and left them to Tim. Altogether more painstaking and restrained than Tim, Dick had been a printer until, as he said when asked why he had left such a good job, 'I was replaced by a machine.' He lived alone and spent most of his waking hours at the literacy project. Any and every event in Tim's home life and each of his emotional upheavals was related minutely to everyone he met, but Dick supplied no details about himself voluntarily, and replied to enquiries as briefly and uninformatively as possible.

'Ah,' he said, leaning back and removing his glasses, ruefully rubbing the purplish groove they'd carved on his nose.

'How are you then?'

At least, Cath thought, she could rely on Kim's discretion as far as men were concerned.

'Pretty well.'

'Enjoying the bachelor life still?' He spoke slowly and with very little intonation. He was a gentle kind of man, Cath thought, easy to ignore or forget, but nice.

'So what do you do with yourself when you're not slaving away for the project?' No one had ever asked her what she did with her 'spare time' when she was living with Steve: that was presumed activity enough. Well it was in a way, more than enough. He probably thought the same way as the police, the doctor: if she lives on her own she must be bored and lonely, living out of tins and liable to invent things.

'Much as usual', she said curtly.

'Good, good,' said Dick, as if to soothe, nodding. There was a silence and then to Cath's surprise he began:

'I've been working on my flat in the evenings, done the kitchen: sanded the floor and moved the sink a bit to the left so that I'll be able to put a decent-sized surface in that corner with the window-wall. And I've got some of those lights that you can swivel around . . . getting quite domesticated in my old age! These lights are good for plants, ultra-violet or something. I'm very keen on plants.' Cath liked plants too, but felt too wary of his sudden communicativeness to say so. There seemed nothing else she could offer as a reply. The conversation at the other side of the table was riotous: they'd been left on their own. She sat quietly making large inroads into her drink. She would go when she'd finished it.

'But you've never seen my kitchen, have you?'

'No.' No one ever has as far as I know, she thought.

A new round appeared, pushed across the table by Tim. Of course, she thought suddenly, Dick's lonely. He's picked on me – why? Because he thinks I am too? Shit. I'm not. Or he thinks he's being kind to me, hell, why can't people leave you alone. She got up abruptly and went to the

124

Ladies, where she sat in a cubicle without locking the door and without unzipping her trousers, just to get out of the din and babble of the bar. She felt deflated and depressed, an unremitting greyness like fur on a hangover-tongue seemed to coat everything she thought about, varied only by odd stabs of pain or irritation. Nothing seemed worth pursuing and nothing worth resisting. 'Zelda – for Zoe always' was written huge above the toilet-roll holder. There was a poem about constipation and a smeared streak of blood, and on the back of the door exactly at eye level a little black and white sticker. She craned forwards to read it: 'If you have been sexually assaulted or raped and feel in need –' Kim's Crisis Line! They wouldn't let you forget it, would they, they were everywhere.

'Shit!' she said loudly, and there was giggling in the next cubicle, the pull of the towel machine and a door swinging and banging shut. Emerging from the cubicle she looked to see if there were bags under eyes, but no, she knew she wasn't tired. Why on earth had Dick picked on her? She didn't look particularly sympathetic now, her large mouth pale and pulled straight across her face like a line that cancelled something out, and the V-necked sweater didn't really suit her: it showed two massive collar bones, the body's beams exposed – she wasn't very good with clothes. She thought she looked pretty forbidding. Can't people take a hint? No one bothered Kim when she scowled.

Back in the garish glow of the bar, Dick was waiting, smiled as she approached.

'You look tired,' he said, sympathetically. 'I expect you've been under a lot of pressure.'

'What do you mean?' she asked.

'Well, all that fundraising and giving that talk, for example. Speaking in public is quite a strain for some people. I couldn't do it . . . I really admire you Cath, the way you just get on with it, whatever it is. Hmmm – determination, that's it. I've always thought you were very –'

She wanted to bury herself away from his attention, sat panic-struck, biting back scathing comments, and arguing with herself: for what was wrong, after all, with being praised? Stop looking at me like that, stop this minute, how dare you. If she could have made him vanish she would have.

'I've often thought – wished –'

Why are you saying all this? Do you want to send me off the rails (but calm down, calm down, he doesn't know). What can I say to stop him, turn him off, drip, drip, stop staring at me, I don't want to know –

Cath dropped the matchbox she had been fiddling with under the table, and as she straightened from picking it up, interrupted him to say,

'Do you want this drink? I can't manage it, I've got to go now.'

His eyes, without wavering, widened a little. 'Wait a minute Cath. I wanted to ask you if you were all right, if something has happened, you haven't been looking very happy lately, has anything –'

'No, nothing. I'm fine.'

She was standing now, but it was difficult to turn on your heel and march out after someone had just expressed concern and still pinned you in a gaze that could swallow you whole. He looks like he's going to cry – no, it's because he's not wearing his glasses.

'I've been meaning to ask for a long time, but never had the opportunity: would you like to come to supper? One night this week? I'm a good cook, and you could give me your opinion on the kitchen.'

'No! No, sorry Dick, thanks, though.'

Dick looked so puzzled and disappointed that for a few seconds she searched for excuses with which to temper her refusal. She must stop snapping or people would think she was going round the bend. After all, what was wrong with him asking her? Why shouldn't she accept, it was friendly. She ought to – but he would look at her, she knew, as he

126

had been earlier; he wouldn't ask again if she was all right but he would be waiting, just waiting for her to say, actually Dick, something has been the matter: capitulation, weeping and bloody sympathy, thick and endless. It would be worse because it was his home and with no one else there he could ask as many questions as he liked. Unbearable. He might put his arm round her, try to kiss her.

'That's all right,' he said evenly. 'I'll see you home, shall I?'

Tim was watching them, waiting his turn to say goodbye and congratulate her for the last time. None of them had ever offered to see her home before, even after really late meetings. Must want to get her away from the others so that he could ask again, or worse, ask why. She knew she was acting like a teenager at her first party, but knowing made no difference, she couldn't bear it a second longer.

'Don't be silly – I'd rather walk home on my own.'

She smiled to try and take the vehemence out of her words.

'OK, OK,' said Dick, aware, she thought, of the others' eyes upon them. With them there, he couldn't argue. She would get a bus. If she approached the flat from the opposite side and far end of the street she had a clear view of the front porch long before she reached it. Downstairs was empty now. She left at last, feeling foolish, but on the whole more cheerful, as if the shock of Dick's invitation had woken her up a little.

Nothing had come from Mrs Anderson after her lesson that week and Cath found herself hanging about, tidying up and reading the small ads in the free newspaper that had mocked her expectation of morning post. There was nothing in the second post either. Perhaps she wasn't well – or the latest instalment of life story was lost in the mail, that would cause a fuss! More likely she was busy, it was getting near to Christmas. Perhaps Sally would send her a card –

127

Cath chided herself for this hope: Sally had never sent her a Christmas card before. She'd not even sent a postcard from the USSR nor written for a whole year when she went to Eire. She knew she must go somewhere for Christmas – she imagined with horror spending alone these dead-quiet days punctuated, perhaps, with visits to the pub and walks for the sake of doing something. Sara, her mother, would be going to Aunty May, and afterwards complain of the unenergetic hospitality: 'too much politeness and not enough to eat.' Impulsively she snatched a sheet of paper and invited herself and her grandmother to Christmas in her mother's home. She went out to the post, feeling as if she had walked out of an argument or consigned an insoluble crossword to the bin. She couldn't stand being on her own there. There was no work outstanding, there was nothing to do. Read? No, her agitation made that impossible. She set out in the direction of the park. She wondered what she would be doing in two years' time, five.

It was only much later, when she found the blue envelope under the mat, that the simmering feeling finally subsided. Why she thought, has Mrs Anderson's autobiography become so important to me? A habit, or a prop? Something to compensate for the fact – she had to admit it – that the project itself no longer absorbed her as it had? Why did she hesitate for a moment, choosing the best place to sit and read it, adding that slight ceremoniousness as if it was a love letter rather than a marking job? Why?

She half lay on her bed, the letter still unopened. You can't open the letter until you answer: why? she announced to herself, and replied: I don't want to open it anyway. It's only more of the same: The Best Times of My Life . . . that awful resilience, ghastly optimism, endurance, almost vulgar vitality. It reproached her. Why couldn't she be like Mrs A, she thought, and then, almost at the same time, why does she never learn, or at least, only the lesson that Life's Like That? Get on with it, get the most out of it.

The letter was open.

'I was working on the buses at the time and I had been thinking if I was ever going to have a baby I'd have to make a start.' Cath's eyes glazed over, she was fighting the words. Something about the third husband. Miscarriage, compensation and leaving the job, no compensation, keep the job, an accident. 'It was a long time before I was right again, and of course a man doesn't understand that . . .'

She thrust the letter away from her. It was more of a letter than part of a book. There were fewer chapter headings now, and fewer mistakes to remind her that she was really reading it only as a teacher. There was a tightening in her throat, almost nausea, as if she had greedily gobbled too many of Mrs Anderson's experiences for her own good. For weeks now she had read them avidly, but all the time fascination had been slowly twisting into a kind of horror. There were so many of them. A lifetime's accumulation of clothing that wouldn't wear out, a depressing wardrobe of variations on a theme. Impossible to justify the expense of anything new, impossible to move with all this to carry.

Part of its power, its awful addictiveness, was its truthfulness. That was what she resented about it now. Herself brooding over so common an injury, unable to stop herself being sucked into its bottomless symbolism and endless iniquities; Mrs Anderson was counting and gloating, slowly, carefully articulating her great list of a life to an audience, like a conjuror pulling an endless swathe of cloth from up her sleeve. They were both of them like mystics in a way, stuck in meditation on a single event that seemed to repeat itself so often as to define the quality of life. She didn't want to be like that. She shut her eyes, she must think herself out of this morass of dwelling on and repetition. But it was difficult. She could see no real pattern, no progress: so much of experience seemed only replication clothed and faced to give an appearance of variety.

Oh God, I can't think. They say women can't think,

intuition not intellect. But how could you, she thought, with that dead weight of repetition pressing on you, obsessive? You would have to get rid of it first. The burden of fertility, the burden of proof, the burden of repetition. A man's life, she thought, doing not done to, would be more likely to provide at least an illusion of variety and a hope of change, a sense of self growing weightier with each measurable acquisition of power. Men's lives seem large and complex enough to require tools of thought: colour-coded pins, computers, secretaries and systems of ideas strong enough to synthesise polarities and calm the exciting panic of choice. She felt bitter and jealous; somewhere in the familiar landscape of womanhood: dunes, she imagined it, a dull sky, edgeless, she'd lost herself and now it was difficult to think, to be ambitious, want, remember.

She lay on the bed, Mrs A's manuscript scattered around her, and shut her eyes in the vain hope of falling asleep. Was that all you could do with life: count the number of times you'd been knocked down and jumped back – or not, as the case might be. Mrs Anderson was so damned resigned; rebellious, yes, but ultimately resigned. But what about me? I'm no better. It must be possible to dissect that awful sameness so that you were mesmerised and paralysed by it no longer. See worlds in a grain of sand, make mountains out of molehills – know your fear like the back of your hand. Then you could go beyond it. That was frightening.

She remembered the time, just a few weeks after they'd moved Steve's things out, when he had arrived one afternoon and overstayed her cautious welcome. She'd stuffed papers randomly into her bag, stood up and then said to Steve in a tone as commanding as she could manage: 'I'm going out now.'

He had drawn his jacket tightly around him as if it were armour against a siege. He'd lit another cigarette, messing about with the matches. There was a wrinkled skin on his coffee: he'd been talking. She stood willing him to leave, it was her place now. He did not look up but said after a long silence,

'I'll go when I've finished my coffee.'

There was emphasis on the 'my', in the memory at least. His hand had circled the mug protectively as if defending it from attack, as if he had transferred his sense of a right to something from her to the flat, then to the mug. Which was technically not his coffee at all, but hers. Coffee with sugar that he had made her give him. She stared at him, desperate. The argument they'd been having was no worse than those they had had when they were together; however it had brought all the others back with it. He fumbled with the handle of the mug, still not drinking. It had become a matter of pride, she realised. Coffee meant he could sit there and talk, now it meant that he could stay there in her home that was hers only when he wasn't in it. He proved as he sat that he could be part of her even if she ran away from him. A foot in the door. A cocked hind leg: but not so blatant; there was a fine slippery distinction that made it harder to accuse him of trespass, for he had come to talk of fairness and love, and even though fairness was sometimes hard and love often cruel, these subjects have status which protects the motives of those who introduce them. He talked of loyalty and consistency and commitment and affection and the Past, which gathered and stretched as the shadow of a mountain. If she spoke of territory and rights and possession, she would be discredited beside such lofty sentiments. She would prove her soul greedy and defensive, she would be the serpent that introduced trade, barriers, exchange, that used. So she answered him words that fought against her. She was trapped.

He had asked for what no one would refuse a stranger: a drink in a mug. He had built on that stolen offering, that lie at gunpoint. He had generated a complicity and won another battle without the unpleasantness of declaring war.

Exasperated she had said, 'You know what I mean, I'm asking you to go.'

'Don't get hysterical. I'll go when I'm finished.'

'I'm not going until I've come.'

∗

When did this feeling he was invading her begin? Or was it always there? Their relationship was like some arcane work of medieval theology where everything prefigured everything else. Any number of trivial incidents held in them the seed of what eventually happened. Rape-seeds, if only she'd recognised them before they grew.

A few weeks later the coffee incident had repeated itself in an aggravated and more intense form, and that was the last time she saw him before he raped her. She had been picking plums in the allotment and he'd walked up, stopped and asked for some. Although she had far too many for herself, although it would have been a friendly gesture, she did not want to give him any. She might have enjoyed polishing them to show off the bloom and presenting them with a slightly ceremonious air of her own free will and in her own good time – not that it was being asked that she minded, not exactly. She'd already given plums to passers-by who admired the fruits, pleased to share the fruits of her and the season's labour with people who could see they weren't just any old plums. The tree, after all, had been planted before she came, she did not feel that she owned it.

When Steve had leaned over the fence, a sudden shadow on her back that made her drop the handful she had just reached for, and said, 'Can I have some of those?', she jumped with surprise. His words were surly and scabbed with his resentment at having to ask at all, harsh with impatience born of the conviction that he had an absolute right to any, however many he wanted. There was no appreciation of what the plums were, of that miraculous thing a plum tree in the city, of the chemistry that made

132

fruit from sun and water, of her regular work and the sheer luck that had produced so many tight burstings of coloured succulence. There was no recognition of anything she cared about, no recognition even that they were plums at all.

'Eh?' he prompted, a stare rotten with the effort of willing her to give graciously and generously – or at least with an appearance of willingness which would confirm his right to have demanded. He had forced the bright flesh of the plums into the shabby dishonest world of the symbolic. To give him just one plum would indicate a willingness to give in in general, it would say she was ready to offer forgiveness, a talk, an apology, a favour, love.

'Those what?' she asked, like a testy mother instilling the rules of politeness. (But you can't have them anyway.) She would rather let every plum on the tree waste than give him one. His presumptions infuriated her. Also, she felt a little frightened, standing stiffly by the fence feeling her own incompetence and the eyes of the world upon her, stuck in the cloying web of this unwelcome complicity, the secret meaning with which he had blighted her plums and which she alone was condemned to understand.

'Those.' He gestured contemptuously towards the basket at his feet. But for the fence he would have bent down and taken one from it, she was sure, and eaten it then and there with conspicuous but feigned relish. She remembered he did not like fruit. Between them crackled the kind of pre-thunder electricity that can turn milk sour. As she said, 'No', she willed it to be enough, but knew she would have to justify and her heart sickened because she did not know how to banish his demands from this innocent-seeming context of a box of fruit. She did not know how to make it clear what she was saying 'no' to, what she was guarding.

'Why not? You've got plenty.'

She was on trial for an offence she didn't understand. An invisible panel of judges, herself among them, waited to twist her words into half truths before they even left her lips, to tint her face with guilty red. The court would dismiss a straightforward answer to the real request – 'I'm my own person now' – as irrelevant, insane, hysterical: the language of litigation would not permit of metaphor, of a plum that isn't a plum. So she was trying to defend a non-existent meanness about fruit, listing what she had done to make the plums hers.

'. . . and I'm making jam, I need them,' she lied.

She ran out of words; it was useless anyway, she was condemned. The court said meanness was worse if you tried to justify it. The court said now we do not accept symbolism, and is not your refusal to give the plums symbolic of your refusal to give of yourself? It is of this really that you stand condemned. Cath felt herself starting to cry. As he walked off he said, 'You always were a tight-assed bitch.'

She saw herself standing by the fence, a large-limbed woman just into her thirties, her solid features, normally composed and inspiring of confidence, crumbling back into childhood as she wailed inside. A woman who had just defended a basket of plums as if it were her baby and Steven an axeman. She looked on the spectacle with contempt. She breathed hard and stopped the tears, not wanting to be mean, or hysterical, or mad, or a tight-assed bitch.

Cath picked a page at random from among those scattered on the bed. Some she had been lying on, and were irrevocably creased. In the half-light she read:

'So that was how he got his foot in the door, so to speak. After that . . .' All too damn appropriate. The next few words had been washed away – two neat splashes diluting the ink so that only the pressure marks remained. Whether they were Mrs Anderson's or her own tears she couldn't be sure. Before she could think what she was doing the thin paper was screwed to a ball in her hand. She put it down and carefully collected the other sheets before drawing the curtains and getting into bed.

9

Cath stared purposelessly at the bookshop notice board. Lessons in Tai Chi, mime, painting, dancing. Third non-smoking person to share. Taxi. Wooden bed for sale. She almost fancied having a tarot reading with Belinda; to ask about the case would be a really good test, settle forever the faint quivering of doubt that preceded her dismissal of such things. Not worth it at £8. Yes, it was still there, the small card like a visitor's card to be carried on a tray: Rape Survivors' Group and a telephone number. The number seemed familiar; she rummaged in her bag for the card Kim had given her, she had kept it along with the receipt for some plimsoles, a prescription for sleeping pills and another for contra-ceptives which it had been awkward to refuse. Yes, they were the same.

The pieces of paper and card in her hand, Cath hesitated by the waste bin. She wouldn't use it, didn't want to wallow, seeing Salter was enough, surely? That was at least practical. Kim might have told her friend about her anyway, and then she'd tell Kim yes, that woman called in the end, and then there'd be Kim's blue eyes wide and melting with secret sympathy, dying to say something, unable to let on that she knew. Unbearable. What could they do any way? Psychiatry? Group therapy, sitting in a circle and pretending she trusted the other strangers, pretending they'd told them everything, pretending afterwards it had helped? Anne once told her she had been to group therapy for her shyness. After the first time she had continued going only because it had cost her so much. Round and round the circle they went, everyone had to speak, everyone had a turn each week except Anne. People burst into tears and shouted at each other. Said things like 'I don't believe you' or 'You're covering up', and then they put their arms round each other's shoulders in a huddle, time was up and they all went home.

'You're parasitical,' someone had suddenly said to Anne, 'you never give anything, sit there listening, take, take, take', and everyone had agreed, but still she had been unable to think of anything to say. 'It was as if I was frozen Cath, I tried to invent something even but I couldn't. I thought I was going to cry and then they'd all put their arms around me, but they looked like they hated me so much, I didn't want them to. I just got up and walked out of the room, never went back. I never once said anything, except hello at the beginning of the session.'

Cath pictured Anne's therapy room, an assortment of people in kaftans and denim sitting in a tight circle on the floor, big thick-painted pictures of spiky shapes (anger) and soft swirls (peace, the womb) hung on the wall. Smell of incense, thin wisps of fraud in the air. All that was middle-class time wasting; recently she'd understood better her mother's contempt for the soul and the psyche, for Analysis and Dwelling on Things, for Hypochondria, Melancholia and Trauma. Poor Anne. Her shyness was really only a kind of inarticulacy, thought Cath, she's not shy with me. People assume you know what's going on, speak their language when you don't and you know they think you're stupid, or dishonest, it makes you all nervous, they should be gentle, not shout at you because you couldn't speak.

But she hesitated by the waste bin and threw away only the receipt. If she was desperate, then it might be worth a try. If it was a choice between the bottle of pills and the phone call, she would probably choose the second, she thought, hurrying out of the shop: she'd only dropped in to kill time before her appointment with Salter; now she was late.

On the desk between them sat the cassette recorder as yet inert, waiting. It would be, she supposed, easier to ignore than having Elizabeth, the secretary, sitting in the corner, her bracelets rattling as she flicked over the pages of her note pad, the studied expressionlessness of her face an invitation to wonder what she was thinking. She stared again at the paper Salter had handed her, headed 'Catherine Sheldon, Background', read and typed and photocopied and filed by Elizabeth who could just be heard typing taped dictation in the other adjoining room. The typescript was amended in Salter's careful copperplate.

'Age: thirty-one – mature time of life. Occupation: professional, secondary school teacher, now literacy teaching, socially useful, voluntary work.

'Unmarried: be careful not to imply that this is because you would find marriage irksome or restrictive. You are a serious mature woman, not a highflyer refusing to conform to the values of family etc which most people in the court will hold sacred. Rather, you are a busy woman approaching a "certain age" who has missed or is late in establishing a family, more by accident than design. Dress to look older rather than younger.

'Past: good character. Work as typist on leaving school, attendance of evening classes and teacher training college, this shows determination, hard work, seriousness, ambition. Emphasise this. Implication: you have had little time for getting involved in the seamier side of life. You have "bettered yourself".

'Politics: your involvement in left-wing politics was on the sidelines only and mostly as a result of your relationship with SB – done out of a desire to help him and out of a general concern for the underprivileged, rather than out of strongly held political convictions. Since your relationship with SB ceased, your political involvement has declined.

'You are compassionate, a little naive in some respects (cf above, voluntary work).

'NB of course you will not be asked directly about your political opinions etc, but it is vital to make sure that your answers to any questions do not imply that you are in any way unrespectable.'

She was aware of Salter watching her as she read. Sketches for an improvisation, points refer to, NB. A pack of lies, an unpleasant awkward string of words she must recite in her head until they became automatic, like learning verbs in a foreign language. Not knowing what to say, she continued staring at the paper.

'All right?' asked Salter. 'Quite straightforward really. But now we'll have to deal with the trickier bits, the things you can be asked direct questions about. Your relationship with Blake is a major problem on two counts: firstly, you will inevitably be associated with his political persuasions which aren't shared by the majority of the population, so you have to work hard to disassociate yourself from that, give the impression that yours was a relationship between two people in which you, naturally enough, took on the whole package without being in sympathy with his ideas for any other reason than that you were fond of him for himself. But, on the other hand, and more importantly, the relationship you had lays the prosecution open to argument vis à vis *consent*.'

And if I emphasise my fondness to cover up my unrespectable views, then I'll make the consent thing worse, Cath thought, feeling the impossibleness of it all rising about her. It was because of the relationship that it had happened, that was quite clear, but Salter was saying that the relationship was something he, the defence, would use, not the prosecution. The categories things were meant to fit into were too crude – the assigned result or consequences of each element were each a bit out, and soon nothing fitted at all. Nothing. And she would be standing there lying. Already here in the office her story had become unrecognisable; it had wiped her blank, empty but for the promise of justice bought at the price of perjury, a kind of monstrous and ever-increasing mortgage.

'On the other hand, his politics will go against him, so it's not all bad news, provided you play your cards right. So try to answer everything I ask you as if you were in court, in the light of what's on the paper, and what I've just said.'

There was a series of muffled clicks as the tape crept into motion, its tiny rotating squeal somehow louder than her own thoughts. The tapes were, he had assured her, wiped and re-used as soon as the interview had been written up. Although she was glad that they were not preserved there was something unsavoury about this, like hospital dressings being washed and used again; it was as if nothing on the tapes could be finally erased so long as they remained intact; in her own silences she could feel the agony of successive afternoons sweated out in the tulipwood confines of Salter's offices, could hear the babble of other people's stories layered on top of one and another, each with its holes and gaps through which those below could be glimpsed, like tatters on an old advertising hoarding.

'Tell me about your sexual relations with Blake, were they satisfactory? Why did they cease? Was it a clean break? Who left who?'

'Mind your own business.' She had raised her voice, but felt the weariness in it as soon as the words were out: as a lobster is plunged into boiling water it screams, not a real scream, just the gas escaping from its shell. Through the rising red, the scalding of hot water, she glared at Salter across the desk with righteous indignation she did not really feel. Her initial relief that there was someone to help her had long changed to a tight useless hatred of him and his office, and to exhausted resignation. This was the horse's mouth after all.

A twitch of impatience briefly disturbed Salter's usual expression of world-weary boredom, giving an almost brutal expression to features normally dissipated, spread into the kind of blandness that Cath guessed was exactly what her mother meant when she described a man as handsome. He was probably about forty, his skin smooth but permanently flushed, as if affluence and a healthy constitution were waging a long and equally matched battle in his flesh.

'As at any crucial point in one's life,' he said staring at the window behind her, 'it comes down to a question of selling oneself. It may seem ironical, unpleasant, distasteful, even dishonest to have to obtain satisfaction in this way, but it is the only way and at least you're not having to pay my fees as well. And you are having help which someone in your position doesn't normally get.' He clicked his pen in and out and continued. 'If the honesty of your evidence and the rightness of your cause shone through your skin and surrounded you like a halo, there would be no need for any part of the Process of Law except the giving of sentences. Or not even that: natural justice, whatever that is, will fall from the skies on to the offender's head. It doesn't happen like that, Miss Sheldon. If you wish to win your case, you have to play the game.'

The pauses in his speaking were longer than those in other people's, as if he had forgotten how to speak to one person in a small room. She wondered how he would write a letter to a friend. Perhaps he spoke to his wife like that.

'As it is, Mr Blake is innocent until proved guilty, and the prosecution, that is the police with yourself as principal witness, is required to substantiate your claims against him. A large part of that task consists in demonstrating that your behaviour and character are beyond even the shadow of reproach.'

But it's not fair! She could whine like a child, but she knew it was useless and would get her nowhere but being treated like one; he was right, he was right and it was awful but what he said was true.

'Unless he himself is free from all blame, a person cannot claim to be considered a victim.' He smiled, she sensed that he was about to pay her a compliment or offer some optimism about the case, something to bring them together again in the semblance of a working relationship. He took two tumblers from the top drawer of the desk and held them to the light.

'The only other approaches available would be to prove that you were of such unsound mind as to be for all intents and purposes a minor. Obviously that is not something the prosecution will be doing in this case.' He smiled at her and poured whisky into the glasses.

'I'm sorry,' she said, 'for shouting. But there seems no sense in it, it's all a contradiction in terms and it seems hopeless. It's not logical . . . to have to falsify things in order to establish the truth.' At least the length of his sentences gave her time to calm down in between the shocks; it was wrong to shout at him, after all, he was only doing what he'd been asked to.

'It is all perfectly consistent within the terms of the Law. Believe me, I do know what I'm talking about and what I'm doing, even if sometimes I don't know how I'm doing it.' He was irritated again, speaking as if to an imaginary person over by the window, an audacious burglar, armed but stupid, who had shinned up the drain pipe, crashed through the window and fallen messily on to the office floor: a little alarming, a trifle out of order, but Salter knew he was equal to it, his ability to demoralise was a sophisticated weapon bound to defeat whatever blunt instruments his opponent possessed.

'You have made your feelings clear. I'm sorry, but these questions do have to be asked. Do you want to continue? If these sessions are too distressing, it might be better not to. And there is nothing to prevent you dropping charges: I can assure you that you will be asked worse things in court.'

Oh to say 'yes, I'll stop', to walk out of the office and into life, pull the well-oiled doors across and become invisible,

141

swooning silently down eight floors and out into the street, to pass unseen through the crowds and on to a train, to rattle down the line and into forgetfulness . . .

'Mmm?' said Salter, sipping his drink.

I could stop it all now, she thought. Change my name, move (how?). Start again somewhere else. Perhaps I'm only going through with it to satisfy other people or maybe it's something I think I ought to do, to prove.

He was looking at her, interested for the first time. 'Selling oneself', he had said, slipping from 'we' to 'one' and 'you' and 'I' and back again to 'you'. From Rape to Prostitution. He sat back in his chair, his shoulders hooked over the top of it, his soft clean hands dangling from the end of the arm rests, his modestly striped tie a little off centre. His eyes were screwed because of the light coming from behind her. He reminded her of the men in Sunday supplement advertisements for unusual spirits or expensive cigars. What was he offering her now? What were the goods? Dignified retreat? Shameful surrender? A truth test? If she dropped charges now, would he be able to think he had never had a case anyway? And would the police, Kim, and her mother think the same? Would there be knowing smiles, embarrassed silences? For she herself often did not quite believe other people's accounts of things she had not seen, held their words in abeyance and waited to see if any subsequent information would confirm or contradict. That's what people would do if she told them; they'd mouth generalised comforts that did not quite fit: 'He ought not to get away with it', 'I sympathise with your distress', have a cup of tea, a drink, a good cry. Until she had proved her case there would be no support for her actual condition, only insurance-policy sympathy for her predicament, the state of limbo awaiting confirmation that would sanction her version of events and license wholehearted commiseration. People would be zealous in minor services, offering phone numbers and enquiring about her health because they knew, like the relatives of a cancer sufferer,

142

that her actual condition, the specific symptoms and pains they gathered into bundles with other things, was worse than the one she herself complained of. Really, you were, on your own, and best keep quiet.

'I would respect your decision in either case,' said Salter.

Why should you care, she thought. What's your respect then? Hypocrite! And throttles had opened in her veins, suddenly she was a choking motor running on pure contempt. She would like to pull the books from the shelves and throw them out of the window to flap clumsily past eight storeys of wide double-glazed windows, banging on the panes to startle conspiracies, frighten deceivers momentarily with the thought they had been seen without their masks, caught in the act; to smash finally on to the street, their pages all splayed for everyone to see the contradictions in terms, the Acts of Ambivalence, the formalised bicker, the ritualised brawl of Law. She wanted to stand up, pulling the back of the polished desk up with her so that the well-fitting drawers would shoot open ejecting stamps and pens, sealing wax and envelopes, diaries, taxi cards, photographs, magazines, contraceptives, bills and certificates – the whisky bottle splurting its corrosive spirits over everything. There would be a spreading stain on Salter's shirt, his face distorted with pain, she would be imprisoned under the weight of the desk as he watched her pick out the tapes from the rubble and strike the match, the whisky would burn like paraffin and –

She could tell that he thought she ought to drop charges.

'No,' she said, 'I want to go on with it.'

A few feet below her window cars, buses and vans crescendoed in from her left, drew to a halt at the traffic lights, ticked over impatiently, revved up and raced away to the right. Headlights streaked across the ceiling. As the night drew on they became less regular but more irritating; there was never more than a few minutes between them. In the distance too she could hear the rattle of trains, some of which set up vibrations she could feel in her mattress. The walls were not thick enough anymore, or the noise had increased; now she couldn't sleep.

She remembered being kept awake by noise when she was at teacher training college, records, arguments, the regular endless squeak of bedsprings enduring sexual intercourse; slamming doors and sudden peals of laughter. Then it had been not so much the noise as the sense it gave her of being out of things: sometimes it had seemed that she was the only person trying to sleep, the only person with nothing better to do. The few years between her and the majority of the other students had made her feel alternately furious at the trivial time wasting of their pleasures (they've never worked in a shit job, or they wouldn't waste their time here), and guilty for being a kill-joy. She would hear the bossy neighbour in her voice as she shouted from her bed for quiet, and it would falter. But you couldn't even shout at the street, there was nothing to do but will herself deaf. There were sounds of people too: the stumbling of high heels, drunken monologues, shouts, wolf whistles, breaking glass – think of something else.

Those days at college seemed so far away. Was I happy there? she thought. Happy? Salter's version: 'ambitious, determined, serious', wasn't too far off the mark really. Not the whole story though, she had been exhilarated as well, for she had got where she wanted. She'd not had to force herself to spend hours in the bright shadowless library filling note pads and exhausting her eyes, it had been what she wanted to do, it had made her feel proud and excited – she could almost remember, almost feel again that satisfaction of effort expended. She remembered walking back from her first day's teaching practice with her legs aching and her back tight, reliving again and again during the evening that moment when the class had suddenly switched from near mutiny to cautious interest and then concentration, and she had done it, she had done it.

She felt nostalgia overwhelming her, the past's

attractiveness so resplendent in comparison to the present that it made it almost unbearable. What had happened? It couldn't have been so perfect. She couldn't for instance remember the names and faces of the other students: she tried but called forth only vague blobs of faces that could be from anywhere. Suddenly she felt on the brink of tears. Stop it, for Christ's sake! She said aloud, and opened her eyes. She felt trapped between her tears and the noise outside, all she wanted to do was sleep, now more than ever since it would stop the memories and the crying. Outside now was momentarily quiet and she waited, tensed for it to be destroyed. A beam of yellowish light burned through the curtains and a couple passed talking in low voices. OK, so she'd been lonely, she was lonely now, it was bound to happen from time to time, wasn't it? She was the type of person who needed props, a sense of purpose. When that went she was bound to feel a bit rough.

When Steve had first come was a time when she could say she'd definitely not been lonely, and look what happened. Perhaps loneliness was worth it? Supposing there was no middle ground between the gentle ache of loneliness and the acute pain which hit you when you woke from the anaesthetic of love to discover that you had excised your right to be alone in an attempt to prevent loneliness, that comfort had become violation? She wouldn't do that again, she wouldn't love again, it was a deceit, was only the kinder preliminaries to an act of complete invasion and complete pain. So would she have to always be numb like a fish in a tank: claustrophobic but knowing the air outside was death, little jerks of pain from time to time reminding her, like the World War One shrapnel her grandfather suffered from in thundery weather, that she had been forced beyond the pale, isolated by experience that lingered incommunicable?

Of course it couldn't go on forever, she would feel better when the case was over. She tried to imagine: 'You have been found guilty: five years', but she felt nothing, it meant

145

nothing, it was magnificently irrelevant. It touched neither her nor him; all she wanted, desperately, was to repossess herself, the one that loss had made seem all rosy and blurred like a lovely dream. If only there was some way, whatever it was she would do it, she would kill him if that would work. It would be justified, one crime against the person of another, an eye for an eye; but it wouldn't work and she couldn't do it.

A crime against the person (why can't I stop thinking about it?) A rape, a little shock-horror word all on its own, like it was only one thing. But oh, it goes on and on. What happened was never only one thing anyway, it was assault and fraud and grievous bodily harm and mental cruelty and theft, and what he took could not be restored by his imprisonment nor his shaming nor his sincerest apologies, nor his money, nor by anything the law could do. It could only be restored somehow by her own efforts. But how, when whatever happened to her just piled and coiled insider her and she couldn't digest it or transform it, when it just warped and hampered her, went on and on? She had to make herself again, tighten her muscles and rub her skin back into feeling – go through the motions until the dead bits tingled back into real life. It could not be that she could let him do this to her.

Should she ring Crisis Line? After all there were other women who had been raped; she was probably not alone nor as bad as she felt. But would the same pain and the same story over and over, the worst bits in slightly different places, make it better? Wouldn't it multiply it so that she would walk out of the room with twenty nightmares instead of one? The alternative, safer and surer she thought, was by clenched effort of will to expunge or expel what had happened. Beat it back.

Cath dreamed she was sitting at a white-painted wrought-iron table under a coloured umbrella, looking out across a green valley. There was a warm breeze that she could feel

146

all over her skin, because she was naked. Next to her sat a woman with broad shoulders and breasts with pale flat nipples like her own. The woman's face was very familiar. Other tables with other women sitting were scattered about, some wore sunglasses. The umbrellas were cheerful looking, all taut and dappled in the patches of sun and shade. The woman opposite – where could it be she had seen her before? – smiled and picked up one of the glasses of wine on the table. They were both very full, one side ready to overflow, the other a little safer because of the light slant of the table. There were concentric ripples in the dark red wine, as if a drop had just fallen from above. Cath picked hers up too, leaning forwards so as not to spill the wine, she could smell its old-earth and metal smell already, she looked at the other woman as she did so and realised with amusement that she was her backwards self. She felt the wine warm on her lip. And then the glass shattered, her body was all sticky with wine, or was it blood? and all around there was the noise of shattering glass. Women at the other tables were standing up, holding one another's faces, trapped in newsprint photographs of agony – blood, or was it wine? was everywhere. She looked back at her companion, saw her face slowly opening into a scream: her own mouth too was gaping wide.

Then she was awake. It was a broken window, there was someone in the room. She couldn't see, she couldn't scream. Dial-nine-nine-nine, she couldn't move.

The glow to the left was the window, she could see the night-whiteness of her sheets, the curtains hung heavy and still, it was not really so dark. Her heartbeat measured out of the room, calming slowly. The room was empty. She turned on the light, pulled back the curtain. Lights were going on in the houses opposite, there was shouting and the sound of distant sirens. The smell of her own sweat, old sheets. She opened the window but it seemed stuffy outside even though it was winter and she knew it was cold. She got back into bed. She would be able to tell by listening

147

what had happened: a break-in probably. False alarm. Bolt the windows, stuff the ears with wax. Blocking and hindering the world's passage in and her thoughts' out, darkening the glass, contracting the possible. Windows that should be flung open, bolted shut, safety in the home. I live alone.

10

Cath sat in the crowded train to Leeds drinking tea from a bulging plastic cup. She wondered what on earth she had done inviting herself home. She hoped there would be no fuss, but wanted there to be something. She had struggled against her mother Sara's coldness in the years before she could leave home, screamed and bitten the stern flesh as a child, but now that visits had regulated themselves to a few weekends a year she could see her as a character rather than an overwhelming force.

When she had been a teenager and people had talked of 'bad vibes' and 'bad trips' and 'freaking out', and when stress and ulcers had been fashionable among the middle classes, breakdowns flaunted and counted like medals, Sara – while aspiring to the material side of middle classness – had maintained a steady contempt for what she called 'nerves'. Particularly against any suggestion that she might have them. 'Two kinds of people,' Cath had heard her say more often than she could at the time bear, 'have nerves.' 'Model girls' who literally starved their nerves into overexposure to stimulus and consequent jangling hypersensitivity, and 'intellectuals' who'd lost touch with all common sense in a tangle of analytic thought and didn't get enough sun and exercise to work up a healthy appetite. The last was directed at Cath whose educational aspirations were a source of conflict. For cases of nerves, Sara expressed contempt and pity in mixtures that varied according to how well she knew the individual concerned: the better she knew them, on the whole, the more contempt and the less pity. Melancholy and insomnia were diseases, and some people brought them on themselves, that was what her mother thought. Cath wondered how she would fare: she had checked her face with her mother's eye before boarding the train, and knew it would be impossible to conceal the circles under her eyes.

Sara herself had always basked in rude health and kept enough flesh to keep nerves – according to her theories – well sheathed. On the few occasions when she spent a few days at less than full tilt, she seemed to suffer as much from shame as sickness, and sought provocation as an explanation. Regular movements. Loose clothes. Good appetite, an ability to get to sleep in five minutes flat no matter what stress she might be supposed to be suffering, a full set of teeth with only two fillings: of these Sara boasted, saying they were the only things really worth having in life. And she had them: you could see it as she walked down the street, like Moses making stragglers part to give her a clear path; you could hear it in the loudness and precision of her speech, her voice a trumpet unmuted by constraints of place, time or respect of persons. It had driven Cath mad, made her hate for years red cheeks, good dinners and health in general and cherish her own 'nerves'.

She didn't hate Sara any more, but she wasn't quite sure what she did feel. In some ways, she was almost sorry for her. The dismissiveness of Sara's philosophy, expressed as it was without the padding of tact or embarrassment, and the way her vigour expressed itself in noisy and unceasing work of the non-finicky kind – beating carpets, moving furniture, cleaning the cellar, spade, axe, mop and elbow grease – made her intimidating to those of a less robust disposition or physique, and a woman often accused of being aggressive. Also, it occurred to Cath suddenly as the train rushed her nearer to the woman shadowing her thoughts, one often envied. But neither was that what she felt.

Memories that the years apart had allowed to surface told her her mother was not made of quite such stern stuff as she had seemed to be. As a girl, hanging around the house while her mother stormed through the housework, too impatient to delegate any of it, she had often seen her – this fearful and monolithic mother – reduced to a lone person struggling in a sea of adrenalin, muscles and vessels twittering powerlessly as those of some half-dead dissected mammal in a laboratory experiment. Her eyes would pop and for a few seconds she would stand robbed of speech, not merely having 'nerves' but existing only as a huge nerve system, overcharged and dangerous. This happened regularly when someone entered a room in which she was alone, behind her back. She would drop whatever she was holding and whirl round, a horror-film cry strangling itself in her throat, her fists clenched but not raised, her face briefly transfixed in the magnesium flare of panic. It's only me, whoever it was would say, and Sara's dislocated face would slowly gather itself into an anger that struck like an overhead storm. But this, she said, was not nervousness, it just went to show how healthy her reactions were.

Cath as a child had grown to smoulder in resentment at having to announce her presence loud and well in advance by banging doors, singing and thumping down the stairs like a traveller in the forest scaring off unseen snakes.

After her husband's death, Sara had had locks fitted to the windows. Sensible precautions. Her mother was as frightened of things as the next person, but she wouldn't admit it. If she did, she'd have to have more sympathy with other people's fears. Cath wished she would; that was what she wanted, all she'd ever wanted.

For the last part of the journey she changed to the small tram-like local train, the same one that she used to take to school. The first day she took the train on her own, she'd sat next to a man reading a pink newspaper held flat on the

151

large briefcase that straddled his knees. She had never seen a pink newspaper before. Her books, ruler, pen and pencil were in a linen shopping bag that was the fashion at the time. What was in the briefcase? Her father went to work carrying nothing that would not fit into his pockets. She willed the man to open the case, squeezed shut, rubber sealed, clipped airtight as a refrigerator, and combination locked for double measure. Secrets, she thought, or clean new banknotes, packed and stacked like envelopes. Anyone could tell what was in her bag from the square protuberances and the dark spread of an ink stain in the bottom corner; there was even a name tape sewn on the handle. She'd like a briefcase, she thought, with secret compartments like the ones in the desk with flowers on in the museum. It would be worth having secrets then. She tried to read the pink newspaper but the print was all jammed together and mixed up with columns of figures. She wasn't good at Maths. There weren't any pictures. Perhaps it was foreign. She slid her eyes round to look at his face. A different kind of man from her father, with a hat covering his hair and glasses hiding his eyes, though his skin, pink, blue, white, was raw-looking and unprotected. That must be the face that went with secrets: it didn't move.

He was going to open it. She sat very still so that he wouldn't notice her breathing carefully, her eyes lowered but staring through her eyelashes at the case. It was a trick; she almost thought there was nothing at all inside it, but if you were careful you could see it was not as deep as it looked from the inside, and he was pulling a little loop of leather and the bottom came up.

But where were the secrets, there was only a pen and a tie and a comic. Why did the man have a comic?

But perhaps it wasn't a comic because on the front of it was a photograph of a lady without hair and black lips: so that was what they looked like under their dresses. But why was she tied like that to the bed? It reminded her of the crucifix in the Mullalays' living room. Perhaps this lady was a Catholic too? Her eyes had opened now, she had forgotten that she must be invisible. What was that man doing standing there? Why didn't he untie the lady? He – the pink hieroglyphics covered the picture, and the briefcase shut. Snap. She dropped her bag and had to chase her pencils that rolled noisily around the carriage floor. The man stared out of the window, drumming his fingers on top of the briefcase in time to the rattle of the train.

Granny met her from the train. Under her thick coat and grey shift, Granny must be like that lady in the picture. She squeezed her extra hard as she reached up to kiss her, to feel if it was true. You couldn't tell; her lips weren't black anyway. Don't get in those little carriages unless there's lots of people in them, said Granny, hasn't your Mummy told you? But she wouldn't say why.

'You look pale. Have you been well in yourself?' That was what Sara would greet her with, she thought, as she got off the train and took unhesitatingly the same route she had taken as a child walking home from school: the same sides of streets and the same crossing places, dictated by long-forgotten superstitions and pleasures. It was the uneasy dusk of winter time, her senses telling her it was evening but clocks internal and external contradicting them, a fretful waiting for real night when the contradiction would disappear. There were crowds out shopping, whole families together: Arnheims, where her father had worked, had caught up with the times at last and gave everyone a full ten days off for Christmas, as he'd always said they should. But it was no use pretending he'd have been pleased; he would have realised, Cath was sure, it was only because demand was falling. There had been lay-offs in the paper only last week.

The residential streets with their progression from terrace to semi-detached to detached-back-off-the-road unwound before her as if she was walking back into a dream or a film;

153

it was always the same going home. So much never changed: even the arrangements of bottles and jars glimpsed through frosted bathroom windows and posters left on the walls of sons long flown the nest remained uncannily the same. Few of the grown-ups she had known as a child had left, though their children, like herself, had almost all gone, and spouses had died. It was all frozen in Time Before.

There were footsteps behind her. She stopped dead and whirled round, and the gesture, though she was not aware of having done it before, was familiar: Sara too seemed to be standing there, both of them caught like rabbits in car headlamps. A middle-aged man laden with shopping passed, giving her a curious glance. Healthy reactions, she thought, but whether I'm well in myself is another question. There was a very precise meaning to those words 'in yourself'. It meant 'periods' and hinted 'infections' and 'emotional problems' which an extensive reading of popular medical lore had forever linked in her mother's mind. Thick white no-nonsense pads, and no days off school. 'It's natural,' her mother said the first time. 'I told you it would happen. Don't make such a fuss.' Of late her own blood made Cath squeamish, she couldn't look.

'You mustn't let it ruin your life,' Sara said, and it was understood that the subject was closed. 'You're not looking well in yourself. We'll have a nice Christmas the three of us. I didn't get turkey, it goes on too long. Sirloin, more of a treat too.' The faint smell of sweat was rising, whether from her mother or herself she could not tell. Probably from her mother because she herself had started using deodorant, which she would have to hide from contemptuous maternal eyes. And how to explain about her recent aversion to meat: the plump brick-red rubber gloves in the meat shop looking among the pigs' tails, blackening liver, marbled chips and curdled mince like some ghastly entrail being marketed as an ethnic speciality. And tonight Grandma

154

was coming. 'I have not told Mother about it,' Sara's letter had said, understood: and neither will you. Grandma was ninety-four and only just becoming tiresome, a reticent but powerful monument to the strength and tenacity which Sara seemed to consider had withered and died in her own daughter.

Her mother's hand was on her shoulder, and their eyes met, briefly. 'I'll make you a cup of tea. Then you can come out and deliver the cards with me if you want.' In gratitude, Cath stopped herself from crying. A display of emotion on her mother's part was worth a suppression on hers.

Why does she never spend any money on the house? She could afford it now she's working and no one to look after. But everything's the same. It was Dad used to persuade her to get things. Cath sat and wrapped presents for Grandma, while her mother worked noisily in the kitchen. The clatter had driven her mad doing her homework upstairs in the small bedroom above the kitchen, but she liked it now. Better than the stealthy cook whom you could feel tensing at the sound of a dropped spoon and waiting for imagined ripples to subside before picking it up.

But nothing in this house seemed to break or wear. Coats hung up, carpets shaken. Paintwork wiped, armchairs taken apart and searched for hidden fluff: all seemed to thrive from attention and nothing aged except perhaps Sara herself. The serving hatch disused now. Opposite it the mirror in which she used to peer at the back of her father's head during breakfast and later suspected her mother of using to spy on her and her boyfriends. She and Peter Brown used to sit sedate and tongue tied on this very settee with its thick tapestry pattern that time and time again printed itself on the back of her legs the summer she wore a mini dress. There's enough room now, her mother ought to make something of it.

Grandma arrived in a taxi, using a cage to walk now but still not in need of glasses. Bags to carry, a rug, a pile of cushions on the largest armchair, kettle on. The thick suit she wore and the one Sara owned differed in colour but were identical in their ruthless practicality. A kiss on the creased cheek that looked dry but surprised with its softness and warmth. A faint smell of lavender water, another bottle of which wrapped in holly-printed paper waited in the heap by the television. Grandma would grumble at the television but enjoy arguing with it.

'You're looking well,' she pronounced, and Sara did not argue.

Since her father's death, the Queen's speech could be watched uninterrupted by his sour comments on the idleness of the ruling classes. 'For God's sake George, I know that, but I like watching it, once a year.' Did she miss him at all? Probably not, but impossible to say. She had been dry eyed at the funeral, got herself a job and spent long holidays with her brother and his second wife, short ones with a variety of old friends rediscovered for the purpose. But then that's how she would be: mustn't let it ruin your life. No.

Sara and Cath pampered Grandma, not just for herself, and not just for something to do when all the shops were shut, the food cooked and the garden too hard to dig, but also to pass on the tenderness that welled up in each for the other and had somehow to be drained like milk in the swollen breasts of a woman who cannot suckle. Waste not, want not.

'So there's no young man?' asked Grandma, shiny-eyed with after-dinner port and ginger wine. The air stiffened and chilled for a moment, as it is meant to do before a ghost materialises.

'I threw him out,' said Cath, her voice completely steady.

'You won't remember, but I threw your father out once, when you were very small,' Grandma said to Sara, and the tiny muscles in Sara's throat relaxed. 'I took him back in the end, and I can tell you, I never saw him drunk again.'

Cath thought it would be so nice to stay, her cheeks hot and her mind softened like wax from the fierce heat of the gas fire with its scarlet unchanging imitation logs, cutting crosses in the bottom of brussels sprouts, catching up on mending, learning to knit again. Doing something useful. She had woken Sara up on the night before her eleven-plus, unable to sleep for fear of failure. Sara got out of bed without a word, strode downstairs, got out the ironing board and a pile of crumpled sheets.

'Do something useful then, and I don't want to see any burns.'

11

Cath had trained herself back into the effortless performance of daily life, and occupied herself with the refining and polishing of its routines and sequences. She slept a deep, cloying sleep that clung to her in the mornings and seemed to be dreamless. It was summer. She did more teaching and less of the bureaucracy at the centre. This year she would get the allotment done properly, and maybe think about finding a paid job. How are you Cath? Forgetting nicely. Sally had sent her a note: 'Don't worry, I'll write properly soon.' But the postmark was illegible. Cath didn't care whether she wrote or not. She considered her life, though neither dull nor uninteresting, fundamentally unaffecting. This wasn't how she used to feel; perhaps it was ageing. The lack of excitement was not unpleasant: it was like returning to an old, well-fitting coat that you could wear without noticing.

Her third interview with Salter disturbed this blank kind of peace, and the days after were involved by vague memories not of the rape itself but of a time long before it had happened, before she had even met Steve: months when her mind had never been still or tired, when she had walked about seeing everything and absorbing everything without trying or realising, when thoughts and decisions dropped suddenly into her mind ready made and well presented like a meal on a plate cooked by an invisible benefactor. Freedom that came from knowing that there was no one she had to tell, that it was up to her if she shared the gift-wrapped feelings and thoughts that presented themselves gratuitously unearned by the terrible struggle for concentration and logic she had used to consider necessary for 'thinking'. Months when the vegetables and flowers she had planted in her allotment grew resplendent, when her teaching was inspired, when she had had endless patience but needed none. And when she had bought the kitten and named it Egg because it reminded her of a freckled egg, when nights stretched out with spoken or written words – spoken with Jean and Sally and strangers or read in books and she woke up hungry in the mornings. It was this that Steve had taken away, this that the visits to Salter reminded her were lost. And the thought made the dull life she lived totter and shimmer as if it was an illusion, but it was all she had. She was getting by. She hated him, and Salter. Hated them both.

Salter sent her back to the police for her statement.

'I came to see if you've got my statement yet.'

'I'll go and see.' He came back with Harris, this time wearing a new-looking flecked grey suit.

'What was it Miss Sheldon?'

'I wanted a copy of my statement, I came in before and you said . . .'

'I'm afraid it's still with the solicitor. Why do you need it Miss Sheldon, have you remembered anything else?'

She didn't want to tell him about Salter. 'No, I just thought it would be a good idea to read it again.'

'I shouldn't worry Miss Sheldon, I'm sure you'll remember everything.'

'But couldn't the solicitor photocopy it?'

He could try, he said, but he couldn't promise anything. Strictly speaking, it was out of his hands now.

'But I'll tell you what I have got for you,' he said, smiling like an eager-to-please uncle. 'Good news. You might be able to get some compensation from the Criminal Injuries

159

Compensation Board. Someone last year got £3,000. I've just found out. Mind you, the injuries were quite severe. But if I was you, I'd take this form and give it a look-over.'

Compensation. It had a better sound to it than Justice, more down to earth. With three thousand pounds, or two, to be on the safe side, you could – what do people do with sudden money? Travel abroad. Wind slowly through Europe to Asia growing brown and lean. If you worked, you could go for a year, or never come back. Egypt. New Zealand. China. Lizards, melons, prawns the size of dogs. Long hot nights, icy streams and thin air: extremes. Passion. Red moons and deserts. For a few seconds her sense of adventure flickered into life.

'No need to look so miserable,' said Harris, already beating a retreat to the door that had to be opened by press-buttoning a lengthy code. 'They sometimes pay up even if there isn't a conviction, so long as it's been reported. Something to do with the legal definition of proof. So you can see, there's a silver lining . . .'

Cath put the form down on the desk and flicked through it. Why would they pay even if there wasn't a conviction? An admission that the law wasn't adequate? A consolation prize? Or a kind of safety net? 'Buying you off.' She heard father's bitter voice, he'd said that about the redundancy money offered in the plant where he'd worked. 'Don't look a gift horse in the mouth,' her mother had answered. There was a guide as to how to complete the form, printed in very small type on white paper, the margins bristling with numbers and letters.

6)c *The board may reduce or withhold compensation if they consider that having regard to the conduct of the applicant before during or after the events giving rise to the claim, or to his character or way of life – and in application under paragraphs 15 and 16 below, to the character and conduct and way of life of the deceased and of the applicant – it is inappropriate that a full award, or any award at all, be granted.*

7) In order to discover if there was any responsibility, either because of provocation or otherwise, on the part of the victim, the board will scrutinise with particular care all applications in respect of sexual offences or other offences which arise out of a sexual relationship.

You had to attend a hearing and organise your own witnesses. She looked up angrily but no-need-to-look-so-miserable Harris was out of sight behind his security door. She pushed the form towards the blob-faced young officer waiting uncertainly at the other side of the counter. Again she hated Salter, he'd sent her back here.

'Will you remind Inspector Harris about getting a copy of my statement,' she said, 'this isn't any use to me.'

He nodded, but wrote nothing down. She knew he wouldn't bother.

The trial was imminent, but they wouldn't say how long it would last. Cath begun shutting down her life and boarding it up as if she'd not be coming back for a good long time.

'So I wouldn't be able to come for at least a month' she told Paul, 'and after that – I'm not sure, I might go away, even move. So she could take over right now if you like or I could go on until the week before, or you could even go to the classes at the centre, it's up to you.'

'What's this court case then? They going to lock you up?'

Paul was smiling broadly, interested, relentless. Fair enough, she'd guessed that he would be either sullenly reproachful or curious, and now that it came to it this was better; she realised she had grown quite fond of Paul, knowing the details of his life from conversations and letters, knowing things that had never been put into words from watching him learn. For him to feel let down would upset her; besides she would have to get used to saying it.

'The fact is, I was raped, that's why I'm going to court.'

She was smiling too.

'That's bad,' said Paul. He took the information in

slowly, silent and focused with the same indefinable physical change that came over him when he concentrated on his reading. Nothing moved, but he looked stiff.

'I was just thinking,' he said – she wouldn't be able to smile anymore – 'what kind of man was that?'

'I lived with him once, a journalist.'

'A white man?'

She nodded. There was another long pause.

'What do you think you'll do? You must keep going with your reading.'

'Rape is one thing,' said Paul, ignoring her question, 'but what I can't understand is when a man goes with a woman and then beats her up.'

She felt herself weakening. She could tell only if she knew she could be comforted, if the listener assumed that what had happened was as frightful as she knew it to be. To have to argue was impossible.

'But it's just the same, the same thing,' she said, her voice a little higher because of the looseness of her throat.

'To beat a woman, that's worse,' he contradicted her.

'How can you know?'

'I did hit a woman once, and that was an argument, but I felt real bad afterwards.'

'But I meant, how do you know what feels worse?'

'A rape, that could come from love, mixed up,' he said, 'sometimes a man . . .'

'I don't want to go on talking about it,' she said, 'I can tell you it's more like beating than love.'

They were both embarrassed. She was scared, thought he was too. Between them in the room was an ugly spiky bomb of mutual incomprehension. She started to put her jacket on, hurrying.

'See you next week,' he said.

The autobiography had settled down into more or less chronological order now, and, as the spelling had improved so the writing had lost its neat, laboured look. It was no

162

longer on the pale blue notepaper Mrs A had favoured, but on A4 ruled feint and margin, which she had been surprised to discover was much cheaper to buy.

'Now selling is a gift, a real gift. Young people are normally best at it – I was thirty-five when I started, but I looked younger, I've always looked after myself.'

Cath could imagine – Mrs Anderson full of postwar hope, her face in carmine and beige, her eyebrows, now thin and dishevelled from years of plucking, pencilled in determinedly, her hair set 'flattering but sensible' once a week. She would wear a black and white dogtooth-check waisted jacket with lapels – in fact, Cath remembered being shown a photo of Mrs A in just such a garment, facing the camera squarely with a background of choppy sea, and in the horizon a blur that was the Isle of Wight where she lived when she was working in hotels.

'It's a gift that most people can't keep for long: like virginity, it's a hard world. Now another thing about selling is that some people buy because they think they want the goods and it's a fair price, but others I should say buy because they like you. So you've got to play it both ways, until you know which kind they're going to be.

'Now I was selling knives, a whole range of knives: pen knives, fruit knives, carving knives, curved knives for cutting up grapefruit, scout knives, any kind of knive.' Cath replaced the v with an f.

'They tried to make me take the saucepans, being a woman. But I said, being a woman, a suitcase full of saucepans would be too much to carry . . . anything bigger than that, of course and you had to just take one to do it all with by order forms, and that would have put paid to me, because of the writing. And really, would you want a man with a case full of knives in your front room? I felt a bit funny too, walking about with so many knives, you felt as if you've done something wrong.

'Now, if I could see that this person definitely didn't want a knife, I'd do a quick guess as to whether they had any money spare, and if they did, I'd stop trying to sell – but leave my case open, and start to chat a bit. The war was a good one: still very fresh in people's minds and either they had lost someone or they felt guilty that they hadn't. Then when I got up to go, they'd look again: you could tell they weren't really looking, pick a knife and pay up.

'There was this man answered the door, he kept me chattering and every now and then he'd pick up a knife and say: "I'm not sure, maybe I'll get this one", and there was something about the way he looked at me made me know he wasn't quite right. So I said, I can see I'm wasting my time, and he said how do you know that, if you play your cards right I might just buy the whole lot. And then I was sure there was something funny about him and I began to feel really scared: he had one of the big ones, a new line, I remember, extra sharp with a kind of wavy edged blade. The All Purpose knife I think it was called. So I pretended I hadn't noticed anything and started packing up the other ones slowly, giving him time to hand it over and I said, not letting on I was scared, well you'll have to make your mind up quick, because they were expecting me back half an hour ago and I was in a real hurry. When I held out my hand for the knife it was shaking like a leaf but he wasn't looking at my hand. He said if I buy this one will you come back and see me again, so I said yes, took the money and ran . . . Well I realised afterward that I hadn't given him the change from the pound note – that was a lot of money then, and so I'd done quite well out of it, but after that my selling got worse and worse, I used to think, you never know, because he had seemed such a nice man to begin with, and that put me off my stroke, really. No one can sell for ever, like footballers, you've only got so long, and models. Then something happens and it's taken so much out of you to keep going would cost too much.'

How could a person stop themselves being bought? Cath wondered. It seemed to be a matter of luck, all wrong, but neither was refusing to accept the situation any solution.

'Well I didn't like bar work, but I liked the manageress and I could see she liked me. Two of a kind we were, though she's had an easier life than me. I'd say she was in the cellars or in bed with a cold if her husband rang when she was off with her fancy man and she'd give me the evening off with pay if I really wanted or slip me a fiver after a hard night. Now this husband of hers owned the place he was meant to manage with her, but he also liked the races. Even when he was there, he never did much except shout if the takings were down. I didn't blame her a bit.

'Well, it must have been about 1965 when he died, and the place came to her. She took me on as manageress, and over a couple of years we turned it into a club, got a late licence, cocktails, French bread and paté, no restrictions. There wasn't another club for miles around and so we raked them in. I've never had so much money in my life and I'm sure I never will again, barring the pools or Fred being in the money when he dies.'

Fred, Cath remembered, was the brother who was going to take Mrs A to Paris in the spring.

'Well early one morning this man in a dark old-fashioned suit comes up to me and Belinda – you two ladies must do pretty well out of this place, he said. Pretty well, Belinda said. We were pretty proud of ourselves I must admit. You want to be careful he said, there's been a lot of trouble round here, that pub in Malvern Road that got burnt down a littlebird tells me that wasn't no accident. Well I thought he was drunk, didn't know what the man was talking about, not even when he spelled it out. What you ladies need, he said, is protection.

'He must have come four or five times, and we never took him seriously. We weren't mixed up with that kind of people and didn't know what it was like and besides, he seemed to be after Belinda and we thought that was what it was all about. Well Belinda wasn't a bit keen, and one night he tried to kiss her. She lost her patience and threw him out. He was the only person we ever threw out. About

165

three months later there was a fire and that was that. The police never got anyone but we got the message. Belinda took her insurance money and went to live in Spain, I came to London and started working on the buses.'

Cath turned out the light, making a mental note about punctuation. She felt proud: Mrs A could write as well as most people, and she felt as if she had completed something worthwhile – and just in time.

The next Tuesday Paul's front door didn't spring open as normal when she pushed the gate. It was his habit to watch out for her, invisible behind the thick lemon-yellow net of the never-used front room: he must have overslept. Cath was dreading the lesson, afraid he might want to talk about the case. She wished she hadn't told him the truth, wished he'd had the tact to change the subject straight away, wished she'd simply not come. Consistency and commitment are vital, she had written in the leaflet for Volunteers, but she'd had enough of it.

She knocked loudly to wake him. He would rub his eyes in deference to convention, but sleep would have already been cast aside as he ran down the stairs. It was his mother who answered the door.

'You come far?' she asked. 'You better come in.'

The kettle had just boiled and Paul's mother added water and milk to a second cup of coffee before announcing,

'He's gone to Jamaica, yesterday.'

'What!'

Paul's mother laughed. 'Well that's what I said, and where did he get the money? I hope there's going to be no trouble. But he left a note, so you must have done him some good: more than his brother did.'

'Dear Ma', Cath read the careful capitals, sloping across the lines on a page of the note pad she had given him, 'I've gone home to find Everard. When I get a job I will send you some cash and I will write soon.'

'Calls it home but he's never been there,' commented his mother, half proud, half contemptuous. 'He'll be back.

Never liked anything different that one. You want a bit of rum?'

Why not? Cath thought, flooded with relief at not having to give his lesson, and having nothing to do until the after-lunch session with Mrs Anderson. There was no label on the corked rum bottle that splurted a viscous dark spirit glinting deep red, like tea. Paul's mum turned on the radio and moved plates briskly from table to sink in between her sips of rum. Cath drank hers quickly because she couldn't think of much to say, and accepted a second glass because she didn't want to go. Jamaica, just like that. What was Jamaica like? She remembered seeing a short film about the island in a geography lesson at school: sugar cane and rum, flowered shirts and white tourists dancing on beaches. She remembered laughing at the commentator's solemn voice, and the inappropriate background of classical music, but not much else.

'You staying?' asked Paul's mum. 'You can slice these up and we'll eat a bit. Getting in a rage always makes me starve.'

'What's Jamaica like?' Cath asked. Paul's mother hadn't seen it for twenty years. It was one of those places she said where you only had to ask and everyone was your friend, or seemed to be. Where luxuries you could afford but necessities got dearer every day.

'A good place for a holiday,' she said, bitterness sharpening her face. A place where the rum and the smoke and the sun made people loving and slow to anger but fiery when roused; where the sea lapped all round and old mansions crumbled and white blocks of the new colonials reared up.

'People here can't dance, can't sing, can't even hardly talk.' Paul's mum had left because she'd thought of England rather like Paul thought of Jamaica, a place where everything would fall just right.

'Remarkable little difference in how you feel,' she said. 'It doesn't matter where you go, you never see the place

167

you're in after a month or so.'

Cath was a bit drunk and cut her finger with the kitchen knife, but it didn't hurt.

'Paradise Lost, everyone's got one,' she said, and wondered where the phrase had come from, but Paul's mother nodded as if she knew what she meant. They ate hot gluey soup, pink from peppers and spice, it sealed the stomach like sleep. Cath stopped worrying about what she would say to Mrs Anderson in the afternoon.

'That's better,' said Paul's mum. 'I don't like to feel hungry, it makes me think of other things I want. You got someone to teach this afternoon?' She picked a small hymnbook from the kitchen shelf and packed it in her handbag. 'I'm going down the road myself.'

'It's the apostrophes', she said to Mrs A, 'Just carelessness. Really, it's only the odd spelling that trips you up.'

'Why can't I get it right? The moment I get carried away, it goes. Why is it? I've always learnt things fast, except writing . . .'

'The red pen makes it look worse than it is – I've put absolutely every mistake and even things that aren't exactly mistakes but just could be better. You've learned quicker than anyone else I've taught, really –'

Mrs Anderson's anger was stubborn. It was as if this was the first thing she had not been able to do; there was something almost childish about her rages, except that even flattery made no difference.

'At school it's just the same, not too long to learn the basics, but years of spelling mistakes, really Mrs A –'

Mrs Anderson sighed noisily, said no more but looked irritated. The lesson was exhausting itself.

'Your autobiography's really coming on,' said Cath awkwardly. 'I feel I really know you, I look forward to getting it every week.'

This was all true, but it sounded odd: she had not said

such straightforward personal things for a long time, now she felt they sounded insubstantial and spineless, like grasses that had grown under a stone. And even on the point of being honest she was being dishonest, padding out and preparing the thing it was necessary to say with things it was not, however true they were.

'It's made me think, actually, how little I've ever told you about myself . . . funny . . .'

Mrs Anderson was settling on the couch, rumpled, but beginning to look a bit more cheerful.

'Well, no I suppose it isn't funny at all, what I mean is –'

'I'm not the prying sort,' said Mrs Anderson.

'This last year has been a bit of a disaster for me,' Cath stared at the vase of white roses on top of the sideboard, 'one way and another . . .' Why did she feel compelled to add this sprinkling of words from an imaginary woman whom she supposed Mrs Anderson would like and understand more than the real one?

'Yes . . . I was raped, just after I started lessons with you, and I'm taking it to court, it should come up very soon. Someone I knew, it was.'

'Nasty,' said Mrs Anderson, 'raking it all up like that.'

'It is – but there doesn't seem to be anything else to do, there's nothing I could do on my own, and I don't think I could forgive myself really if I didn't go through with it. But it is nasty, you're right.' It wasn't what she'd expected.

'Happens all the time,' said Mrs A. 'I wish you luck dear, but the most he'll get is a couple of years, you see it in the papers every day – three years for shoplifting, eighteen months for rape – and you've had all that worrying and waiting. I wouldn't do it myself.'

Cath's hopes of the scene shrivelled, and she tried to fight the feeling that Mrs A was actually hostile. There was something so dismissive, more than just uninterested, that it seemed malicious, yet really the woman was only telling the truth as she saw it, and what was wrong with that? Perhaps some residual bitterness about such things, buried in resignation, made her resentful at Cath's raking them up? Perhaps she thought it was weak and silly to make such a fuss? Or was it that there was a generation gap, a moral code that Cath had unwittingly blundered into? Mrs Anderson had been very frank about herself but, Cath realised, nearly always by innuendo. Perhaps the rape was a shame one couldn't actually name.

'After the case, I'll be going away, I hope, so Anne will take over the lessons, if you think you still need them, and –'

'But what about my book? What's she like? I wouldn't want just anyone to see it, not before it's finished,' interrupted Mrs Anderson, scandalised and betrayed, rising out of the sofa.

'I was going to say, I'd like you to go on sending it to me. I'd miss it – When I go away, I can give you my address . . .'

'Tell me,' said Mrs Anderson nodding her relief and approval of this plan, 'do you think it's changed much between where I started and the last bit? Do you think it's getting better?'

Cath had imagined telling Mrs Anderson would right the imbalance between them, cancel out a debt – yet it seemed only to have estranged them; and now Cath was no longer sure, even, if she liked Mrs Anderson: she likes to do all the talking, she thought, she's too full of herself to bother with anyone else. Like a child. I only told her because I had to anyway.

Mrs Anderson held new sherry glasses up to the light, but Cath didn't want to share in the ritual. The overheated flat, all pink and polished, seemed hideously uncomfortable, sickly as parma violets. Mrs Anderson was trying out a new aerosol furniture cream and there was a faint smell of meths from it.

'No thanks, I'll be off now,' said Cath, feeling already dismissed.

12

Once Cath dropped a bottle on the way to a party, and after it left her hand but before it actually hit the ground, she saw and heard it smashing and bleeding on the pavement. Then, a split second later, it all happened again exactly the same, for real. In the same way, when the bell went unexpectedly in the late afternoon, she knew: it's Sally, saw her, opened the door and saw her again.

'Sally! Where have you been? One grotty little postcard in nearly a year – call yourself a friend, I dread to think what enemies are like – '

Tumbling up the stairs was Sally; a bit slower than usual? Was she ill or tired or something?

'Where haven't I been would be a better question. Most recently drinking gin. Have you got any tea?'

Cath boiled, measured, stirred, waited in silence. Sally watching her like a thirsty but polite dog. Her hair had grown longer, it had become a mane, quite different from the no-nonsense feathercut she had maintained with nail scissors ever since she first went to Ireland. Cath pushed tea towards her, handle first.

'I did get a postcard – before that I called round and Max said . . . I was worried about the flat, but –'

'Fuck Max,' Sally interrupted. 'I daresay you put two and two together: I walked out. The little green-eyed monster

171

reared its ugly head, I cut it off, it grew another six. He started bringing her to the house: expected me to just disappear, lock myself in the toilet or something . . . '

She pulled a face and pushed something invisible away from her, a parody of fastidiousness, by which Cath was to understand: subject closed.

'First I went to stay off the fat of the land in Den's parents' place in Cumbria – beautiful, but I thought I'd go really mad with nothing to do and nothing to talk to bar the stones and trees and so on. So I went home to my Irish grandmother's, she needs the help. I'll go again soon. Everything's up shit creek here, I only told them at work I was taking a week's leave . . . '

Sally was hunched, inhaling the steam from her tea, her face loosening in its warmth. 'What about you?' she asked, and then, she said: 'Look Cath, I'm pregnant. Don't know who, don't care. *DON'T WANT IT*. So, yes, I'm getting one. That's what I'm here for. All under control. But Cath – excuse me if I go on, I am pissed, you know – but every day that foetus gets an inch bigger and nearer to being a Baby Jane, I know it doesn't really, but I catch myself feeling like a murderess. But I'm going to do it – this is the last-ditch battle with the god-fearing rosary-counting mother of fifteen everyone wanted me to be. And of course, everyone out there conspires to make you feel guilty as well, not that I've told anyone but you. You just know, you can tell from the things they say . . . except Gran, maybe, she's even had a few herself, but you know Cath, she's really not at all well, that's why I went there in the first place. She's got some kind of anaemia, really she can hardly keep awake but she will try to keep the garden like a front parlour and the chickens like well-scrubbed children: anyone'd think she'd still got a family to feed.'

Sally was crying, huge-eyed stricken face with her mouth gone loose and snail tracks of tears stretching down the sides of her face. It was almost another face, Cath realised, shocked, not hard at all, this Sally, come to collapse in her kitchen, dissolve on her cushions and exude the soft foam of self-pity around them both. Whether she should be glad or not, she was. She hugged Sal close and said when are you having it, it'll soon be over, see, we marched for abortions and now you're getting one, that's good. I'll come with you, I'll hold your hand, money? Another cup of tea, plenty more where it came from if you change your mind, better this way –

'I'm glad I came,' said Sally, 'I almost couldn't face it.'

'I am too, glad you told me.'

'You were going to say something, Cath, and I do believe I interrupted you –' Sally pulled her head back, dealing with the tears and acting like there was no more to be said.

'Come on,' she said, 'tell.'

'Steve raped me,' answered Cath, 'after Jean's party.'

'What?'

And it was almost a pleasure to say the words a second time, Sally had not known, she had not known.

'He raped me. When I got home from the party. He was at the door. Said he was passing through and could he come in. Then it happened. Said he thought I owed him something, and he said he wouldn't go until he came. I phoned the police. I phoned you too, not remembering you'd still be at the party.'

'Oh Cath, I wasn't there!'

'Well of course you weren't, silly, that doesn't matter.' And suddenly nothing mattered but mixing this river of tears between them. You swim in mine and I in yours but which is which is impossible to tell: the same salt's in both. Neither of us was there. If I had been there Cath, if I had been there Sal, it would never have happened, there would not have been or have to be the alien metal breaking into your cunt, poor flesh; you'd not have to scrape your insides out and start again, to lie your story and fix your face to hide your nightmares even from yourself, if I had been there. There was a buried reservoir of grief that had been waiting to leak and squeeze itself out through the crevices

173

of their faces and the pores of their palms, push and gasp through heart and throat: that reservoir had been buried a pool and grown to a lake, the original pain growing with the drip, drip of others like a stalactite swelling and compounding itself inside.

We weren't there. I didn't know, or imagine. And the shared parts of this sadness made the sum of it both of theirs, larger, but also lighter.

'I keep getting drunk, hoping I'll haemorrhage and won't have to go through with it.'

'I'm frozen up inside, I can't tell anyone, I thought you might not believe me, and I don't want to remind myself –'

'Inside you, like your body's been appropriated without permission.'

'Like it was never really yours in the first place.'

'And I thought, Cath this *can't* have happened to me, just because it was the last thing I wanted. I almost believed I could will it away: it hurts my pride that I can't.'

'And I keep thinking about it, and is there nothing I can do to get it back, get back what he ruined? I feel missing, gone missing, but I couldn't think of anything to do except get on with my life and wait for the case.'

'And no one can kid me it won't be worse before it's over; Cath, you know I'm not cowardly, but I'm frightened of the pain. There might not even be any, it's probably all modern and safe, but I'm frightened I might die.'

'Go mad. You think you can forget, but really you can't.'

Cath and Sal, all huddled and damp on the cushions by the

174

fire, their arms as indistinguishable as their words, fell silent. Cath took her hand from where it was cradling Sally's head and turned on the fire. It was here, she thought, right here that it happened, but she felt safe so long as she didn't move.

She noticed with surprise that there were black mascara streaks on Sally's face.

'When your case is over,' Sally was saying, 'we could go away, on holiday. We could go to the place in Cumbria. It doesn't cost anything. It's halfway up the hill, just on the edge of the woods, the quietest place I've ever been, it'd be lovely if there was someone to talk to. And there's everything there, they only use it a week a year but it's got ironed sheets and a fridge and a fire – one of those aga things . . . we could go for walks, when do you think it will be over, your case?'

'I'm not sure: soon, but they don't really tell you till the week before, and there's no way I can find out how long –'

'It doesn't matter: I can go any time. I could send you the keys so you could go straight up there as soon as it was all over. I'll be at Grandma's. You could just drop me a line as soon as you're ready.'

Cath hesitated. It was so unexpected, so uncharacteristic that it felt dangerous. Sally persisted.

'Or if you wanted to, go on your own for a bit first? Communing with the wilderness and so on. Then I could come with my little carrier bag of duty-free whisky and my nasty cigarettes and my radio – what's the matter with you? It'd be something to look forward to!'

'Wouldn't it be tricky to get there without a car?' said Cath, feebly. How near the surface was this fantasy of The Place: the little cottage on the hill where time stood still or even flowed backwards – where the world was vanishing in a flurry of blown leaves, the slow rhythm of the day and night lengthening and contracting, balancing the hours. It's very sentimental, thought Cath, on the point of denying herself.

'You never would come anywhere with me.'

'You never asked me before. You just disappear, then don't write letters. Then it's all over by the time we meet again, just a sentence to describe a year.'

'I asked you to come to the USSR.'

'But I had to give up *everything* to do it. I remember you said –'

'That's true,' Sal said. 'This is different. Not me going off to find the Big Answer and wanting you to come and find it too; just a holiday.'

And Cath thought of the smell of woods, of cool air and the peculiar light of cottages: small deepset windows, and at night low-wattage bulbs shining from odd corners, caressing a glaze of undisturbed dust that bound all colours together, whatever they were. And of waking in this strange light to silence or the sound of wind, not the rumbling of engines and the slamming of a million doors. She looked at Sally who was being charming, putting herself out to persuade, whereas before she had issued ultimatums: 'take it or leave it, this is where I'm going you can come if you like'. That Sally, too, should want this old pipesmoke dream, to be in a bubble of lamplight with Cath her friend, and that she should admit to being even temporarily tired of being hard and being busy – it was a sudden twist that linked up the years between then and now, time that had begun to seem almost lost. Once they had kicked stones slipping out of the school gates to Outside, where there wasn't really much and you wouldn't have bothered if it wasn't for having your friend. Egging each other on. Now, they could slip away again.

'Let's, then,' said Cath.

Sal stretched over the cushions for her bag and extracted a crumpled packet of Irish cigarettes.

'Shouldn't smoke when you're pregnant,' she said, lying on her back sucking loudly in a parody of inhalation, defiant.

'When is it?' And how long had she known? How had it

happened? Didn't she use? – inevitably the wrong questions surfaced, but they were in someone else's careful King's English accent presenting a woman's story to the world; Cath knew they were not worth asking and their irrelevance would offend.

'Tomorrow. I don't want to stay over if I can help it.' Sal pressed the flat stretch of denim between her hips as she spoke. Was that where it was, was that the womb? thought Cath. You couldn't really tell. A period pain, she thought, was a peeling pain – a suffusing pain somewhere inside: it didn't have a source, no lump you could feel through the skin. And your vagina: that could be a tiny hint of a space or it could be enormous, and at the end of it was the womb – even so, you couldn't really tell how far up it was: perhaps it moved too. It was strange, almost frightening to think that –.

'It's OK about coming with me,' said Sal, sitting up in one movement, strong from years of swimming and carrying things, small body with straight hard edges. 'I'd really rather you didn't. But thanks. I just want to go there and grit my teeth till its over, then blot it out. Some things are worse if there's someone else there. I just want an end to it. And then I'll bore you sick with it afterwards.'

Cath said nothing, feeling a fine dust of salt crystallising on her face, feeling happy.

Cath imagined Sally lying naked from the waist down, straining silently in an empty room. Though she knew better, she imagined her with machines, drips and dials, something metal – really it was a simple operation, though it was difficult to believe it wouldn't be painful. Sally would not cry, she was sure of that. There would be anaesthetic. She remembered reading in a dentist's magazine about a drug they give to women in labour that not only lessened the pain as it was happening, but also wiped it from their memory. Who are they? That way, the article said, a woman would not be traumatised by a difficult birth. Not

177

traumatised, she thought, but tricked.

She hoped Sally wouldn't forget. Perhaps it was best not to have anaesthetic. If she had gone with her, forgetting would have been out of the question.

Painful things always happened when you were on your own. They made you alone, perhaps they made you what you were. Was it fear or was it pride made you want to forget? That it happened to me! That I was powerless to stop it! That it couldn't be undone! She knew what Sally had meant. It was a kind of pride, but atrophied so that you only knew it was there when it hurt. How could you get back something you'd never known you had?

An envelope came, covered in a mosaic of small denomination stamps, reinforced with sellotape.

'Airport,' the note was headed. 'Lots of palaver before and after, but only bad for about ten minutes.' There was an address in Cumbria, another in Eire, a coach timetable, an old-fashioned key. Cath held the key, warming it. She put the note in her desk, as if it were a love letter. Despite its brevity it recorded a startling change: a deliberately planned escape together instead of an accidental meeting on return journeys from seperate spheres. The letter proved it to be no idle plan conceived in an afternoon of too much drink and too much crying: there was the timetable, the key, the little map. Evidence. Muscles around her mouth pulled, and Cath brought her hands to feel the outside of the smile. She did not like to think back, she did not want to imagine what was to come but there was a sense of something breaking through, a message, indecipherable as yet, from inside.

The week before the case was due to come to court everything normal came to a stop, and Cath rattled in a capsule of empty time. Each day she telephoned to check that the date of the hearing hadn't been altered. Tapping the barometer: no change. She had an appointment with Salter the evening before her case, and Sara was going to take the dawn train on the morning itself interrupting one of her visits to a distant relative. Hours and days to tick off, to trick into passing. She almost wished her mother would come earlier, though she suspected the atmosphere would be awkward when she did. In preparation she ironed her bedlinen and bleached every available surface in the kitchen and bathroom. Her mother had never seen her home before, she felt the desire to make it as like as possible the one she had been raised in.

She bought butter, tinned ham, a frozen half-cooked loaf that you could finish off in the oven. She went out again for grapefruits, bacon, a chicken, chocolate biscuits and some peas: none of these she normally bought. She tried to remember what foods Sara particularly liked and, never quite sure, bought more and more as things occurred to her. She would have to roast the chicken as her mother did, rather than in a casserole with wine. Stuffing mix. They would have neat dinners with everything in separate little piles on the plate; no pasta and no peppers and no garlic. She bought tinned fruit salad and jelly to make a trifle. 'Afters'. Gravy browning. Cocoa, chops. Potatoes. Mint sauce: she bought more food than she could afford, and more than could possibly be eaten, determined that should Sara say, for instance, 'Is there any marmalade?' she would be able to say yes, here you are. Everything there, everything full and clean, I do very nicely thank you. Baking powder, roasting dish, tinfoil, tea.

The stretched carrier bags clunked on the tiles of the step with a sound she associated with guilty drinkers, and she rummaged for her key. Still no one had moved in downstairs since the Browns went –

'Miss Sheldon?' A man in a dirty suit held out a large triangular package swathed in bright paper and curls of ribbon emitting the sharp crackle of cellophane as he handed it to her. Flowers! But she didn't know anyone who'd send flowers, she held them at bay. The man was not amused: it happened too often. That was the whole point of a bouquet: as a surprise, he said, acidly. It was her name and address, wasn't it?

Upstairs she slit the envelope before unbinding the flowers. On a small card printed with a border of violets she read:

'To cheer you up if things get you down. A small token of thanks for all the help you have given me so far. Good luck, yours Celia Anderson.'

Cath hurried to the sink to cut the flowers loose. To thank you for what you have done so far, and probably in the hope that you'll go on doing it, but never mind I will anyway, she thought, reeling under the dazzle of flowers; piebald carnations, miniature roses, mimosa, big yellow roses, fern, chrysanthemums, freesia, and a small white flower she did not recognise that looked like a delicate scattering of froth and smelt stronger and sweeter even than the freesias. Cut the stems and pound them. And a couple of grains of sugar in the water, wasn't that right? Vase? Jug.

The flowers looked good on the mantelpiece, but the fire would shorten their life. By the window, the incoming light dazzled so that they were nothing but a spiky bundle. On top of the desk, they only caught the eye if you were sitting at it. She carried them into the bedroom and put them by her bed. She would move them back into the sitting room when her mother came.

This is the last time I'll see him Cath thought, only half hearing Salter as he spoke. They sat in a city pub amongst a crowd of six-thirty drinkers trying to miss the rush hour on the trains in favour of the one in the bar. Large suited men with their ties loosened, big soft hands curled round glasses of whisky, thrust in and out of pockets. It was very noisy. They probably think I'm his secretary, she thought, noticing how few women were there and that none of them were drinking on their own, but then she caught a glimpse of herself in the painted mirror on the wall behind Salter's

180

head: overgrown haircut, cold-blotched skin, and a line shaped like a child's representation of a flying bird across the middle of her forehead, and decided no one would take her for an up-and-coming secretary. That was her first line and she had not noticed it growing, had had no chance to think of retarding it with creams or facial jerks, no chance to panic or to meditate upon what this second coming-of-age meant. It had had a head start, and caught her unawares.

'A calm witness is a bad witness, in this kind of case,' Salter said.

'I'm not likely to feel calm.' But right now she did feel calm, so utterly empty and washed away. She stole another glance into the corner of the mirror. Perhaps there were other lines, maybe at the corners of her mouth – Salter coughed irritably to regain her attention. He was in a hurry to catch a train.

'How you feel is immaterial. You have to give them something concrete. Otherwise how can they know what you feel? Certain things are to be expected of a woman in your position: describing in public such a traumatic event, the presence of the defendant only a few yards away: it would be only natural for there to be some form of visible distress . . . reliving the event . . . it would greatly add to the credibility of your version of events . . . integrity . . . and, of course, sympathy.'

She swilled the thick sickly orange juice he had bought her at the bottom of its too-large glass; she felt so tired that even her accumulated hatred of the unpleasant truths he told had evaporated. He was obviously a good barrister, a good man to have on your side, one to give hot hints and good tips: my advice is, put on a good show, let it rip. Told you the tricks of the trade, the way to get on. She supposed it wasn't his fault that things were the way they were.

'Mind you, not hysterical. I would go so far as to say that how you conduct yourself in the witness box will be as important as anything either you or the defendant says,' he persisted.

But even though it wasn't his fault, it was obvious that he felt no particular frustration at the dishonesty of it all, no desire to change the system: indeed, he actually seemed to enjoy the convolution, bluff and double bluff of what he called 'the process of justice', much as her father had used to enjoy dealings with the tax office or the DHSS.

This 'process of justice' she imagined was for Salter a kind of ritual combat, a game played for high stakes in sombre casinos where nobody's honesty – and least of all the dealer's – could be taken for granted. Playing by the rules was a mug's game, worse than trusting to luck.

He was waiting for some kind of acknowledgement, eyes frozen unblinking.

'I see, yes.' Her vocal cords felt brittle and perished like old rubber bands, and she was surprised that the sounds seemed to emerge clear and steady, and that Salter seemed satisfied and looked away, taking a sip of his whisky as if something had been concluded. 'I see, yes' – had she committed herself with those three words? Were they a legally binding contract? After the hearing would he come to her like a vengeful god: 'You contracted to weep, to tremble and to blanch; you broke your oath, herewith I institute proceedings for breach of promise . . .' She knew she would not, she could not perform as he had suggested, and not only because her hackles rose at the idea that she must become a textbook victim in order that people might believe something wrong had been done to her, but also, she thought, because I couldn't, I just can't afford to, I mustn't. Salter, his brain a strange hybrid of the actor's and the crossword puzzler's, was drawn and driven into the fray by the smells of blood and money, loosened into brilliance by the pale gold Irish whiskey. All his instincts and drives were harnessed in the service of his career. His advice was sound, and if she didn't follow it she halved her chances of success. But –

But to do so would be to disintegrate, not merely as he suggested to 'relive' but actually to *become* – in the worst of

182

places and circumstances – what had happened to her. To shudder and weep and suffer – even for a moment to lose that slender distance, that secret passive arrogance that had hovered with her even as her body and will were held and crushed, would be to drown in her own powerlessness, in an anger that confused itself with shame:

That I let it happen to me.

'Well, that's all. Good luck, and try and get a good night's sleep.'

They shook hands.

'Thank you for your help,' she said coldy, and he nodded, looking down and watching his fingers twisting buttons through buttonholes, the first time she had seen him embarrassed. It was cold outside and Trafalgar Square was almost deserted. Salter walked briskly to the subway, raised his arm with his back still turned, and disappeared for ever. A late-night delicatessen-cum-supermarket had opened next to the souvenir shop by the bus stop. Its neon brilliance switched everything else into invisibility and she found herself staring across the road at the well-stacked shelves inside. Was there anything she needed? She had fifteen pounds for the next two days. She crossed with some difficulty and examined the window display of bottles in rush baskets festooned with hay and livid plastic grapes. Tequila, Martini, Vodka, Chianti, Campari, the names like the shapes of the bottles, exotic and self-contained. Piat d'Or, rosé, brut, crème de menthe, retsina – for ten pounds a bottle of hot cactus juice that would send her reeling into sleep: better by far than the sleeping tablets Doctor Ross had prescribed. There was something comforting about the display of bottles, the ancient crude but pure amnesiac, fruit fermented to rottenness and distilled into fire. Spirits. The Demon Alcohol lying sealed in glass, cork and wax to await the luxurious gesture of opening, the drowning of sorrows or the incitement to song. She pushed open the supermarket door: brandy perhaps, the traditonal comforter, for medicinal purposes.

Eau de vie. Or whisky, stiffener of the upper lip. But perhaps it was not a good idea: she might turn up in court late with laddered tights, red eyed and reeking, swaying in the witness box . . . the wrong kind of performance entirely. A staccato hiccuping sound emanating from her throat surprised her, she must have laughed aloud and the thin young man restacking shelves and watching her out of the corner of his eye swung round to stare at her properly, his ticket gun held pointing at her midriff. A kind of distraction seized her, a frilliness about the edges that made her muscles twitch and her voice fretful and high.

'Have you got champagne?' she asked, and took the first bottle he showed her.

The bus was very slow, she could not keep still, couldn't read her paper, it seemed to shake in her hands. The suspension was bad. The bottle of champagne, initially cold to the touch, grew warm whilst she herself grew steadily icy and lost and forgotten muscles, flexing and jumping, set feet and fingers through strenuous routines. She ran from the bus stop, the crepe of her shoes making a faint sticking noise, her breathing louder than the traffic and the wind. Even indoors her breath seemed to follow her, a shadow that disappeared when she turned to confront it. A slight whistle on the in-breath and exasperated crescendo on the out, ssh hah ssh hah ss – for a minute she held her breath as she walked around the room looking for her one remaining wine glass, but it fought its way noisily out again. It might help to talk to herself, but there was nothing she wanted to say, and besides, her throat was too tight. She switched on the radio, music. The telephone, like the voice strangled inside her, strained for sound yet resisted use, wound in on itself and sat awkward and heavy as a lump in the throat. Now there was an arts programme: slow, braying voices she could not listen to long enough to discover the subject of the discussion. She took the still-tepid champagne out of the fridge and braced her thumbs against the cork, pushing till her nails went white, relaxed, pushed again, twist push relax twist push until it seemed to move. Rotating the bottle heavy between her knees after each even gentler pressure, the cork crept then hurtled out of the bottle, hit the ceiling then the table, the back of the sofa, and she rushed the foaming bottle to the glass. There was a hiss of tiny bubbles, like faint applause.

'To the judge, I mean the jury. And to luck. A bribe before the event,' she toasted aloud after the first mouthful, and as if it had been waiting for a signal, the telephone rang, two calls in swift succession: her mother with details of the train she would be getting (she would only have fifteen minutes to spare) and advice not to wear too much, it was bound to be hot, and then Kim.

'I'm fine,' Cath told them both. 'I'm just going to bed.'

She took the phone off the hook, turned the radio on and the light towards the wall. Only a couple of glasses and already she felt quite reckless; the constriction in her throat was losing its grip and she caught herself humming to the symphony on the radio, always a fraction of a beat behind and more than a fraction out of tune. Briskly, but with lapses of memory and repeat journeys to the wardrobe and chest of drawers, she assembled her dress, bra, tights, knickers and shoes for the next day. Almost the very same outfit she had worn for degree day eight years ago. Sunday's Best, also worn for weddings, christenings and funerals, without discrimination. Clean underwear in case you get run over. Wear a nightdress to save the sheets and a vest to save your blouse, pack a dressing gown when staying overnight. Thank god no one wore hats anymore.

'Shouldn't think they'll take me for a "high flier" in this', she said and mimicking Salter's measured tones: 'I advise you to dress to look older rather than younger.' She giggled. It was indeed rather similar to degree day: the flowery dress, champagne, a pompous apportioning of blame and praise on what seemed pretty arbitrary grounds.

Her father, George, had been alive still – just – at degree day, visibly proud. Thinking, she guessed, the thing I never had my daughter has got. Against the odds. Living proof that hard work can get anyone anywhere. Food for optimism, flesh of his flesh, a bridge from the factory to the professional classes, change from the bottom upwards, but don't forget where you came from, little Cath. She found herself weeping a little, salt with the acid of the wine, at this infrequent and always inconvenient remembering of her father, and she was shocked too to realise that time had turned him into a caricature: a dignity-of-labour socialist, a hard-work no-nonsense union man, leather jacket or brown worsted; both he and Steve had no time for the same kinds of things and she never realised it until now . . . Her father proud as punch at smart flowery dress and a squiggle on a piece of water-marked paper, what would he have thought of this, then? Would it have been 'How dare he', 'Anyone who does that to a daughter of mine deserves to be hung'? Or would it have been 'There's no point in crying over spilt milk, no need to go dragging it through the courts'? Would he even have been ashamed, or would there have been ambiguous silence then her mother, stern-faced, saying: 'Your father's wept. I never saw him cry before'? She could not even begin to guess, but she was glad he was not here: belief or disbelief, support or desertion would amount only to another element in the cacophony of judgement that she felt gathering round her. The rape, it seemed, had been only the first in a series of acts of judgement (not to be confused with justice, nor assumed to be accurate) pursuing her in relay. His would have been another pair of eyes which, for one reason or another, it would be difficult for her to meet.

A little champagne spilled as she poured the last glass. There were hardly any bubbles left and it tasted both sweeter and more acid.

'Bastard!' she shouted suddenly. 'Look what you've done, you rat.' For it could make you mad, to be in a world where suddenly everything seemed to depend on other people believing what you said: friends, relatives, strangers,

186

acquaintances, if they did not believe, if they did not think you were right, the world fizzled away like a drop of water on a hot plate; if they measured up the truth and it was the wrong size for them – what then? How could you contradict? Tomorrow – no, not tomorrow but at the end of the week, she would know. Maybe longer. The jury could lock themselves up endlessly, twelve people probably never raped using her predicament as a metaphor – an esperanto with which to battle out their conflicting prejudices, deciding in the end only out of boredom, exhaustion, thirst, the best of three, perhaps. Twelve men good and true. Pinnacle of the system. She might hope and she did – somewhere the figure of justice stood on a roof pointing at the sky, shining still and conducting bolts of wisdom to the jury chamber, decent people doing their best – but it would be disastrous to anticipate or to expect that everything would come out right in the end.

'What a world', she addressed the room with a casual gesture of the hand just as if it were a person seated opposite. But the walls had neither ears nor tongues; and oh the damn tears again, not the gentle ooze of alcoholic melancholy but rough dry heavings in her chest and stomach like being sick, but worse, as if what was inside was alive and desperate for air but too big, so enormous, that the whole of her torso must dilate to let it pull itself out, and the whole process a race against time and asphyxiation.

If only it would stop. I'll never know what I want again, just what I hate. I hate you. I would break you if I could. Steven Blake. What a mess! You did this. Why?

But it makes no difference why.

You did this.

I hate you.

If only it would be over.

But the room was senseless, not a womb to rock in but a cell too small to sit, lie or stand in. There was not even an echo, the carpet was dry, the walls were motionless, nothing changed but the same air going in and out of her lungs and the same wire and rubble in her throat.

As soon as I can breathe properly, she thought, I will phone that number; and the thought itself seemed to soothe her lungs.

'Women's Crisis Line, this is Melanie . . .'

'Melanie?'

'That's right.'

'I'm going to court tomorrow, I was raped – ' She waited a second in spite of herself, in case Melanie wanted to say anything, though she didn't want her to.

'I thought it was all OK but suddenly now I feel really crazy. I had this bottle of champagne and I can't stop crying. I know I'll feel awful tomorrow. So stupid because it's important; it's taken so long and now I'm going to make a fool of myself. It must sound silly, it's not as if I've just been raped or anything, I am sorry if . . .'

'No, it's not silly. Anyone'd have the jitters. We get women ringing up years, literally years, after they've been raped, so don't worry about that. What were you saying?'

'I don't want to drop charges or anything I'm just so worried about what's going to happen. I won't be able to sleep.'

'Is anyone going with you tomorrow?'

'My mum's coming. But that's, well, it's a bit awkward somehow. I wish she wasn't, I . . .'

'Would you like some of us to come too? We could meet you early and show you everything, get you somewhere decent to wait and help with your mother, if . . .'

'Do you believe me?' asked Cath, realising she hadn't told Melanie anything, not even her name, except that she was going to court; but even so there was sense in the question, there was only one right answer and 'what do you mean?' would be no good. She held her breath. A headache was developing, she must drink plenty of water and bathe her eyes before she went to bed.

'Yes, of course,' said Melanie. There was a pause.

188

'Would you come to court tomorrow then? I don't even know where to go or anything. I –'

'We can sort all that out if you tell me which court it is. We can get there early and check it all out. You know, you haven't told me your name . . .'

Cath told her it had been the man she had been living with, about her mother, and about the idea of going away with Sally afterwards. She told her about Paul disappearing to Jamaica just like that, about the literacy project. She told her she thought the rape was something to do with revenge. Melanie agreed. Melanie said she used to be a teacher, until she had a baby. They talked about the news. Cath had lost track of it. Sleep and dried brine gummed her eyes, her voice could hardly climb out of her throat.

'I should set an alarm,' said Melanie, 'just in case.'

13

Cath's period, three days late, woke her before the alarm went off with scouring pains and a sense of total surrender to gravity. On her sheets a heavy red that seemed to have more substance and life than the body from which it came. She dressed slowly, but still left with enough time to forget something and go back for it if necessary.

The tube was bleak but its anonymity was comforting: everyone isolated in their particular desires for the day, wanting to get their journeys over, avoiding fellow passengers' early-morning eyes, breathing in and tensing so as not to touch. It was a place designed for the efficient endurance of the unpleasant in-between parts of days and lives. She passed along the tiled corridors effortlessly, like something discarded carried on a tide, walking slowly with her shoulder brushing slightly against the curved wall. Her legs ached a bit. A busker, as yet invisible, could be heard strumming and wailing below. What a bad time to play, she thought, and felt in her pocket for change. But when she turned the corner he'd stopped playing. He was sitting on his jacket on the floor and looked up at her as she passed; her eyes twitched away but it was too late. He picked up his guitar and began to sing again: she knew he was singing his horrible love song to her, she could feel his attention crawling on her and she wanted to run. But she kept her pace, and forced herself not to look back. Never show your panic to its cause: dogs, ghosts, strange men, they all smell fear and it only makes them worse. . . As she turned on to the platform and the sound was cut off she loosened her grip on the coin in her pocket and her back slackened a little. She checked through her things: court papers, piece of foolscap with important points written on it – she'd taken those from Salter's recommendations, which she felt would be somehow incriminating to possess – tampons, crossword book, money, ticket. An apple left over from earlier in the week.

The apple was beautiful, its colours turning smoothly through scarlet and orange to a sharp vibrant green dusted with yellow and gold speckling that meant it was completely ripe. Out of habit she started to rub the red side on her coat, to give it a shine. The apple's smell rose heavy, so strong she could almost see it. She wasn't sure if she wanted to eat it right now. A crumpled leaf was still attached to the stalk. For no reason at all, she felt her eyes prickling. 'Pull yourself together' one part of herself muttered to the rest of her that wanted to curl up and weep for the simple loveliness of the apple. She would eat it then, rather than go sentimental about it. She bit, wondering why the trains were taking so long to come, the platform was packed now. She took a second bite before she had finished the first. The acid searched out the recesses of her mouth and teeth, smarted everything into life. It was the best apple she'd ever tasted.

'Sorry?' she said, her mouth full: someone had asked her something. She turned and saw a smallish, pulpy-faced man dressed in an open-necked shirt patterned with 'Gay Paree' and navy-blue Eiffel towers, and tightly belted beige trousers. A sizeable belly had collected in the bottom of the shirt, to jut above the belt like some bizarre piece of civic regalia. A large smile stretched his lips, at variance with the dull challenge in his stare.

'Can I have a bite of your apple then?'

She turned her back to him. The train was coming.

'Enjoying it, aren't you?' he shouted after her. 'Go on, give us a bite.'

The polished gold statue of justice (Justice was a lady) shone despite the overcast sky. There were a lot of statues in this part of the city – one, standing in a garden by a church, she noticed in particular: a man's legs with a huge bull's torso and erect penis. Most of them though were dignitaries or allegories: but then perhaps the bull-man was an allegory as well.

There is no reason at all why everything should not be all right she told herself. Melanie had said last night the police wouldn't have bothered if they didn't think there was a reasonable chance of conviction. The Magistrates' Court had been a piece of cake, the lady of Justice was bright: if omens were to be believed, yes, it would all come right in the end.

Cath stood on the court steps. There was no sign of Sara, but then it was very early. She consulted the diagram of the courts with her entrance marked on it. She'd walked past before, but never realised how many rooms the building contained, nor tried to imagine how many people were in there and why. She pushed through the turnstile, finding herself suddenly in a crowd. Someone searched her bag. Someone in blue and gold she had to follow. The little man who looked like a caretaker flapped a pair of panelled doors shut, extinguishing the uproar of the waiting hall.

'It's postponed, your case,' he said, 'and you came so early, what a shame. But they want to have a word with you, tried to get you on the phone yesterday but – '

Cath stopped walking, half of the long corridor stretching behind her, half in front. There was a faint smell of disinfectant, an echoing and shuffling from unseen feet.

'Detective Inspector Harris told me it was absolutely definite,' she called to the blue-uniformed man forging on down the corridor. 'It can't be cancelled, it's impossible.'

192

'There's definite and definite – it happens all the time in this game. . .' She had to trot to catch up with him to hear what he was saying. 'The Inspector's here anyway, so. . .'

He delivered her to a small group of men waiting in an alcove, smoking and laughing.

'We did try to get you yesterday,' said Harris, 'another case dragging on longer than expected. But it'll definitely be tomorrow – or Wednesday at the latest.'

Harris wore a firmly knotted tie, and a triangle of white handkerchief poked out at the top of his breast pocket; Cath saw him as from a great distance, wondering how she would get through all the time between, minutes and seconds like an impossible pile of potatoes to be peeled, hours like rocks to be heaved away.

'This is our barrister, Mr Lindell, Miss Sheldon.'

A white hand softer than her own offered itself from among swathings of black and pinstripe blue. He wasn't in the slightest like Salter to look at, he was all cheekbones, and insubstantial beneath the layers of clothing, a body nothing but brittle bones.

'Delighted,' he said. 'Don't let the delays upset you. The important thing is to give your evidence clearly and calmly. I don't think there's anything else.'

Salter had told her a calm witness was a bad witness. The babysoft hand took hers again. He would be in his chambers, he informed Harris – it was Harris's case – as he shook it, and Harris said to her, 'If you could stay at home, then we can let you know new arrangements over the phone. We might even get a different judge, and that wouldn't be a bad thing.' A Silver Lining.

'I'll just go home then?'

'Good girl.'

Cath felt foolish, embarrassed at how much it upset her to be delayed, all confused and worried by her glimpse behind the scenes. Performance cancelled, so did everyone scuttle back to change their costumes? She caught sight of Mr and Mrs Brown in the entrance hall peering at a notice board; she couldn't face telling them, panicked and managed to walk behind them without being seen.

She sat in the tube train again, going home, her face outwardly composed even calm, whilst her insides wrenched in the wake of two forces straining for supremacy: a firework one that wanted to scream and kick, to go back to the court and insist, to start running until she fell asleep or got to the sea; and a clenching one that was self-control, less spectacular but very strong. These forces balanced and lurched like arms pressed against each other, a tiny, deadly battle, the intensity of which seemed to propel her home. Home where Mrs Anderson's flowers quietly shed their pollen and petals. Home with its mortise lock, chain, spy-hole and smell of last night's champagne. She must stay home because of the phone. She opened the window.

She should have thought to sit in on a case, any case, just to see how it happened. Where people stood and so on. She could have done that today, except now she had to be in for the phone. They should have given her a time: what state did they think she'd be in after waiting all day and night for a phone call? 'Give your evidence clearly and calmly'! Self-control said tears would be debilitating, there was no point getting angry now. Self-control won for a while.

The instant the phone began ringing she realised she had forgotten about her mother.

'I know it's postponed but why didn't you wait for me? Did you forget I was coming? What's the matter with you? I've got a very heavy bag . . . I had to get up at five o'clock to get here, I could have done without it. You wanted me to come.'

But she hadn't, not really. Perhaps she'd forgotten her on purpose? Cath broke out into a sweat.

'Are you all right? Nothing's happened?'

'I'm fine Mum. I'll come and meet you straight away.'

'Do you want to go shopping?'

'No, not really.' Or did she? It would fill the time.

194

'I'd love to look around Lilywhites and maybe. . .'

Looking around the shops. Sara would do exactly that: look. She would examine every object, compare it with memories of similar objects seen in her own shops or with expensive ones from the past and pronounce it 'scandalously steep' or a 'bit steep' or 'trash'. With her pensions, legacy and insurance she was probably better off than she had ever been, but she would not buy a thing: all she purchased was basic food and train tickets. At the end of a day's comparing and adding she'd feel content because she could, if she'd wanted, have got most of the things cheaper back home, and what she couldn't have wasn't worth having in any case. Cath now bought everything without looking at the price or counting in her purse and, as near as possible, as soon as she saw it. Each purchase still bought with it a sense of relief that she had acquired it without the endless talking, weighing up and deciding she had endured as a child, following Sara from store to store.

'I'll leave my bag at Victoria.'

'I'll meet you when you've finished.'

She wouldn't look at the time, not yet. It must be about eleven. Perhaps the Crisis Centre would phone. She hadn't seen them, she'd been too early. But perhaps they hadn't come anyway, too good to be true. Her mother would now be consuming a buttered currant bun and a pot of tea (not strong enough), before setting out for the West End. To save being hungry later on, in the expensive parts of town. What should she do then? Everything was already tidy. If it wasn't for waiting for the police to call she could have gone to the allotments and seen what had grown and died, what had survived the frost: time always passed quicker out of doors. She changed into jeans, hung the flowery dress up on the back of the bathroom door and washed her tights. She called the Centre. Melanie was just back, they said, taking off her coat. Melanie had been to the List Office and been told the case would definitely not be on before tomorrow at ten and it was 'very unlikely' to be postponed beyond tomorrow afternoon.

'Very frustrating,' said Melanie, 'you get all geared up and then – nothing. It nearly always happens.'

'I felt like kicking something,' said Cath, surprised at herself. Melanie didn't comment.

'I saw Lindell,' she said, 'I told him you'd want a private room to wait in. Otherwise you'd be sitting in this sort of corridor and all the defence witnesses and friends and so on, and maybe even the rapist, would be there as well. Did you know?'

'I don't really know anything about what happens in court.'

'You can have two people wait with you. Anyone else has to go in the gallery. But you need someone in the gallery to see what actually happens.' Sara, thought Cath, would sit tight-lipped and stare at Melanie until she left. She would not approve of calling strangers.

'My mother's come down,' she said.

'Shall we go in the gallery then, unless we hear any different?'

Cath agreed and thought she would get her mother to go in the gallery too.

'After you've given evidence,' said Melanie, 'it depends. Technically you can just go, but sometimes they call you back. If you have someone in the gallery, you can meet them at breaks to find out what's happened.'

'How long do you think it will last?'

'It depends on the defence. How many witnesses, how long the speeches. The more doubts they introduce, the longer the jury will have to be out. But at least it's happening now, the end of the road, and it can't happen twice.'

Something like a bubble of indigestion gas rose in Cath's chest, dissipated in her throat, leaving her feeling weak. Was there anything else Melanie or the Crisis Centre could do? Could tell her? Did she want company, did she want distraction, did she want –

196

'No, I don't think I want anything. Except, I want to go out and the police told me to wait for a phone call.'

'I'll ring them.'

Melanie was all right. She was practical. Time had started to flood, it was one o'clock. She would have to rush now to get to the allotment and back and change in time to meet her mother. Melanie didn't seem like Kim at all. Or maybe Kim wasn't so bad anyway; she was glad she'd used the number, and Kim had given it to her.

The spade slid into the damp clay matted with months' growth of weeds and last year's dead leaves. Cath sweated, working effortlessly as a machine. Fat clusters of earthworms writhed away from the unexpected light. Everything was overgrown or overblown, here and there remaining one of the tight white cabbages she had been so proud of, turned into a bunch of untidy leaves sprouting from a thick woody stem. There was no one there, it being work time. The spade hit an old brick and split it neatly in two. She watched the spade and her foot kicking it into the soil; as time went on, she noticed smaller and smaller creatures, skinny orange centipedes and mushwhite grubs, little red spiders and leaping things with shiny wings. She thought of nothing, nothing at all.

Sara looked tight-lipped on the journey back from Victoria, irritated, or perhaps just tired: she'd got the early train after all. The tube struggled along the line, stopping between stations, straining to open its doors as if the burden of weary passengers was a disease gradually getting the better of it. Cath thought that she should have arranged for tickets for a 'show': the evening at home could only be filled with talk or silence, each equally daunting. They carried Sara's holdall between them; it was exceptionally heavy. Cath remembered it from family holidays, years ago.

'I could show you my allotment, it's not much out of our way,' she said. Though there would be little to interest her mother: dark, shining, just-turned earth strewn with fragments of desiccated weeds, a few tiny plums on the tree.

'It's nearly dark,' replied Sara. 'Let's be getting this bag home.'

'Well, I suppose we'd better be getting some dinner into you,' Sara said when she had washed and put her slippers on. She brought the holdall into the kitchen. It was mostly filled with food: neat newspaper-wrapped deep-frozen packets just going soft and damp. Cath began to laugh – there was enough food now to feed the whole of Battersea – but stopped abruptly when she heard the squeak in her voice like wet hair pulled between the fingers. Her mother unloaded methodically, handing Cath the packages – 'That'll need to go in the fridge', 'That'll keep', 'Careful with this'. The sharp rustle of screwed paper, the sudden sharp ring of two jars touching emphasised the silence between them, filled it for Cath with a kind of despair.

The truth was, neither of them was hungry. The kitchen groaned under its excess of potential meals. Cath wished her mother had not come. She probably hadn't wanted to, and it could have been prevented. Perhaps, she suggested, we could just get some chips later. Make some tea. Sit quietly or chat or go to bed. Play cards. Dominoes. Television. The more she attempted to present her mother with acceptable phrases and normal comfortable things to do, the more a babble of absurdities gathered in her head, threatened to fill the room with the desperate flappings of hysteria.

She'd be glad to get away from this room. So many overcharged scenes had used it: the nights she'd told Steve to go, the night he raped her, the day Sally came back and now her mother – it no longer supported ordinary life. From now on it would change every movement into a gesture, part of a drama; it would amplify each change of mood and project it for an imaginary audience. When she came back, she would paint it again, move everything.

198

'Nice flowers,' commented Sara, putting down her tea cup.

Cath nodded. There was a long silence.

'Will it be in the papers?'

'I shouldn't think so, I don't know.'

Briefly the idea of phoning Sally burned away the dampness in her head. She wanted to yank up the receiver and say, 'Do you know. . .they postponed it!' What do you think of that? 'Do you know they expected me to sit in a room with his relatives?' 'Do you know they expect me to be calm and not calm at the same time?' And Sally would be horrified, good heavens, that can't be right, they shouldn't be allowed to. The trial was something real happening at last and people would believe it without effort, the things to complain about everyone would understand: their sympathy could be tapped. But she would have to phone the pub next door for someone to fetch her, and then phone again ten minutes later. It would be too expensive, and awkward with her mother there. She was surprised and pleased to find herself wanting to talk, despite the frustration of not being able to. She felt something smouldering and spluttering that might almost be excitement. The End of The Road, Melanie had said, or, The Last Chance. Or the Beginning. Either way, the waiting was nearly over, the tongue-tied burden-carrying time-wasting months were all but done. She smiled at her mother.

'Shall I get the chips now? And then I'll probably try to get an early night.' She'd take a sleeping pill, but she didn't mention that.

14

Cath sat in the cream-painted waiting room with the high ceiling and no window, unable to think back or forwards, unable to speculate as to the outcome of what was about to happen: frozen by the momentousness of what was about to take place. She was alone – Sara had complained, but accepted she would see more from the gallery – waiting in the state of shocked vacantness that had overcome her periodically as she'd reached various milestones in her career as a woman. Cold hands, butterfly heartbeat: she's got to tell her teacher her periods have started; her boyfriend fumbles with her bra straps in a dancehall; a man puts his hand between her legs as he kisses, and so it has progressed to this, the feeling of exposure and scrutiny protracted over weeks and months and punctuated with long periods of waiting, torturing her with the poised violence of the inevitable.

The door opened suddenly, making her jump. An oldish man in a slightly tatty uniform – a caretaker perhaps – a man with the combination of bulk, pallor and tiredness which suggested a gentle, bumbling personality. He stood awkwardly, his hand was not quite steady and he was trying to prevent spillage from the saucerless cup he was carrying, a finger and thumb gripping the handle too small for the finger to go through, his other fingers splayed. The cup was of white porcelain painted with pink roses and nipped in at the middle. It made his hand look pulpy and ridiculous. He brought his other hand up to hold it from the bottom and held it out to her, she could see the tea opaque and orange coloured in the artificial light.

'Nervous?' he asked.

'No!' said Cath, drawing back the hand she had held out for the tea.

'You look a bit peaky. Thought you might like a cuppa.' The man's gentle stare was unnerving. Did he know what she was there for?

'Thank you,' she said wanting him to go. She didn't recognise her voice: it sounded sharp and echoed unpleasantly. The handle of the cup was hard even for her smaller hands to hold. She put it on the lino-tiled floor. The man stayed standing in front of her for a few seconds then walked slowly out, leaving the door ajar. She had forgotten to wind her watch, but it couldn't be long now.

Another man came in, this one spryly dressed in navy and gold with red cuffs. Cath followed him downstairs, along a corridor, up identical stairs. It was like walking inside a body or a brain. She guessed they must have walked underneath the court – Court Seven. They stood by a pair of swing doors.

'Not yet,' he whispered, and propped the door ajar, keeping his arm across the gap as if he feared she might rush in. Cath could see large leather-covered desks with several people writing frantically, beyond them part of what must be two rows of people sitting in church pew-type seats with little angled writing desks in front of each and to the left at the back there was a raised platform strung round with thick tasselled maroon ropes like a boxing ring: and though they were in woollen-suit material she knew immediately the legs she could see were Steve's. She stepped to one side to try and see more.

'It's the Plea,' Red Sleeves turned to mouth at her, his finger to his lips.

'. . .or Not Guilty. How do you plead?'

In the pause between question and answer Cath felt herself bloating with hope: 'Guilty' he would say – she craned her neck again – if she could make him see her and their eyes met – if he said 'Guilty', just that, the world would come back, the court would vanish as in a fairy tale and they would all find themselves standing still and bemused in the street outside; they'd rub their eyes and take their bearings then go about their separate businesses, carried away by the crowd. A sign might be left perhaps, a scrap of paper to be blown away by the wind, an item of clothing to be picked over by tramps or tossed in a street sweeper's cart. Oh say guilty Steve. I could forgive you, I would forgive you, I would. I would try to understand it even, after all I loved you once, if you only said 'Guilty'.

'Not Guilty,' he said, in a voice as clear and confident as a bridegroom taking vows.

'Not Guilty.'

The last chance was gone now. He took a few steps back, turning a little as he did so, so still she could not see his face, only the straightbacked danger-tense body. And how he was dressed to kill: a flecked oatmeal suit, tan polished shoes, white cuffs of a bright new shirt; he was playing for high stakes, he was her adversary – in the flesh now, after all these months of phantom life. He was something new, Mr Hyde spawned by his barrister: 'Dress to look respectable' his barrister would have said, have a haircut. And there she was, Cath Sheldon, in her flower print dress buttoned at the neck in memory of Queen Victoria, on her legs a fine second skin of machine-spun fibres, neatly laced half-heeled shoes that ached, brassière straps already cutting: that was the price you had to pay to have it understood you were not a loose woman, you had to keep your self strapped tight and pulled up, to show you wouldn't lie. Oh surely, none of this was real? Man and woman, they were two cardboard dolls cut out from cornflakes packs, dressed in paper clothes with tags to hold them on. And the men in black gowns and yellowing wigs, they were from the television or the tarot pack, none of it was true.

Now the jurors were shuffling about. Twelve names picked from a box. They rustled papers and polished their glasses, unwrapped sweets and coughed unrestrained before the silence set in. None of them looked at each other. They couldn't, Cath thought, be ordinary-people-picked-at-random, they were too clean and too well dressed. Eight men and four women, some faces self-important, some blank, some averted, ties and ironed blouses. Something of an occasion for everyone, she supposed, fancy-dress clothes that made you feel good for half an hour then grew progressively more uncomfortable as you slipped out of role back into your real self: nothing fitted then. Cath reknotted her belt and glanced at her nylon-sheathed legs, checking for ladders.

One by one, the jurors were committing themselves to large words: Duty, Ability, Honesty – so help them God. She would have to do that too. Their voices rang out like glockenspiel (she must remember to speak clearly), an octave between the highest and the gruffest, some dry with nerves, others firm with conviction and solemnity. A straight-standing man in his sixties with iron-grey hair and a scar on his cheek pulled to attention as he spoke, nodded when he'd done. There was a sense of arrested motion: was she imagining it, or did the sound come a fraction after the movements of his lips, like thunder after lightning? She watched the next juror carefully, a woman younger than herself whose long chamomile-blonde hair was already straying from the pins that held it in a knob on the very top of her head. Something glinted at her throat, a locket or crucifix, half covered by the white ruffles of her blouse. The woman plucked nervously at her neck as she spoke, shook the hair out of her eyes. Yes, it was a crucifix.

What could you tell from a face, a tie, a dress? Nothing, she told herself and yet her eyes strained to see into their hearts as they swore themselves to judge her fairly. She read and shuffled the clues they'd chosen to display. If we met in the street, what would she think of me? Which newspaper does he read? Those eyes come from temper, that face from spite –

There was a dark-skinned man with a thick burr of blue-grey hair, his voice rumbled the long words as if he were in church, faith and song and far places over the sea filling the sounds so that they almost made her shiver. 'Religious', she decided, at least two were religious. Was that good or bad? What did the Bible say, the Ten Commandments? No killing, no coveting, no stealing, no adultery – there was nothing about rape, you'd have to argue sideways to get it in: you coveted a bit of me, you stole my person, you adulterated my self-respect.

A plump but hard-faced woman with an efficient haircut read from the card as if it was a grocery list – she's not religious, thought Cath. She would be a local government officer perhaps, or a supervisor in the Social Security. She wore a pale pink shimmering silk blouse that contrasted vividly with the granular, allergic-looking skin on her face, no make-up.

While jurors she couldn't see swore their oaths, Cath continued staring at the woman, feeling she oughtn't, it was rude to stare at people, but fascinated and irrationally convinced that this woman would be crucial in deciding the verdict.

There were squirtings and shiftings in her intestines; the acids must be held in, must not seep through to spoil her dress or crack her voice or distract her concentration. The jury had finished swearing. She could not fight off a sense that the issue was already decided, if only she could read the twelve faces correctly she would have the answer without all the length and formality: whatever was said or done it was they who would decide, they would pin down truth on the basis of proof. It would all happen in a room where no one could hear them, where she would not be able to argue or to check they'd remembered right. Cath felt someone stepping on her grave, an awful despondency.

Salter was right.

One of the wigged men at the largest desk rose to his feet – it was Mr Lindell; for a few seconds not a paper rustled and she could hear the faint sound of traffic in the street, and – oh – the rhetoric of gesture, the way he held his arms out straight on to the little wooden lectern and looked slowly round the court, meeting pairs of eyes one by one: surely it was not upon these black-and-white, silence-in-court histrionics that she had to depend?

The man with red sleeves turned his head and nodded slightly, his arm still across the door. The back of her legs started shaking, her throat stuck rigid halfway through a cough, she wouldn't be able to speak when the time came. Hurry up, hurry up; she was invaded by fear, raw and rough, so overwhelming it might have been sexual. Her mind bleached away everything that went into it.

'. . . I shall also be reading the evidence of expert witnesses, ladies and gentlemen of the jury. Such readings are permitted, provided that both parties are in agreement, and it saves time and expense. These expert witnesses will testify conclusively as to the presence of clothing fibres and bodily secretions likely to be those of the defendant being found on the victim when she was examined by a doctor at the police station, and of clothing fibres from the victim's . . .'

'The victim', she thought, that's me.

'. . . But, ladies and gentlemen of the jury, before I call my first and principal witness, Miss Sheldon herself, I must ask you to remain aware of the traumatic nature of such an appearance in court for a woman in her position, especially for a woman of good character as is Miss Sheldon . . .'

Woman of a certain age and a good character. Ex-teacher. Voluntary worker. Dedicated, a little naive. No time for the seamier side of life. Hard-working. Modest.

'Ladies and gentlemen of the jury, I am asking you to imagine, in so far as you are able . . .'

205

What kind of cue is this? What does he expect? Should I follow his lead, or do what I think's best? Under the lights and she wouldn't hear the prompt, she'd say another woman's lines –

She wished Red Sleeves hadn't left the door open, her legs wouldn't move, her mind wouldn't think. No cameras, miss? Tape recorders, guns or bombs? Bags please. I'm a witness! She knows they're trying to catch her out.

'Call Miss Sheldon.'

'Miss Sheldon.'

'Nothing to be nervous of,' Sara had said on the way, 'it's not you that's on trial' – but of course it was, Salter had said as much and he was right. Pull yourself together, no time for stagefright, it was grand opera before the emperor and she an ordinary woman who'd blinked and found herself on the stage expected to sing, stuttering before ranks of upturned faces.

Red Sleeves had lowered his arm and now he touched her shoulder. Cath held back still a few seconds looking into the room she was about to enter. Fear sheathed and contained her, cut her off from remembering why she was there, from knowing it would end, from the rest of her life. As if all that was her had never been, she stood trapped and naked in the fine strong mesh of the present; this was all she amounted to, all there was and would ever be – and there was nothing she could do to escape.

Cath held the book and, reading from the card, swore to tell the truth, the whole truth and nothing but the truth. As she spoke the trembling jerked its way to a halt. She would be all right, Lindell would be on her side after all; this was her chance. Mr Lindell's lips twitched at her before he spoke. He stood an unnatural distance away. The fat one next to him must be Steve's barrister – they heard everything you said.

'. . . It will help if you can address the answers to my

questions to the jury rather than to me. . .' he spoke very slowly. She turned to the jury, now she could only see him from the corner of her eye.

'And also,' interrupted the judge, 'speak as loudly as possible, so that I can hear you clearly.'

His voice was smooth as faded velvet folded round the steel of an inherited sword. Beside it, even Lindell's carefully modulated voice was the upstart squeak of scratching chalk on a blackboard. Cath turned back again to look at Judge Barford. He was tiny, sparse-fleshed; he had little creases round his mouth, and large, irascible brows.

'It saves time,' he said, and there were other things in that voice: cornered foxes and the King's War, childbirth in stifling rooms, Father Right and Landlord Right, blood on the stairs. It came from another world, hopelessly different.

Successfully she gave her name, address and age.

'Where was it that you were walking home from that Saturday night?' Lindell asked, and the words came effortlessly to her lips.

'From a small supper party at a friend's house in Broomfield Road.'

'What was your first reaction when you saw the figure of a man standing in the porch?'

'I was alarmed. I screamed.'

'Do you often walk home late at night?'

'No.' She was going to be all right.

'How far is it between Broomfield Road and your home?'

'About a mile.' She felt herself warming to Lindell, almost convinced herself that she liked him; she was grateful, he was making it easy.

'Since the forensic evidence is conclusive, I think we can limit ourselves to what was said by the defendant and the complainant.'

They were reading from the same script: her statement.

The facts would speak for themselves, there was nothing to worry about, nothing at all.

'And when you brought in the sugar, had Mr Blake moved?'

'Yes.'

'Did you think anything of it?'

'Not really. It was warmer on the cushions.'

She had been staring at the woman with the silk blouse, now she let her eyes stray a little, though she kept them away from an invisible line beyond which there was a possibility she might see Steve. In the centre of the ceiling an old-fashioned four-bladed fan had worked loose in its housing and rotated queasily, like a bent record. She glanced at the woman with the crucifix, who was looking at her knee, then at Mr Lindell carefully setting her statement aside, page by page as it was dealt with. Remembering the instruction to speak to the jury, and conscious that looking away might be construed as a sign of lie-telling, she began again to examine the jurors one by one. None of them was looking up. 'Look me in the eye,' her mother had used to say, 'and tell me that again.' But if you focused both your eyes on the inside corner of one of theirs, you weren't really looking into their eyes, and you could speak without the slightest blush.

'And how long was it before you phoned the police?'

'I'm not quite sure exactly. I was in a state of shock. I lay on top of my bed, perhaps half an hour. Then I ran a bath, and while it was filling I realised I should phone the police, and that I shouldn't have the bath until –'

'Please speak more slowly,' said the judge. 'I take everything down in longhand, as do the clerks of the court.'

She had not expected it to be quite so formal, so old-fashioned. The clerks' heads bent earnestly as they wrote. The waiting ushers stood motionless, their buttons burnished bright. Outside, above the big mahogany doors, was the golden lady of Justice, serene and untouchable above the messy street where crime took place. The polished enunciation of that antique language, slow spoken and well padded with subordinate clauses, was somehow comforting as old things are: it could not be a part of confrontation, it almost soothed.

'How much time elapsed between Mr Blake moving out and the events of the third of November?'

'About six months.'

'When did you last see Steven Blake before the incident?'

'I saw him once when I was working in my allotment, by accident.'

'Were there any other occasions when you saw him after he left?'

'Just one other, when he let himself in while I was out.'

'And how long before the incident would the last time you saw him be, the time when you were working in the allotments?'

'About three months.'

'And on either of those two meetings, was there any talk of the possibility of a reconciliation between you?'

'No.'

'And was there any physical intimacy between you?'

'No.'

'Thank you, Miss Sheldon. That is all I wish to ask.'

For a moment she thought it was all over, but no, of course now there would be the cross-examination by the other barrister. There was the sound of many fresh pages being turned, loud and dry in the panelled still air of the court. Games we play as children, shouting and silence and summary execution.

Steve's barrister, a large man whose oversize gown hung askance on his shoulders, rose slowly. On the desk before him was a thick ring binder with an improvised index system made of scissor-cut cardboard tags sellotaped to the pages.

'Miss Sheldon,' he said, and there was a huge pause, long as an opponent's thinking time in chess. 'Mr Lindell saw fit not to deal very closely with your movements in the sitting room just prior to the alleged rape –' Another pause paralysed the court, pens reached the end of their sentences and had to wait. It was no longer an 'incident' or an 'alleged incident' but now an 'alleged rape'. Why? Did he think that to have alleged – falsely – a rape was worse-sounding than to have alleged a mere incident? Or was he just trying to show how straightforward he was, how he called a spade a spade?

'When you brought in the coffee –' ought she remind him it was tea, but – 'where was Mr Blake sitting?'

'In the armchair in the middle of the room.'

'And where did you sit?'

'On the cushions by the fire.'

'It would perhaps assist, your honour, if you and the jury were to have a copy of the plan of Miss Sheldon's flat.'

And everything was suspended as one of the uniformed men slowly distributed the plans. How had he got the drawing? From the police? Steve? X marks the spot.

'The position of the cushions, as found by the police, and that of the chair are marked with a circle and a square respectively . . .'

'I see,' said the judge, the muscles around his eyes moving visibly, symptoms of an alertness so constant and so acute as to be almost neurotic; no dozing justice this. The barrister continued:

'So then –' oh, it was all so slow, slowness that confused and dulled – 'you went out for the sugar, and when you came back you say Mr Blake had moved to the cushions.'

'Yes.'

'And where did you sit then?'

Did he pause so long on purpose to unnerve her?

'I sat on the cushions where I had been before.'

'Did you not think, Miss Sheldon, that Mr Blake's moving to where you had just been sitting was an unspoken invitation, and that your sitting next to him could only be construed as an acceptance of that invitation?'

'No, I did not.'

'And *do* you not think, on reflection, that what I have described may well have been the case?'

'No. It was only natural to sit by the fire.'

'It is rather unusual, is it not, for a woman not to be aware of the subtler forms of communication under such emotionally charged circumstances?'

The question was indigestible but it was impossible just to spit it out, she had to say something, she could feel her hesitation turning guilty, like milk going sour.

'I suppose it's a matter of opinion.'

'Were there any problems in your sexual relationship with Mr Blake?'

'Not "problems". We stopped sleeping together, or nearly, during the last year or so.'

'Was it you, or Mr Blake, who instituted this change?'

'I think it was me.'

Why was her voice squeaking like that?

'Would you not agree that such a change was likely to be distressing and confusing to Mr Blake?'

All of a sudden he was speaking quickly, each question breathless on the heels of her last word, as if the questions were more important than the answers.

'You say you had been to a party on the night of the alleged rape. Had you been drinking alcohol? Is it not well known, Miss Sheldon, that alcohol tends to increase responsiveness to sexual stimulus, particularly after a period of celibacy or abstinence?'

Lindell was on his feet.

'Your honour, my learned friend is, by implication –'

'Yes, yes. There is no need to answer that question Miss Sheldon.'

But it had been said. And the interruption seemed only to increase Cath's growing sense of congestion and confusion. He seemed to be leading her up blind alleys, and as soon as she realised where they were going and how she ought to respond, he had flicked the pages of his file, and suddenly they had jumped a year and started all over again.

'When, prior to the alleged rape, did you last visit a doctor, Miss Sheldon? Why did you do so? I must press you, Miss Sheldon. Did you complain to your doctor of depression?'

She could see the page he was referring to, close written, with its paragraphs underlined in red. He was better organised than she was. Cath was running out of steam, finding herself unable to deflect the course of his questions; she felt him inch by inch making her help him tell a story that had her in it, plausible, but a lie. And it seemed that however clever her answers, his words and tone sketched out a contradiction of them, and in the end, who was to be believed would be a matter of faith, or prejudice. How long had she been standing there? It was as if something had broken down inside her, like a running muscle that's stretched and pulled until it's sprained, and now she was just waiting for him to stop. The pauses, the sudden accelerations in pace, the shuffling of papers and adjusting of posture seemed to be dragging it out longer and longer. All about her were coughs, dropped pens, whispers making it impossible to concentrate.

'What were you wearing, Miss Sheldon?'

She could just see the front row of the public gallery, but her eyes wouldn't focus and she couldn't straighten out the white blur that was the clock. She couldn't see Sara. How many had come from the Crisis Centre? 'Support' they'd said. But what could they do? They almost made it worse, another audience tangling everything up with their hopes and expectations. They want me to win, she tried thinking to herself, but it brought no comfort.

'Why did you scream, or try to, Miss Sheldon, when you saw the figure on your doorstep, before you recognised it as Steven Blake?'

'It is true, is it not, that when you recognised Steven

212

Blake, you were relieved? Even pleased?'

Every eye on her made it worse. And all she could say was 'yes' or 'no'.

'You say, Miss Sheldon, that you were aware that Mr Blake ejaculated. Did you yourself – I hope the court will pardon the indelicacy of the question – reach a climax?'

You'll be asked far worse things in court! It wasn't embarrassment though, but outrage which set Cath's hands twisting and clenching, longing for a communication cord to pull so that there would be a grinding of brakes, a jolting into ominous silence, sirens, bells, the bustle of a bomb scare, and she could disappear in the panic, the walls falling down on the court to bury it for ever. For it seemed there was no limit, she had absolutely no rights, and no respect since Steve had forced himself in her: now she was public property, her words, her actions to be mauled and pawed at, turned this way and that by any fool who cared to.

'I put it to you, Miss Sheldon, that whether or not you expected it, you were not displeased at the sexual developments that took place between you and Mr Blake that night. Is that not the case?'

It would be easier, he'd said, if you wanted me. It would have been. And had he laughed, or was she just adding that, it wasn't in the statement. Or was it? But she remembered him laughing at the shock on her face. For the first time since the questioning began, Cath became acutely aware that Steve was in the same room; it damned him forever that he could let this happen to save his skin or his pride or whatever it was, and she wanted to interrupt the questions, look up at the dock and curse him like a mad woman free in the street. She wanted to shoot him but she couldn't do that, she must content herself with not letting him see her weep inside and saying yes or no.

'No. Nothing could be farther from the truth.'

'And afterwards, is it not the case that you felt your feelings towards Mr Blake could not be admitted, since you had previously rejected him? That it was then, and only then, as you were running the bath and thinking about what had happened that you decided to call it "rape"?'

'No.'

'Thank you, Miss Sheldon. I have nothing further to ask,' said the barrister, his voice solid with the satisfaction of someone who believes he's laid a ghost forever.

Contrary to their plans to meet for lunch in the tea shop nearby, Cath and Sara went straight home in a taxi, sitting in silence all the way. Cath couldn't bear to look at her mother. The afternoon slipped featureless through her mind as clean as a handful of dry sand. There were cups of tea and sheets and light through the curtains, distant playground sounds, the build-up of traffic as the dusk drew in. Sara was cooking the chicken, and at six o'clock she fetched Cath. It sat between them naked and silly-looking on the kitchen table. The gravy Cath could have picked out from thousands as Sara's from the way it poured and stretched across the plate. Cath found she was hungry.

'This is nice,' she said, swallowing the first chunk of meat and immediately filling the space it left with another one, lest too many words bolt out at once.

'Hungry?' asked Sara, seemingly reassured when she nodded. They ate.

'You did very well,' Sara said suddenly. 'Your voice was very clear, you stood your ground with that second one, the things he asked, I'm surprised he wasn't stopped. What a dirty job! What can his wife think of a man who does a thing like that for a living?'

Cath ate slowly, glad of her mother saying these things since she didn't trust her own tongue and had mislaid temper.

'And I didn't think he'd be there all the time –' her mother hesitated, uncharacteristically embarrassed, as if unsure she should have reminded Cath of Steve.

'– It's not fair, when it gets to his turn he could change his story to fit in. He kept writing messages and a man – in

214

a suit not a uniform – carried them over to the man asking the questions, the solicitor –' Sara packed a potato into her mouth.

'Barrister,' corrected Cath. Sara finished chewing.

'But I'm sure it'll be all right, he just showed them up, asking things like that. Everyone was on your side, you could tell.'

With surprise, Cath realised that her plate was empty, and she picked a strip of meat from between the chicken's tiny ribs.

'No need to pick, have some more. There were a lot of people in the gallery,' continued Sara, cutting second helpings of chicken as she spoke. 'It'll be a bit raggy, I'm afraid – yes, there was a group of girls all together, some of them writing everything down. They didn't look like reporters though. What do you think they were up to? I nearly said something, if they're there tomorrow I'll go up and ask them. I made a trifle while you were asleep, it's in the fridge.'

So the Crisis Centre women had written it all down as well. What a quantity of words would have been written about that night in the end, back and forwards scanning the same story that was there already, printed indelible inside her, but no one could see. Another few transcripts, another few versions, what the hell.

'It's all right: I know them.' Her spoon glided through the glistening custard-coated mound and emerged with a small sucking noise, bearing a neatly striped sample of the trifle's strata.

'Nice,' she said again; she was beginning to remind herself of her father, he'd never once omitted to praise even so much as a piece of toast put before him.

There was a telephone call from Melanie.

'How are you feeling then?'

'I'm sorry, I just went – I couldn't stand to wait around after. I've been asleep. My mother's here and she made something to eat. I feel a bit better.'

'Oh, so long as you're all right. The defence was pretty grim, wasn't it? Some of the things he asked seemed really out of order, I don't know why the police barrister didn't take them up. I thought maybe he didn't bother because you were handling it well – it was better to let you answer than let him say what he was saying anyway and not give you a chance to reply . . .in a way I think it was probably all for the best, I'm sure you gained a lot of sympathy, and he lost it.'

'Mum said that too.' Don't hope, don't hope.

'We'll just have to wait and see. This afternoon they had the medical evidence, and then the people who used to live downstairs, and that's the end of the prosecution. So tomorrow the defence barrister – he's called Petrone by the way – will introduce his case and then they'll bring out their witnesses. After that there's another speech from each side, and the judge's summing up. Then the jury go out. Do you want to come to court tomorrow, or shall we meet you afterwards, or lunchtime?'

'Is the cross-examining always like that?' interrupted Cath.

'More or less,' said Melanie. 'But honestly, you handled it very well, I don't know how you kept so calm and collected.'

For a few seconds the distaste Cath had felt for Kim's effusive sympathy returned, but it did not overpower her, and was soon dissolved in a stronger feeling of sheer relief that Melanie and the Crisis Centre existed.

'Well, I'll be at court, but if you need anyone there will be someone in the Centre, and they'll know all about it. Oh, by the way, which one is your mother? She doesn't look like you.'

Melanie's voice was quite low and steady, but not solemn. Cath couldn't remember her face, only her dyed red hair. But she liked the sound of her.

'That was one of them,' she informed her mother, 'the

women you were talking about, I'll introduce you tomorrow.'

They gave the cat the rest of the chicken and went to bed.

Cath dreamed she was standing at the other end of the court in the red-roped dock, and she was scratching all over, as if swarms of invisible flies were attacking her or as if she wore something rough and matted and too tight next to her skin. It was something she'd put on for the occasion as a protection but oh how useless, it had woven itself into a penance. And she mustn't scratch, she must stand still and look as if nothing at all was happening. The discomfort grew to fever pitch and then she suddenly went blind, and a slow, patronising voice began to explain why it was she was itching: it was her own fault and should not have surprised her at all. And what are you going to do about it now? the voice asked, echoing like a BBC rendition of the Almighty, you're wasting your time here. Her hands were clenched behind her back. You might as well *just let go*, the voice said, savouring the words, you might as well *do yourself justice, put up a fight, give yourself the satisfaction.*

She opened her eyes to escape the voice. Everyone was turned to face her, desks and chairs put into lines. They were all waiting for her to answer a question she hadn't even heard. She was on fire.

Cath got up in the dark and tried to consider what had happened objectively. Melanie and Sara had both said that Petrone's insinuations and tactics were so gross that they did more good to the prosecution than to the defence. They'd said her calmness turned his venom to her advantage. But Salter, who lived in the filtered fishtank world of the courts, breathing precedents, exceptions, arguments, arraignments and applications, he said: 'A calm witness is a bad witness'.

A dull pain in Cath's bones muttered that he was the one more likely to be right and that she would lose, that Petrone's words were weedseeds scattered on well-prepared

217

soil. However well she had acted or spoken, she had not stopped him tangling the facts up and strangling her story. Salter, she had known all along but tried to forget, was absolutely right: it boiled down to the impression you made and the kind of people you had to make it on. She should have contradicted Petrone not with denials, mere syllables so much more easily forgotten than his fluent paragraphs, but with tears, incomprehension, breakdown; with the startled stuck-eyed white-wiped face of how a victim should be.

The irony was that all that panic had been in her but she'd swallowed it, she'd had to. She had known she couldn't, wouldn't cry; couldn't, wouldn't use that cleverness that consists in playing dumb or mad: she would have found it too confusing. She felt that she was just beginning to understand certain things: about the law, about the rape, about her mother, about herself – a tangle of thin threads she must be careful not to drop. It was important not to complicate matters. Through this legal warping of her experience she was at last able – being forced – to describe what had happened, to herself and to such as were able to listen. And that, she was sure, could not be done at the same time as conniving with those who were not. From this point of view her conduct in court had perhaps – whatever anyone said and whatever the outcome – been sensible. She was reconciled to it: 'You did very well, your voice was clear', that was some kind of real compensation, in its way.

Mrs Anderson's flowers had to be thrown away, and Cath wrote thanking her and reminding her about the autobiography, since none had come for at least two weeks. But she left the envelope unsealed, so she could put the verdict in; she did the same for the letter she wrote to Sally.

Dear Sal
I'll set out for Cumbria at the end of this week. I know it'll be very awkward for you to leave your Gran just like that so I won't

expect you till at least the following Friday. I'll be quite happy on my own. I think I'll bring a transcript of my case for you to read. It is an eye opener for me in more ways than one, I'll try to explain all that later.

Hope your Gran is no worse, and that there weren't any problems when you got back from London.

Can't wait

Love Cath

PS. Fri – he was acquitted.

15

In my sitting room where, nearly a year ago, it had happened, in cafés, in the Crisis Centre's offices, Melanie, my mother and I poured over the transcript after each day of the trial. Or rather my mother sat, unusually silent as Mel supplemented the neatly charactered pages with details of how people had looked and how long silences were and what had been whispered in the gallery. Sara couldn't read shorthand, and besides that, I think she felt at least to begin with that it would be better if I had as little information as possible, so that I couldn't dwell on it.

'He was sweating a lot,' said Mel of Petrone, 'hangs on like a leech.'

I was reading Petrone's cross-examination of Mr Brown:

'During the time in which Mr Blake and Miss Sheldon were cohabiting were there ever disturbances, such as shouting, during the night?'

'We were often kept awake by them into the small hours.'

'Maybe once or twice,' I said, 'but he's blown it out of all proportion!'

'And your barrister Lindell hadn't asked them about it when you were living together, he just asked if the shouting on the night of the rape sounded as if it was "in earnest". And Brown said that it was difficult to tell, especially after so much time had gone by. Petrone picked up on that by asking them if they'd considered phoning the police, and they said no.'

'What did the police say?'

The police evidence was off-putting to read, whole pages uninterrupted by questions.

'They read from their notebooks. You came in at such and such a time, what you said, your statement, pretty routine. Oh, Petrone asked –' But she stopped because I had stopped listening. I'd found a bit of dialogue and was reading:

'When the statement was taken, I said to Miss Sheldon: you are aware that rape is a serious allegation, and she said yes. She signed the statement, and I offered her a cup of tea which she accepted. I said you had better see the doctor now and she said all right.'

I didn't recognise it at all, I kept reading it. It was so different from what had happened that it was hard to remember the truth, there was no similarity at all.

'This is all wrong. I had to keep asking for a doctor, he said there was no point me seeing one unless they were sure it was rape. It was ages. He did offer me a cup of tea but that was long after the statement, they just kept asking me things like had I thrown him out or was it the other way round, and why did I ask him in for coffee.'

I flicked through the pages. 'There's none of that here, none of it.'

'No, he didn't say anything like that,' said Sara. Melanie sighed.

'It happens all the time,' she said, 'but there's nothing you can say about it without discrediting your whole case. Well, if you did, the whole thing would grind to a standstill. If it looked like they hadn't believed you from the start Petrone would say well, you know –' She shrugged and looked up at me, her small sallow face managing to express both hopelessness and encouragement, rage and sympathy.

The defence case took one day to present. When I met Sara and Melanie in the entrance hall to the court, I was overwhelmed with a sudden and acute perception of every small line on my mother's face. I had often seen her angry, but what drained and pinched her features now was not anger, on which she almost thrived, but a mixture of indignation and confusion that seemed to shrivel her.

Melanie steered us to the door. Outside it had begun to rain, big drops that hurled themselves on to the pavement. The air smelled of disturbed dust. I thought of home: streaked windows, the cushions, the bed.

'Can we go to the Centre?' I asked.

I could see the curled pages of Mel's writing book poking out from her bag on the floor, harmless-looking as schoolgirl notes. I wanted to know what Steve had said, I knew it would be awful but I needed to know precisely how awful, in the way perhaps that people will read about the details of a violent crime that makes their innards scream, in order to force themselves to accept that such things are possible. My mother broke the silence.

'He said you smiled at him as you sat very close to him on the cushions. In his statement he denied saying the things he said. He said nothing at all was said while you were on the floor or in the bed, but in court he said you had cried out but he had not heard the words and once he thought it was because he was crushing your leg, and the other time he thought it was –'

'Pleasure,' said Melanie dryly.

There was a silence, and the contents of the room – three settees, a woman on each, rugs, kettle amidst a huddle of mugs on a table improvised from a bread crate and a sheet of plywood, a canvas bag on the floor – seemed to shrink, as the atmosphere blew out with anxiety. They found it hard to repeat what had been said, but they were also frightened of me reading it. I took the transcript from Melanie's bag. My mother got up and stood looking out of the window. I found the place but did not begin reading. I began to feel resentful that they did not want me to read it, me whom it concerned more than anyone – I was about to say I'd take it to read at home when Melanie too walked over to the window.

'Don't worry,' I heard her say quietly to my mother as I began to read.

Petrone called Steve his 'client' and indeed treated him gently, almost obsequiously, as if he were a rich and respected patient at a private clinic.

'I thought we might make love but I wanted to be spontaneous. It was only when she sat next to me that I was sure.'

'When you were – making love – was there at any point any doubt in your mind as to Miss Sheldon's willingness to do so?'

'None at all.'

There is something particularly shocking about seeing lies about oneself written down, and these were not little disquieting ones like Salter's politic exaggerations made for my benefit and by means of some kind of consultation with fact: they were the sort designed to knock my truth flat. And I, in my turn, wanted to obliterate them, to destroy the script.

'How would you describe Miss Sheldon's temperament during the time you lived together?'

'It seemed to vary.'

'Would you say she was prone to extremes of mood, that she was inconsistent?'

'Yes.'

'When sexual relations ceased between you, did you accept the situation with good grace?'

'Yes. There was nothing I could do about it.'

Mr Petrone, I thought, was capable of both crudity and subtlety, and of choosing his moment. I imagined him looking up from his cardboard tag file, his large face expressing an almost mystical solemnity as if he had just spoken one of the weightier passages in a Shakespearian tragedy. I realised he was a better barrister than Lindell, who seemed to operate on the level of fact and contradiction, or maybe it was that all barristers performed better in defence and better still if they knew in their hearts the defendant was guilty: perhaps the sheer weight of truth was like a mountain they must climb and conquer, sticking their flag in to fly in the teeth of the wind that knew different.

'If, as you say you believed, you had just "made love" to Miss Sheldon and that pleasure had been mutual, why did you, Mr Blake, leave so suddenly after the event?' Lindell asked in cross-examination and Steve replied,

'I had an urgent appointment in Glasgow the next day, and had to drive through the night.'

'Why then did you, as you said subsequent to giving your statement to the police, visit a friend of yours before setting off on this long drive?'

'I'm not often in London and have to take the opportunity to visit my friends when I can.'

'Why did you not mention this visit in your statement to the police?'

'At the time I didn't realise it would be important; it didn't seem to have anything to do with what they were asking me. I was shocked and confused.'

At this point I put the transcript down: it was obvious that Steve was a match for Mr Lindell as, in argument, he had always been a match for me. I was tired of reading and wanted to ask my mother or Mel who this 'friend' mentioned by Petrone and then Lindell was, but when I looked up I saw that Melanie had left the room, and my mother was asleep on the sofa, sitting upright with a saucer on her lap, her hands just losing their grip on it and her lips parting.

The friend, of course, was Max. Max was not Petrone's

'client' and so he treated him more functionally:

'Did you have a conversation with the defendant in the early hours of the morning following the alleged incident?'

And Max replied, yes, he did. It struck me that you could call this evidence uncorroborated, since no one but Max was present and there was no way of knowing whether it was true or not.

'And did Mr Blake mention that he had just seen Miss Sheldon? What was said?'

'He said I paid Cath a visit earlier on and I said how was it, and he said we went to bed.'

Equally there was no way of knowing if this conversation took place, or if this is what was said, or all that was said: I skimmed the transcript convinced that at some point someone ought to have pointed this out, but there was no challenge, only Lindell asking about hours and minutes and how long the two men had known each other, and whether they often talked about their 'personal lives' with such 'candour'. I left the room quietly to look for Melanie.

She and two other women sat in a room much smaller than the upstairs one and crammed with brightly painted cabinets and other office paraphernalia, bookshelves and three telephones. There were no windows, but the room managed to be cheerful in spite of this; it reminded me a little of the literacy centre. Melanie was writing, one of the other women sat on the desk talking to the third who was mending a pair of jeans. I'd seen them both in the court.

'Jill and Caroline,' said Melanie. 'Have you finished it?'

'Yes,' I said and then, suddenly aware that here if nowhere else I could be precise and still listened to . . . 'Well, I had enough of it. My mother's asleep.' There was a pause. Melanie offered me a chair and Caroline pricked her finger and swore.

'I've got a feeling we'll lose,' I said. 'Petrone, well, he seems to have put more into it than Lindell, seems to have got away with murder really, and I keep thinking of the people on the jury, they all looked as if they could so easily believe the sorts of things he suggests, somehow.'

I was surprised how undisturbing it was to admit aloud that I thought Steve would be acquitted; just as since that moment in court when I had realised quite how much the man I used to love – the man I had been capable of feeling responsible towards and guilty about, even after he had raped me – was prepared to crush me, I had found it easy to remember him again and to use his name at least in my head, as if he was a figure from history with whom I had a certain familiarity, but no intimacy at all.

'The dice are loaded,' said Caroline, 'not just in this case but in every bloody one. Like having to corroborate something that always takes place where no one can see. Like having to be absolutely clear about all the details when you've been scared out of your wits.'

'Did you notice when he said he forgot to tell the police about visiting his friend because he was too "shocked and confused"?' Jill said. 'I almost spat. But a lot depends on the speeches tomorrow, especially the judge's. People tend to remember the last thing they've heard.'

Mr Lindell spoke first, then Mr Petrone and then the judge. This is the prescribed order of things, a chivalrous gesture towards the defence that they might have the second to last word, before the very last words spoken by a figure supposed to be disinterested, intelligent and experienced. Each speech was about twice the length of the one preceding it, and the whole thing lasted over two hours, with no breaks of any kind; it was all over by the time I'd woken from the longest night's sleep I had had in weeks. I wonder what exactly happened to those twelve ordinary people, no more gifted in their powers of concentration than myself, as they listened to Petrone's address, spoken in a language of which they probably had only a passive understanding. I imagined it would be rather like skim-reading a text, the significant parts of which would be already underlined for them by the stress and modulation of Petrone's well-oiled voice. Only certain well-emphasised phrases they would actually hear, remember, write down:

'And, as you all know, it is no part of the jury's responsibility to pass judgement on morals, on the ways in which individual adult men and women conduct their intimate sexual relationships.'

'Miss Sheldon may have been genuinely confused; she may even have acted out of malice.'

'To convict, you must be sure, sure without the least shadow of a doubt, that what took place was rape, and not sexual intercourse. Ladies and Gentlemen, in the light of the evidence you have heard over the past two days, you cannot be so sure. The prosecution's case that the sexual intercourse – which no one disputes actually took place between Steven Blake and Catherine Sheldon – was non-consensual, that is, it was rape, rests on two things alone. These are Miss Sheldon's word, which I must remind you, Ladies and Gentlemen of the jury, is only as good as Mr Blake's, and the evidence of Mr and Mrs Brown, who heard Miss Sheldon shouting. Now, you have heard, Ladies and Gentlemen of the jury, Mr Brown testify on behalf of himself and his wife, saying that in the two-year period during which Miss Sheldon and Mr Blake lived together as man and wife, by mutual consent – such an arrangement used to be called "a common law marriage" – shouting similar to the shouting heard on the night in question often disturbed them. From this we must conclude, Ladies and Gentlemen of the jury, that such shouting was a regular feature of the consensual relationship between Miss Sheldon and Mr Blake.'

And of course they would remember the end.

'And so we find, Ladies and Gentlemen that, on the contrary, the prosecution have offered no evidence which is not at best ambiguous, no evidence which is capable of being called proof, and I scarcely need to remind you that it would be wrong to convict a man on evidence which did not constitute a completely convincing proof of guilt, let alone in the face of the defence evidence amounting to proof of his innocence. If you were to convict, Ladies and Gentlemen, in this case, you would *be convicting an innocent man, a man who is already the victim of Miss Sheldon's confused, or even malicious feelings towards him, or even one who simply misread and misunderstood the situation she was in.'*

The little connecting words, so carefully picked for their unobtrusiveness, their suggestiveness or their ability to balance a phrase so that it passed smoothly from lips to ear to brain, would have died like mayflies almost immediately they had hatched from Petrone's lips, and with them would die their stings shot unnoticed. The cloud of dubious assumptions, the 'musts' and 'wes' and 'therefores', the rhetorical questions attached so tenuously to the matter in hand, the underhand brutality with which Petrone suggested that the jury imagine themselves as innocent victims of circumstances: all this, the real bones of Mr Petrone's argument, would not have time to stand scrutiny.

I read the speeches alone in my bedroom, aware of Melanie and Sara in the other room who sat frozen waiting for me to join them in their indignation. But I had a feeling in me like the ringing in the ears that follows noise, like the running deceleration of a machine after the power has been cut. I answered every sentence in my head as I read it, almost shocked by my own articulateness and understanding. For a few seconds I thought surely, surely, the jury would likewise contradict.

Judge Barford spoke slowly in his steel and velvet voice, slowly for the tired jury, not used as he was to dealing with such a density of words, such a welter of truths thrust upon them like unwanted gifts; slowly enough for the clerks to copperplate each word in longhand and for him to consider his next sentence in the pauses in between one phrase and the next.

'You have to hold yourself back from shouting: it's like being bricked up alive,' said Melanie. 'But it doesn't help if you shout, they just drag you out and do you for being a disturbance and the jury disapproves or overcompensates

228

for not disapproving.'

So Judge Barford spoke uninterrupted. His summary was the end of a process designed to establish truth, yet it was the final twisting of a key that locked truth forever away, as far as justice was concerned.

'Firstly, I am obliged by law to advise the jury on the matter of corroboration. All the witnesses in this case have given evidence. Corroboration only occurs, however, when one witness's evidence confirms that of another, for example if one witness were to testify "I saw her run after him" and another witness said "I saw her running after him". In cases of rape, where the sexual nature of the offence increases the likelihood of, and motivation for, false allegations, it is extremely inadvisable and very, very rare, for a jury to convict on the uncorroborated evidence of the woman, that is, on her word alone and uncorroborated by other evidence – although to do so is not in fact prohibited in law. As I review the evidence in this case I shall remind the jury of this, and discuss each item of the defence case in such a way as will make it clear whether or not it constitutes corroboration. For now, it will be enough simply to remember that independent confirmation of Miss Sheldon's story of some kind is what is to be looked for.'

Judge Barford described me as: a self-possessed, calm and determined young woman who gave her evidence with great clarity. He remarked that I now live alone and gave a brief summary of my statement to the police. Though they were not marked on the page, I could hear inverted commas in his voice:

'Miss Sheldon said she then lay on the bed for about half an hour, got up to run a bath and then decided to telephone the police . . .'

If you were being raped, Judge Barford, I interrupted as he read, I suppose you would plot your most sensible course of action even as you lay pinned to the floor and rammed up inside? You would not need a bath to wash him away, to numb the pain, unstrangle the tongue and mind before picking up the phone?

'*The defence ask you to consider the previous relationship between Miss Sheldon and the defendant. Whilst I leave it up to you to decide upon its precise implications, I must bring to your attention its obvious significance as a factor which renders the question of consent particularly acute . . .*'

'Acute' – you mean dangerous and fatal and nerve twisting as a tightrope, a stretched hair; walk this stretched hair without breaking it and you're innocent; jump in this pond with lead in your boots and if you don't drown you're a witch: why don't you say what you mean, Judge Barford? And this was what I had struggled with in the library all those months ago, what I had not quite been able to imagine when I read 'thorough corroboration of the evidence of the prosecutrix is not essential in law; it is, however, always looked for and it is established practice to warn the jury against the danger of acting on her uncorroborated testimony', and discovered that the 'burden of proof ' was mine. Now at least I know the score.

'*In attempting to establish Miss Sheldon's frame of mind on the night in question, the defence point out that she had suffered from depression in the past and Mr Blake says she was subject to changes of mood. She had been to a party . . .*'

So, is this your famous objectivity, the impartiality of that carefully balanced procedure: argument, counter-argument, summing up, verdict? 'Calm' and 'changeable', 'clear-minded' and 'deranged': am I so little a person you can give me any contradictory characteristics to suit the purpose of your prejudice? No, that was not me, I was not a screwed-up woman past her best, living on her own. That night I was walking home, fingering my key and thinking 'Soon I'll be home', I was happy, happy from the party and seeing Sally (but no, I was not drunk), I was experiencing a rare and precious sense of limitless potential. I was excited and glad to be going to the home that held the archives of a life I was suddenly pleased with again, where I would sit on the cushions by the fire and drink a toast of tea to the future, move the chair and change the sheets to celebrate.

230

There was a wind rising that stirred up the smells of wet earth, and the darkness was as smooth and unyielding as skin and me in it, my blood suddenly volatile as if it had absorbed by osmosis the freedom of the wind. I walked with my arms swinging, my pupils wide as the night blotted jungle shapes in gardens and purple shadows behind tremulous curtains, the stirring of marvellous dreams in sleep-sodden rooms. I knew this exhilaration and self-satisfaction and hope would disappear in daylight, as names and facts marshalled themselves to contradict – but somehow that seemed as irrelevant as distant death and the tolling of pompous bells, for surely the longer I played in this fountain, this meeting of rivers somewhere lost like paradise within me, the stronger its music and its memory would be, and the easier to rediscover?

That was my state of mind on the night in question.

Then I saw a man at the door and screamed, the loose warmth of flesh suddenly contracted to a small stone of fear. Keys in hand jangled uncontrollable and a voice said run, go for his eyes with the keys, scream, talk him out of it, give him the money – run – but no sounds would come out. And then the man spoke and I knew it was him, Steve, the defendant, and I was glad it was him and not the stranger hiding in the porch . . .

'Both the defendant and Miss Sheldon state that they initially had frequent sexual relations when they lived together, and the defence argues that this shows Miss Sheldon was inclined to be attracted to Mr Blake sexually . . .'

And in fact I stopped, does that not show the attraction had ceased? Doesn't it?

' . . . inconsistent, and argue that Miss Sheldon may well have realised that sexual intercourse might take place or even been expecting it when . . .'

I counted the pages dealing with the prosecution case, mainly the summary of my statement, the police notebooks, and the Browns,

' . . . who heard Miss Sheldon shouting. Whilst the

231

prosecution offer this as evidence substantiating Miss Sheldon's version of events, the defence in cross-examination show that Mr and Mrs Brown had in fact been regularly disturbed by shouting in the past, and did not attach any particular significance to it on this occasion. Ladies and Gentlemen of the jury, it will be an important part of your decision to establish whether or not in your opinion the shouting on the night in question does or does not constitute corroboration.'

'Corroboration' means: you are a liar unless you can provide a witness to what was done to you by a man in a four-walled curtained room, locked and private as the grave.

'That Miss Sheldon had at some recent time been penetrated by a man of the same blood group as Mr Blake is the extent of the conclusions to be drawn from medical evidence, and it is my duty to point out this does not constitute corroboration, and neither is it in dispute that this man was Mr Blake.'

So that second time – metal and glass, respectable white-cuffed hand with only a cellophane skin between it and rape, that humiliation suffered in order to establish the truth for others to see – even that he pushed aside. There was the first rape, I thought, and then the medical rape and now the court rape.

'The defence point out that Mr Blake's conversation with Mr Maximillian Jackson is hardly consistent with the behaviour of a rapist . . .'

What is the behaviour of a rapist? Apart from raping, does anything mark him out? If so, I missed it when I was living with one.

' . . . according to your understanding of the facts as they have been put before you, and acting upon your own judgement. If you believe that it is proven that Steven Blake had sexual intercourse with Miss Sheldon knowing it to be against her will, then your verdict will be guilty. If however you decide that what you have heard in court does not amount to proof that this was the case, then you will acquit him.'

It was obvious that Judge Barford felt that he had no duty

towards me. I was only a witness, after all. I lay and watched what happened to my person, but that does not constitute corroboration. Judge Barford, I suspected, felt sorry for Steven Blake. Judge Barford would talk about the case at dinner, as a man of the world, and his guests, double chinned and fur coated like the members of the SPL, would swirl brandy in their glasses and hang on to his words. But he knows nothing, I thought, nothing.

It took the jury half an hour to decide that rape had not taken place. By implication, I was found guilty, among other things, of lying and wasting everybody's time and the government's money.

'There must be something wrong with the people on that jury. Can't you appeal or something? It's a scandal –' My mother was indignant.

'I wouldn't want to.'

'You couldn't anyway. No one can be tried twice for the same thing once they've been acquitted.'

'Really, they only did what the judge told them to,' I said, thinking of the hard-faced woman in the silk blouse. And it is true: within the terms of the law they performed perfectly, for it could not be proved, not 'without a shadow of a doubt' that I did not consent, not in my heart of hearts, even as my lips shouted No and my flesh crept with loathing. Could not be proved, that is, so long as the law assumed me likely to be a mad woman or a liar. Even so, I know which way I would cast my vote in such a case, however many times I was reminded of precisely what constitutes corroboration. I would seek to hinder the enshrined prejudices of the Sexual Offences Act with my own, I would insist that the man was likely to be guilty, and that his defence was likely to be lies.

'What are you going to do now?' asked Melanie, and I told her about the holiday.

'After that, I'm not sure. I've got so cut off from everything. I don't think I'll go back to teaching.'

'You've got the Centre's number still? And here's mine.'

Perhaps Melanie was raped herself. I will ask her one day. In any case, she is an acute and sensitive woman, and probably guessed that at the end of all those versions of that story – many of them I don't doubt photocopied and catalogued and kept – and of all that forgetting and remembering, I would eventually want to write down my own version. Even if I have had to write as if it happened to someone else, here, in the account I have given, at last I recognise what happened to me. I am back in the first person. And, of course, this time I expect to be believed.

16

I bought Sara a sherry while we waited for the train to take her back to Leeds.

'Thank you for coming, Mum.' I felt almost gay and clinked the beer mug against Sara's pinch-waisted sherry glass.

'I hope it's not going to upset you. Like your friend said, it was just a technicality, everyone there must have known.'

There were a couple of deafening thumps, I started and turned away. A group of musicians who had been plugging themselves in and blowing into microphones burst into sound. All I could hear was one hundred per cent loudness; as if a cook's hand had slipped adding chilli – it made any qualities the music may have had indistinguishable. It was so loud that it was silence, it put the ears to sleep. When I turned back to Sara I saw she was crying. She was saying something too, but it was impossible to make out the words. I put my arm around her and squeezed, aware that my own eyes were pricking and that I was also smiling. I'd never seen my mother weak before: that she had permitted it to happen, or rather, not been able to prevent its happening, was somehow more comfort than being comforted. I finally knew then that she believed me and I would always know it.

Soon I would be away myself. All over now. I felt as if I

was stepping off the edge of the world, riding into a dream; I was catching a train rattling into the blue clear at the end of the tunnel.

The song came to an end.

'No, I won't let it get to me,' I answered, still holding her tight. 'I've had enough of that.'

The wind was rushing through my hair, sailing away, running, running. I had been still so long: heart, hopes and limbs frozen deep, waiting for the kiss of life. Little girls stand in the asphalt yard holding the sides of their navy blue skirts and pulling up and out with all their strength as they count carefully, their voices showing the strain as they reach two hundred; and then they let go, feel their arms rise and float, each too preoccupied to observe if they really do, if it's really, as the game is called, 'levitation'. Release. Oh, how the world's colours intoxicated the eye, how the aches in back and neck suddenly transform into sensation rather than pain. It's over, it's over.

'It's all over now.'

My mother's face has scarcely changed over the years, she's never worn cosmetics and so she has aged without that sudden shadow that comes over some women when they change their style of decoration to declare the crossing of a line they have drawn across their lives. For all that she is a woman whose tongue has for years proclaimed the matter of fact and dismissed things ambiguous or introspective, her face has the surface tension of one consumed by both. Its lines come not from the simple collapse and drying of skin, but from some kind of effort that's left its tracks on her face, from something she's doing and has always done. That's why she seems to have changed so little.

'Never seen you crying before,' I whispered in the sudden absence of noise.

'Don't know what's come over me,' she replied, but made no effort to cover up the lapse. For a few minutes we watched a small middle-aged man in a woolly hat scraping his feet vaguely across the floor and swinging his jacket from one extended arm as if it were a partner, and then we walked through the darkening streets, lost but found, arm in arm and struck dumb by something that had happened to us – or had it? Like little-girl levitation, it was something you felt but could never hope to prove.

I returned to pack my wellingtons, sweaters, and transcript and, just before I left, remembered the book stolen from the library, retrieved it from where I had hidden it and parcelled it in a plastic carrier from under the kitchen sink. It seemed an odd thing to have done, and I certainly hadn't taken it to read: that multiplying of humiliation was more than I could have sustained. The theft seemed to me then, as I stood still undecided whether to take the book with me, a premonition: as if I had known somewhere for the second it took to slip it into my bag that one day I would want to read it, and as if I had felt that it was mine and no one else should see it until I had finished with it. Perhaps Sally would read it? I packed it, turned off the gas, locked the door and stood outside for a moment before walking away from what had been my home for so long. Would there always be ghosts there? Or would the rooms grow back to shape, cleanse themselves in my absence?

Next to me on the coach sat a youngish man and woman equipped with sandwiches and several paperbacks for the journey. The clothes each wore sat a little uneasily on them, and I guessed this was the result of bearing each other's taste in mind when buying them. Both wore wedding rings in a pale metal, white gold I suppose; his was considerably thicker than hers. They seemed as if they had been married longer than they had been alive, each unhesitatingly completing the unfinished sentences and actions of the other, each knowing precisely when to let the syallables die in their throat so that the other could have the satisfaction of having the last word. Tasks and habits as familiar as furniture, as comforting as cocoa. They reminded me of my own parents as I saw them as a small

237

child: Mum-and-Dad. How did it happen, that hand-in-glove fitting together? 'Marriages just don't happen, they're made, my girl.'

So I had failed then? A disastrous relationship ending in rape, not wedding bells, not ever and ever till death do us part. And yet I'd always expected that I would live like that with some man: not married, but fitting, living with and knowing the man like daily bread, absorbed and absorbing, passionless but substantial and necessary. I watched the couple next to me with the same squeamish acknowledgement I feel when I am shown photographs of myself as a child. The man finished the last sandwich, which she had left for him and he had taken without asking her. He folded the paper wrappings together and gave them to the woman, then offered her a can of lager. Simultaneously they began to read their books. Straining my eyes, I could read the title of the woman's: *Victim! Victim!* For a moment I was shocked, it was like suddenly meeting in waking life a face you have dreamed about and tried to forget. Behind my competence and calm, I'd thought of rape daily; I'd hidden these thoughts as soon as they were born among a clutter of others, forgotten them if possible, or relegated them to nightmares. I had told myself that my preoccupation was understandable but it did not reflect the outside world, rape was not, as I had felt, everywhere. Yet the woman in the beige sweater, tights and checked skirt sat clamly absorbing *Victim! Victim!* (on the cover a woman stares out, her blouse ripped across to show her breasts, a trickle of blood running down from the corner of her mouth) and later she would pass the book to her husband as matter-of-factly as he had just passed her the sandwich wrappings. The couple huddled up close as it grew colder, pressing and smiling. 'Truth is stranger than fiction,' Mrs Anderson had often said knowingly, and I knew what she meant but I thought maybe it was truer to say of relations between the sexes that fiction was even less strange than truth. Maybe it's all the same story, all varieties of excitement are at base the frantic

238

compulsion that comes from a sense of imminent trespass: a conclusion that creates its own ghastly suspense time and time again, gathering force and momentum till the only reply is a convulsion that's nothing but face-saving consent in the teeth of the inexorable.

The woman, sitting calmly in the dim light, was obviously undisturbed by what she read. She turned the pages rapidly, but her face was still, almost vacant. The book, after all, described her own experience and mine, merely adding to it a sheen glamour and omitting some of the drabber suffering. Watching her, I was struck suddenly by an understanding that we are trained to be or act as victims, to be, just as Salter had bluntly told me I should be, prepared to weep. We listen daily to the same story: thrill of the chase, victim! victim! which, told again and again, makes itself into truth. Some of us resist its droning more than others: in a blind kind of way, I had fought quite a bit myself, but until now I hadn't seen exactly what I was fighting, or why. That story's a constant noise you grow deaf to, but you're hearing it just the same, and even if you refuse your lines the police and barristers, the judges and obedient juries: they all stick to the script. That story even hooks itself inside you and grows unnoticed as you pass from child to girl, learning what to expect and blood every month that seems to prove it. You read that story and your little-girl cunt mouths capitulation and you think, this is it, I'm a woman. If there were other stories it would be different and we would protect ourselves better.

I looked along the two rows of seats, stopping a moment at each woman's head. We've got all the evidence, I thought, but we're so used to it that we don't see: sipped in small but increasing doses violation tints the world and paints our faces and becomes as unremarkable as any other condition of existence. Part of life. The woman reading yawned. We've heard it so often it's even boring. I ought not to have been so shocked at what happened to me: in retrospect much of my life's been a red light warning, but I never saw it till now.

My thoughts were accompanied by a slow rising of astonishment that I was escaping: oh no, it wasn't going to happen to me again. Then I asked myself: would I ever have noticed the commonness and significance of rape if it hadn't happened to me? Was Steven Blake even now responsible for the path my thoughts and life would take, simple and humiliating as that? Or would I have put it together in any case, the rape a catalyst that brought me to conclusions earlier and sooner? I'd never know for sure. I stretched my legs and shut my eyes, deciding it was a useless question, as unanswerable as whether the things we touch really do exist.

I woke up when the coach stopped for its meal break and wandered disorientated into the service station cafeteria: a huge room carpeted in a once-brilliant pattern now sludged together into a dull orange. The coach drivers were together in a cheerful huddle in front of a huge television set delivering the late-night sports news, turned full on to drown the sounds of cutlery and fruit machines. Leather- and parka-jacketed youths in two distinct groups stabbed at plates of chips, tired couples picked the cherries out of small slices of fruit cake. I bent my face low over the mug of tea to steam my eyes open.

'Going on holiday dear?' It was the round-faced white haired woman who'd offered me a boiled sweet earlier, squeezing herself with difficulty between the table and the stool riveted to the floor with only enough space for the 'average person' between them.

'Yes. Near the lakes.'

'Well the weather's not too bad; mind you, it can bucket down up there. Have you got family there?'

'No, but I've got a friend coming.' She winked at me.

Having those few days alone would be just right, then Sally will come and we'll go walking even in the rain and talk ourselves dry.

The couple with the books were at the table in front,

their arms entwined, watching the figure skating on the television. As the skaters twirled themselves into applause and a commercial break, two women in high heels and very short skirts walked slowly across the cafeteria, scanning it with studied boredom and a hint of desperation. The bony women in blue overalls dispensed them fizzy drinks. Drivers winked knowingly among themselves and the youths pulled faces. I felt very remote from everyone in the cafeteria, and even from my own immediate past, which seemed like something idly read in an old newspaper found on the train. A smallish column it would be, dwarfed by the Mafia, Royalty and smuggled guns, lost in the litter of experience. It was difficult not to get carried away thinking of the future which, in contrast, filled me with a new kind of excitement that had nothing familiar about it and inspired no dread.

It was three o'clock in the morning when the mini cab finally arrived outside the cottage. The lock was stiff, and momentarily I fancied there had been some mistake with the key. I was very tired and put my blankets on the bed right away, noticing little but liking what I saw: the old range and neat stack of logs in the kitchen, a rust-coloured earthenware jug with teasels in it, a telephone, a postcard on the mat for me already: Sally, explaining how to get to the village. Her writing was careless but also very large, so easy to read. She writes her name just the same as any other word, without flourishes or underlinings. I propped the card by the mirror and prepared for bed.

I'd locked the doors, but on the point of shutting the bedroom window I hesitated, smelling trees and the wetness of the land after rain, listening to a silence that was almost humming, tingling with anticipation that was exhilarating without being enervating. I took long slow breaths and pulled the bottom sash right up so that I could see the night unconfused by reflections on the glass. Apart from the dim triangle which framed my own elongated shadow, there were no lights visible at all, not even a glow on the horizon. The thought of standing outside, of walking through such utter dark gave me a kind of vertigo; for a few moments I felt afraid as a single human being in the midst of so much other life. I heard the trees stretching as the wind carried the signals bustling through their leaves, and water dripping as hidden planes and surfaces shifted and twisted. I heard the dry whirr of wings, the tiny persistent clatter of insects on the move. I heard my own breath strong and smooth as cream, and the fear was gone. I had been observed and accepted with indifference.

I left the window open and lay in my dressing gown on top of the bed. With the light out now, I could see the sky was a different darkness to the land, slightly purple and softer, less consistent. Between the two darknesses I lay and felt safe. My fear of the night had surprised me, but, I thought, it came not from any actual threat, but rather from the sudden sensation of being without the defences I had trained myself into over the last year. It was the shock of meeting the world without protection and precautions between me and its touch. My skin shrank a little from the cold.

At first when I touched my body it was with a kind of curiosity, as if opening a package of old letters hidden long ago because they were too painful to read. Lying on my back my stomach was flat, but I could tell I had put on a little flesh: like the wrinkle I had found on my face before the trial, it had grown without my being aware of it. 'A woman of a certain age' – perhaps I was becoming one after all. A little fat would keep me warmer in winter; new flesh for old was better than shrinking away, I thought. It was warm and resilient beneath my hands, a tractable expanse between the hard curves of my pelvis on either side. My breasts too had changed: now they spread to either side as I lay. I stroked them, surprised by, then drawn into, the intertwining sensations in my fingertips as they travelled across the stretched flatness of my chest and into the heavy curve of the breasts, and in my breasts which welcomed

242

that touch and strained towards it. As I touched I felt my curiosity tense into a wanting that was almost painful: a need to touch all the parts of my body not only for pleasure but also for reassurance, and to repossess them. The pale parts, the tired parts, the muscles and the places where the bone stretched the skin, the wet parts, the places where hair prickled its way through: I had forgotten them so long I had not dared to visit this my own land, how long. And it seemed that my flesh had its own memories, locked in its parts that had functioned unceasing, never letting on that they knew and noticed, and now it woke immense and hungry, sweating out the fevers that had circulated obediently tame in veins and arteries; it woke and broke its silence crying and laughing all at once. The hair between my legs so thick it supported my hand, like sleeping on heather I thought, and I could smell heather and bracken and the sea; I let my hand lie there stroking out the hairs that had strayed inside to disturb the perfect smoothness there. My cunt was wet all over, I was wet and the bittersweet smell of sweat was good; at last I stretched every muscle, I felt myself opening inside, I felt awe at the powers of this my body as if it was not quite me. I thought I could give this, but no one will ever take it from me, oh no. And I was making my cunt grow, pushing the night gently into new places. So simple it would be, if by the gentlest of rubbing circles, we could set all that is in us free to shift and grow, if we were clever enough to find just that spot where everything could be rubbed beautiful, like that, the stupid and the cruel could be smothered and coaxed to rise elsewhere transformed, oh yes.

My body exhausted its memories and its prophecies, I held my hands over my cunt and slipped a finger in to feel its moving from both outside and in, that rhythm that was mine again.

Other new fiction from Virago

UNION STREET
Pat Barker

Union Street could be any street, anywhere. But in this powerful novel it lies at the heart of a city in the industrial North-east of England, a wasteland of decaying streets and partly demolished houses. It is the winter of 1973, a cold winter of unemployment, the year of the miners' strike.

This is the story of the women – and their men – who lived in that street, in that year, at that time. There is Kelly, eleven years old, bright, funny, engaging, a tough child of the streets; there is Joanne, eighteen, pregnant, unmarried; there is Lisa, mother of two, pregnant again, her husband out of work. Then there is Muriel, breaking her heart over her dying husband, comforted – but not for long – by her growing children. Central to the story are Iris, formidable mother and grandmother, the matriarch of the street, and Dinah, the local prostitute, knocking on sixty but still on the game. Last of all there is Alice, seventy-six now, fighting for that last and most precious freedom: the right to die in her own home.

Other new fiction from Virago

BLOW YOUR HOUSE DOWN
Pat Barker

A killer is roaming the streets of a northern city, setting off a wave of terror. He singles out prostitutes, and the face of his latest victim stares out from every newspaper and billboard, haunting the women who walk the streets.

But life and work must go on. Brenda, with three children can't afford to give up, while Audrey, now in her forties, desperately goes on 'working the cars', protecting herself as best she can. A city and its people are in the grip of a deep sickness, and when another woman is savagely murdered, Jean, her lover, can only find the strength to counter evil with evil. It is Maggie, the survivor of an attack, who finally outlasts the malign and terrifying presence, and recovers her capacity to love.

Other new fiction from Virago

EVERY MOVE YOU MAKE
Alison Fell

June Guthrie, Scottish and working class, is a child of the 1970s counter culture, idealistic, committed, insecure. She arrives in London at a time of electrifying political antagonism – and possibility. The odyssey of the urban nomads becomes hers: squatting and the fight against evictions, the occupation of the Electricity Board, battles and jailings – and the tightrope balancing of her needs against those of her two lovers. Everywhere June sees oppositions growing up around her – between reflection and action, utopianism and compromise, autonomy and dependence – until they tear her apart and she suffers a breakdown. Slowly she rebuilds her life around her young son, and her work on *Womanright*, a women's magazine collective, until a turbulent affair with a passionate, unstable man once again throws into question her fragile independence and her strategies for survival.

'Alison Fell travels fearlessly . . . She sees shadows, and demands we take them back as our own. But she is still daring to hope' – *Sheila Rowbotham*

Other new fiction from Virago

A MEASURE OF TIME
Rosa Guy

'Like a lady. That's how I stepped onto that train.' Dorine Davis, sassy, spirited, hustling, is leaving behind her the harsh racism of Alabama to take Harlem by storm. Black Harlem in the 1920s is a kingdom of tree-lined avenues, glittering nightclubs and luxury apartment buildings. Dorine wants it all. She becomes a 'booster', pulling off store heists with class. And she takes as her lovers the dreamers and schemers of Harlem. Yet through all these heady years there's the tug of home and of 'Son', being raised as her sister's child . . .

After a spell in prison Dorine comes out to a Harlem whose heyday is over. But out of the ghosts that haunt its decaying streets rises a new generation of the 1950s – amongst them 'Son' – who dare to dream a different dream.

'I (was) so overcome that I fell to weeping . . . This is an encouragement to every Black person under the threat of racial oppression . . . We will read this book and weep, and then we will rise' – *Maya Angelou*